EVIL QUEEN

THE ROYAL COURT · BOOK 2

REBEL HART

EVIL QUEEN

THE ROYAL COURT - BOOK TWO

REBEL HART

1

NATHAN

The blaring of my alarm in my ear was a wholly unwelcome sound. I wouldn't say that I enjoyed my winter break, but regardless of the constant headaches, frequent upset stomach, and generally being on the verge of a mental breakdown, not having to think about school for a whole two weeks was a nice escape from at least some of my problems.

Just getting to winter break had been intense. No one said much about what happened, and Cherri dropped off the face of the earth. When The Royal Court met for lunch, we sat in total silence, and we didn't speak much in class either. They were all still upset with me, and I deserved it, so I didn't push them. By the time the holidays and the two-week break came around, it was a double-edged sword. We all needed the break, but the weight of everything that had happened dropped on us like atomic bombs, and the wreckage was difficult to sift through.

With my arms stretched above my head, I cracked my neck to the left, then to the right, then reached out to my right and put my arm down. I expected it to find purchase on another body there, but I found only the comforter of my bed. Glancing over, I noticed that there was no one there. I'd be lying if I said I was surprised, but midnight slip-outs were something I was increasingly becoming used to. To be safe, I flipped back the covers, climbed out of bed, and padded my way out of my bedroom and down the spiral staircase to my kitchen and living room. I glanced into the kitchen, and though there was no one there, there was a fresh pot of coffee steaming in the coffee maker.

I walked over and lifted the pot from the machine, then whispered, "Thanks, Nikki."

With a small smile on my face, I poured myself a cup of coffee, only mixed in a small amount of cream, and then carried it back upstairs with me so that I could get ready for school. Ordinarily, I would spend an insane amount of time picking out a carefully coordinated outfit to wear, probably even messaging Kyle and even Brayden to tell them to wear something similar, but the fact of the matter was, I didn't have that energy in me. Though I would likely catch a glance of myself in a mirror at some point throughout the day and be disappointed with what I had on, I couldn't be bothered about that for the time being.

Instead, I grabbed the first respectful top and pants I could find and carried them into the bathroom with me. I started the shower, ripped off the pajama pants I was wearing, and climbed in. An involuntary sigh came out of my mouth as the heated water blasted the top of my head. Showering was my least favorite task as of late because I didn't want to get in, and then once I was in, I didn't want to get out. I'd found that, ever since my mom died, my dad disappeared, and my estranged half-brother went on the chase, it was the base-minimum, keep yourself alive and kicking tasks that I struggled with the most.

Thank God that Nikita had been with me most of the winter break to see to it that I ate and bathed.

After about twenty minutes in the shower, my

head started to hurt. It was something that had been happening as of late, likely because before my dad left, if I spent more than about ten minutes in the shower, he'd be in the bathroom, screaming about the amount of time I was wasting away. Nikita had slowly worked with me to try and break me out of my ingrained habits, but they weren't dying easily. Sometimes, I still felt like I could hear my dad's loud, demanding voice, screaming at me, telling me I was a disappointment to him.

Who was the disappointment now?

It only took another two minutes for my headache to overwhelm my sense of pride, and I washed my body free of the soap I'd lathered onto it and then turned the water off and climbed out. The digital clock that was built into the mirror on the wall opposite the shower read that the time was four-fifteen in the morning. School didn't officially start until eight o'clock, and during the break, if I woke up too early, I could just go back to sleep, but if I tried that now, I'd oversleep and miss the first day back. I wasn't being forced to study business, practice my languages, or listen to lectures about being a man.

What did normal students do in the four hours before school?

I got dressed at as slow a pace as I could justify

and then walked back into my bedroom. With a slump, I dropped down onto my bed and stared at the wall. Part of me told myself to go to sleep, part of me told myself to grab my laptop and work on business matters, and part of me told myself to just leave and drive until I got somewhere interesting. Nothing sounded good, and nothing had for a while, but only one of the options I came up with made any real sense, so I stood up, grabbed my backpack, slung it over my back, snagged my coffee, and made my way back downstairs.

I stepped down into the sunken living room couch and fished my laptop out of my backpack. It whirred to life as soon as I lifted the lid, but then I was met with the infamous updates screen. A sigh blew out of me, but it wasn't all bad. I set the computer down on the couch, stepped back onto the main level, and walked into the kitchen. I wasn't a chef, so I kept my fridge stocked with quick-grab items that I could eat without any preparation. When my parents were still around, they used to have a world-class chef prepare me breakfast every day, but about a week after they were gone, I caught him celebrating their absence and fired him. I grabbed a banana and topped off my coffee before walking back into the living room and sitting down next to my computer to eat while I waited.

Eventually, the updates finished, so I opened up my emails and let out a hiss of frustration. "Shit."

The inbox was jam-packed with people contacting me from my father's company, wondering what they should do next with my dad MIA. He was the president, sure, but weren't Fortune 500 companies supposed to have an entire hierarchy so that they could continue to function if the head got lobbed off? Hell, knowing my dad, there had to be more than one person waiting for him to keel over one day so that they could rise up and take his spot.

Were they really so useless without him?

It wasn't like medical supplies needed active selling. All hospitals, prisons, and schools were in the market for them, not to mention the department stores and insurance companies with whom we had multi-billion-dollar contracts to be their go-to supplier. All they had to do was keep showing up and doing things as they always had been. How hard was that?

I started to type a thorough, extravagant email to the president of the board of directors, who was the main person contacting me, but after about six paragraphs, I just picked up my phone and called.

It was still early in the morning, but I didn't care. If a group of grown adults was going to bug a high-school student non-stop about how to run a business, they were going to get advice on my schedule.

"Mr. Loche?" Arden Taft, the president of the board, greeted. His voice was groggy as if he was just waking up, and I could hear a second voice grumbling in the background. "Good morning."

"Good morning. Also, call me Nathan."

"Yes, sir." There was some shifting, and then I could hear Arden moving, likely climbing out of bed. "What can I do for you, sir?"

"Arden, I realize my dad is MIA, but I cannot wake up to fifty emails from you guys. I'm still in high school. I start school again today. Why is it so difficult to continue operations with just one man missing?" I was snippier than I wanted to be, but I was also irritated.

"Sir, you have to understand, your father didn't allow *anyone* other than himself to make decisions. He doesn't have any protocol for what to do if he isn't around, only to defer to you. Now, we can both imagine that he assumed that wouldn't come into play as early in your life as it has, but it's where we are."

My neck cracked as I twisted my head to the left and then the right. Nikita's voice skated across my mind, telling me not to crack my bones, but what else was I supposed to do if I was stressed and felt tight?

"Listen," I started. "I get that my dad isn't a very trusting guy, and believe me when I say I am aware of the fact that he forced all channels through him because he's paranoid, but that doesn't mean there isn't at least one person there who was listening when he talked."

"N-no, there are, of course, many of us who know your father's plans for the company well, but what of the open contracts? Many of the emails you received contained contracts that need approval."

With that, I pulled my computer onto my lap and started to sift through for anything with an attachment. "Okay, this QILR contract looks good. I know my dad has a signature stamp, so tell his assistant to use it to sign the contract and return it. If it's an e-signature, she has my permission to sign his name." I flipped to the next one. "Hertfeld County is trying to low-ball us, so I'm sending this one back. Please have Caitlyn call their purchasing manager—I believe his name is Doug—and tell him that for a county supply, the complete package that they're looking for runs a two million minimum. Our machines don't even fire up for less than one and a half, but I want five."

"Yes, sir," Arden replied.

Clicking through the rest of the contracts, they all seemed pretty reasonable. "The rest of these look good and can be signed. Please ensure they're added to the quarterly numbers and review them at the February board meeting. As long as we're trending up or maintaining, I'm fine."

"Well, sir, with all due respect, I really do think you should be at the meeting," Arden said. "Our board is desperate to get some face time with the next person in line."

I rubbed my temples. "I'm not the next in line. Connor will be back soon. It's just a matter of holding until he returns. Do you think you can manage that?"

Arden was silent for a long time and then sighed. "Yes, sir."

"Good. I'll be in touch, but for now, please have people route their concerns and questions through the CFO. I still want signing power, but he should have the prowess to handle anything else."

"Oh," Arden said, and there was a heightened relief in his voice. "I can do that. Thank you, sir."

"Yeah. Bye."

"Bye."

The line went dead, but no longer being on the phone didn't help ease any stress I had. For as long as I had no idea where my dad was, I could continue to lie and say that he'd be returning, but the truth was, my half-brother Deon was searching for him, and we were both hoping to end his life. It was either him or the people we loved, and we'd fight to protect them, regardless. It probably made sense that Deon was doing the dirty work while I was attempting to keep the company afloat, but I still wished I knew more.

I lifted my phone again and navigated to Deon's phone number. We finally exchanged phone numbers when everything went wrong in the fall, but I hadn't used it once. Deon would definitely contact me if there was a development in his hunt, but I often found myself wanting to talk to him, hopefully, in a way that wasn't nasty or aggressive. Our father-induced differences aside, I always cared about my brother. When I first learned that I had a brother, I was over the moon, and that year he lived with us was one of the best of my life. After everything that happened, would we be able to salvage our relationship now?

Maybe I should call?

My phone rang in my hand before I could make a decision. I fumbled around and nearly dropped it from shock, but I caught it and answered without checking who it was.

"Hello?"

"Hey, man," Kyle's deep, bass-filled voice responded. "I was kind of hoping you were still asleep."

I snapped my laptop shut and tossed it over to the couch cushion next to me. "Nah, still waking up around four these days."

"Well, let's make the most of it, then. Want to meet me for breakfast? I know this awesome diner. I always wanted to take you, but I don't know, it felt like it might be below you."

A different person might have been offended, but I just laughed. "Yeah, I get that. Sure. Text me the address."

"Cool. See ya soon."

"Bye."

I ended the call, then stood up, collected all of my things, and made my way toward the door. I grabbed the keys and was just about to head out when I remembered something and turned around. Taking the steps two at a time, I made my way back upstairs, went into my closet, pushed aside some of my piled clothes, and grabbed the box of Cherri's things that I'd been hiding from Nikita.

Cherri was a bit of a sore subject between us.

My hope was that I could get the box back to Cherri without causing too many issues with either woman. With the box in my hand and nervousness sizzling through me at the thought of returning to school after everything that happened, I left.

2
____

NIKITA

My breath billowed around my mouth in a cloud of opaque smoke. As my feet crunched through the snow, there was an ever-present chill on the tip of my nose and ears. At least, that would be my cover story for why they were glowing bright red in the wake of a *"Good morning, my life"* text from Nathan. He was headed to breakfast with Kyle, which was good. My face was the only one he'd seen for the past two weeks, and on top of that, I still hadn't sorted myself out enough yet. I loved Nathan so much more than I thought possible, but there were more than a few reasons why I was struggling with that. It was good for him to see someone else and, hopefully, work his way back toward normalcy.

"Hey," a dusky voice called out to me.

I looked up and rolled my eyes at the scene. Jaxon was there, but he was wearing his typical skinny jeans and black boots. He'd also donned a red flannel, half-buttoned, and a sleeveless, acid-wash jean jacket that certainly wasn't enough to protect him from the cold of the snow all around him. At least he had a black beanie pulled down, hiding his black hair and covering his ears. He was sitting on top of a picnic table at a park not far from Postings Proper High. It was our favorite place to go when we ditched or just needed to meet up, and he had a lit cigarette balanced perfectly between his lips.

"You're gonna freeze to death like that," I called out.

He shrugged, and I laughed. If there was anything I'd learned about my best friend in the time since Nathan brought him into The Royal Court, it was that it took more than a few trivial discomforts to rattle him. His naturally tanned skin from his Filipino heritage was covered in scars and scrapes, which he considered trophies. He was the kind of guy who could easily survive if the world went ass up and we had to revert to caveman tactics.

I kicked my legs over the bench of the picnic

table and climbed in to sit, ignoring the frigid feeling on my butt and legs as I did so. I laid my head down on Jaxon's knee next to me. He bent over at the waist and gave me a gentle headbutt, and I snickered.

"By the way, I don't like not seeing you for two weeks, so let's not do that shit again, okay?" he huffed.

"Agreed," I replied. "What'd you do with your time off?" He didn't respond right away, so I looked up at him, and he flicked his head over toward the parking lot. I looked back over my shoulder at his black and green Lamborghini and noticed there was another person sitting in the passenger's seat. Though totally bundled up, the short, pixie haircut was unmistakable. "Colette. Is she asleep?"

"Yeah. She needs it, so I didn't wanna wake her up."

"How did she end up with you?" I asked.

Jaxon snuffed his cigarette out on the picnic table and flicked the butt off into the snow. "She's been calling me pretty much all winter break to sleep with her." I raised an eyebrow, and he shook his head. "No, not like that. Literally, sleep. Just hold her and talk to her until she falls asleep. She only gets a few hours a night, so I'm doing what I can, but..." He sighed. "She's not doing great."

I carefully watched Jaxon's face and noticed how sunken his eyes were and how weary he seemed. He was normally an aloof, unemotional kind of guy, but he seemed truly pained by the anguish Colette was experiencing.

"It's kind of shocking," I said. "I mean, it's not like I thought she was totally unattached, but I didn't expect her to take it so hard. I didn't even feel like Cherri liked her all that much."

He shrugged. "Yeah, I tried to get her to explain it to me a few times, but I don't think she really knows what it's all about. I just think The Royal Court means more to her than she realized, and now it's so fractured. She can't deal."

"I understand that deeply," I replied.

Nathan and I grew up in the same neighborhood and became friends pretty quickly. It's said that kids don't understand romance at a young age, but I always knew that I loved Nathan. He was the one I always wanted to be around, the one I cared most about, and the one I would do anything for. When my grandmother finally saved me from my father, who was molesting me, and my mother, who was allowing it to happen, my therapist at the time, Sistine, saw how attached to Nathan I was. She stepped down to foster me, and my grandmother bought us a house to live in so that I could stay close to him.

Nathan promised to always take care of me, and he always did. When he established The Royal Court, he invited me in as a knight and kept me close. How important The Royal Court was to him made it important to me. I'd never been a big fan of Cherri, for obvious reasons, but I cared about her as an extension of this family I'd built.

Now it was broken, and I wasn't entirely sure how to proceed. Nathan hadn't spoken to anyone from The Royal Court other than me in the two weeks that we were all off on winter break, and Cherri hadn't spoken to any of us at all. The last time I saw her, she was denouncing all of us for dragging her away from Deon, who was chasing after Connor. I empathized with her position. When I first found out that a bunch of them knew that Nathan was missing and hadn't told me for hours, I was so livid that I punched a hole through the glass of my driver's side window.

Leaving Nathan behind at that cabin and not knowing if he was going to come back was the most difficult thing I'd ever had to do, but at least I had the choice. If someone had forcefully dragged me away from him, I'd be pretty pissed too.

"How did everything get fucked up so quickly?" I asked. "All it took was one tiny thing."

"Well," Jaxon replied. "We found out Nathan had a brother and found out his dad was on some sadistic, force-machismo shit with his son, and a teacher threw herself out of a third-story window. All of that wasn't one tiny thing."

"I guess."

I was only one of two people in The Royal Court who knew about Deon before he suddenly resurfaced earlier that year. Connor had suddenly dropped the bomb on Nathan that he had a brother and that this brother was coming to live with them. It was pretty much just Nathan and me at that point, and I can admit I got a little jealous. Deon showed up, and Nathan was crazy about him. All he would talk about was his new brother, how cool his new brother was, and how much fun it was, having a new brother. Things that would ordinarily just involve Nathan and me suddenly had this new person hanging around, and it wasn't long before Deon started to make friends, so our circle slowly grew.

I didn't like how much Nathan loved Deon, and then when Deon decided to just drop everything and leave, Nathan was heartbroken, and that made me like him even less. Only Kyle stuck around from the friends that had gravitated toward Nathan thanks to Deon, and it was Kyle and me who made the leap with Nathan from his post-Deon days to when he established The Royal Court.

"Tack that onto the long, growing list of reasons why I feel guilty every single day," I said. "I knew Deon existed, but he left a lot of that story out, especially the part about Cherri."

"Yeah, fuck, that was the biggest reveal, wasn't it? Nathan went and got Cherri because he *knew* she was his brother's girl? That *is* a little twisted. I'll give you that," Jaxon said. "He's obviously in love with you, though. Who knows how much of that shit was manipulated by his batshit dad?"

"A good amount of it, I would imagine."

"How's he taking all of it?" Jaxon asked. "Nathan."

"As good as can be expected," I replied. "For those first few days of the winter break, I literally had to force food down his throat. For being a spoiled, rich brat, he's fucking strong."

Jaxon laughed. "You think ol' Connor was going to leave weight training out of the equation? He was trying to grow himself a little trophy."

I laughed, though it was far from funny. "I might have expected it." My face started to burn, imagining Nathan handling me in the bedroom. "He's…strong."

Jaxon looked down at me, poking my cheeks, which I was certain were bright red. "Slept with him again, huh?"

"Yep," I replied.

Jaxon sighed. "You said you weren't going to."

"I know," I responded, "but I love him."

"I know, kid." Jaxon set his hand on my head. "I know you do. What if—I don't know, what if you just went for it? Just put the past behind you and looked forward?"

I glanced up at him. "You know why I can't do that."

"I know. All that shit with your dad, but Nathan isn't like that. Your dad was a monster. What he did to you…" His hands balled into fists. "I wish I could kill him for it. Nathan's not that guy, though. Nathan's not a monster. We've all said it. He just snapped."

"So snapping makes it okay for him to rape someone?" I asked. "Cherri didn't deserve that."

"Of course not," Jaxon said. He opened his mouth and tried to say something, but he stopped. "I don't know. I'm not defending what he did."

"You're not?"

"No," Jaxon barked. "I'm not. I know what he

did was fucked up, and no, it's not okay that he snapped. Cherri got the brunt of it, and she didn't deserve that. I'm just saying, are things like that the end-all and be-all for someone? That's all they get? That one fuck up, and it's all over?"

"You think they should get more chances to do it?"

"Nikita, you're starting to piss me off," Jaxon said. "You know that's not what I fucking mean."

"Then what do you mean?" I asked.

"I mean, people like your dad, lock them up and fucking throw away the key, but people like Nathan? He's *not* a bad guy, and you know that. Is there any reality in which people make that mistake, as horrible as it is, and then pay their penance and get to move on and be in happy, healthy relationships? Does this one thing just define him for the rest of his life? Fuck how smart he is. Fuck how much he loves his friends. Fuck his sense of humor. Fuck his business prowess. His dad applied more and more pressure until he broke, and now that one thing just defines who he is forever? There's nothing left for him? Eighteen years old, and he's done?"

"He made that choice," I replied, a lump of emotion settling in my throat. "I…" The image of me standing in front of an obviously cracking

Nathan, telling him to punch me or fuck me or do whatever he had to do to alleviate his stress, whipped across my brain. "There were other options."

Jaxon started to gently rub my head, and I could see why Colette called him to comfort her. He was oddly good at it. "Are there only two extremes in this situation? There's no redemption?"

My parents popped into my brain then. Poor, sobbing young Nikita, begging her mom to listen and cowering from her dad. I would never want my mom nor my dad to be happy for as long as either of them lived. With everything that had gone down with Cherri and Deon, I could only imagine Cherri felt the same.

"For Cherri's sake and mine, I certainly hope not."

"Damn," Jaxon said. "Then, I'm sorry, but you need to start moving on."

"Yeah," I replied, tears coming loose and sliding down my cheeks. "I don't know how, though."

"It's gonna be a teaching experience for us both," Jaxon said, "but you know I'm here for you, right?"

I nodded, smiling up at my best friend. "Yeah. I know."

He glanced from me to just past me where his car was sitting. "I don't like seeing the people I love hurting."

Part of me wanted to ask if that was Jaxon's way of admitting he was in love with Colette, but I decided not to disrupt the moment any further. I laid my head back on Jaxon's knee and let him slowly and softly caress my head until we eventually had to leave for whatever hell-storm awaited us at school.

3

NATHAN

Where Kyle and I grew up in South Postings was much different from where Deon and Cherri grew up in North Postings. South Postings was the posh part of town compared to the more slum-like surroundings of North Postings, and Kyle was right. If he'd invited me to a diner there six months ago, I absolutely would not have gone. I, not unlike most rich kids living in their own world, bought into the narrative that North Postings was too dangerous to go into, but then my father tried to frame my brother for murder, killed my mother, tried to kill me, and threatened to hurt the people I loved most all in the span of about two days.

Funny how life puts things into perspective.

My car was far from being the nicest one on the

pothole-ridden street that I parked on in front of the small mom-and-pop diner that Kyle directed me to, and unlike the way people often stared at me regardless of where I went in South Postings, as I climbed out of my car, those who could see me didn't give me more than a quick glance of aware- ness. There was the laughter of people standing around despite the frigid temperatures outside, and when I passed them by, they all smiled and nodded. No one ever did that in South Postings.

"New around here?" a man with pale skin and rosy-red cheeks asked as I passed.

I glanced down at my designer jeans, Doc Martens boots, and flannel under an expensive down jacket. "What gave me away?"

"You're Kyle's friend, right?" he asked.

My eyes widened a little bit. "Yeah. How'd you know?"

The man nodded toward the diner. "This is my place. His mama and I go way back." He held out a hand. "I'm Gerald."

I took Gerald's hand and shook it, and the firm welcome in his grip was comforting after spending months alone in my cold mansion. "Nice to meet you. I'm Nathan."

"Yeah." A frown crossed his face. "Listen, I know you been through some stuff. Kyle didn't tell me everything, but he told me enough. Said you need some of ol' Pop Gerald's comfort food. If you ever need anything,"—he motioned to the group of people around him, an eclectic mix of older and younger people of all types—"we got you covered here."

For the first time in a very long time, I smiled. In my world, strangers didn't give a shit about you. It was strange.

"Thanks," I said.

Gerald tapped my shoulder with his hand. "Head on in. Kyle's at his favorite booth about halfway back. They'll take your order, and I'll hit the grill for ya. Order whatever you want. On me."

My jaw dropped. "Uh, I'm really not trying to brag or anything, but I can pay for it."

He laughed. "I know you can. It's not about the money. Sometimes, we just need to look out for each other, you know?"

I nodded. "Yeah. Thanks."

Walking away, I almost expected to hear an insult grumbled under his breath or a judgment thrown from one of the other people he was talking to, but he huffed, "Yeah, that's a good kid. I feel bad," and everyone agreed.

Was this the care and concern of other people

that I was missing, locked up in my world in South Postings?

Bells on the door to the diner jingled as I opened it and entered the small restaurant. A few tables were scattered in front of me, and to my right, booths were situated all down the wall toward the back of the quaint diner. I could throw a ball from one end to the other, and because it was so early, there weren't many people inside. As I scanned the few occupants, a hand went into the air, and I noticed Kyle sitting about halfway back along the row of booths. He smiled as I walked over and stood up to greet me with a hug. His chocolate skin was well covered under a black bomber jacket and a black beanie, but I could see that he was wearing one of his designer sweaters underneath and had a classic pair of tan Primo Castagna high-tops on his feet. His wrists and fingers were still covered in all kinds of jewelry, and a set of wide-rimmed glasses still sat on his nose.

Why I was anticipating seeing something other than the typical Kyle, I wasn't sure, but it was good to see he was still really and truly himself.

"Hey, man," he said. "I'm glad you came."

We broke our embrace and dropped into opposing sides of the booth. "Yeah, me too."

Kyle was my best friend. We didn't meet until

Deon came to live with me, but when he left, all of the friends we'd made together ditched me except for Kyle. He said that I was a good guy and that he liked being friends with me. Gaining and then losing Deon gave me more than a few trust issues. By that point, I already assumed that everyone who was sticking around me was doing so for some benefit, even though Kyle and Nikita both had long proven that it wasn't the case.

Along with everyone else in The Royal Court, I'd avoided speaking with Kyle, but he was the one I missed the most. He knew me better than nearly anyone else in my life, and I think the idea that he'd see through me terrified me. It was already bad enough that Nikita was hanging around, taking care of me while still silently riddling me with guilt, and I figured that having just one of those people in my life while trying to figure out what was next for me was enough.

Just like back when Deon left, Kyle had stuck around, and he'd gotten very little from me in return. Seeing him gave me that familiar, finally-home feeling, and I hated that I'd avoided seeing him for so long.

Looking through the window to my right, I could see Gerald still chuckling with the group of people he was talking to. "I met Gerald."

"Oh, yeah. Pop's a really good man. He and my mom have been friends since childhood. She lived around here, growing up, but moved to South Postings during her residency, and well, that doctor's salary allowed her to start a family down there. She always made sure to bring me around here a lot, though. This is my favorite place."

"He's…" There was a shake to my voice I wasn't expecting. "I get why Deon wanted to come back here."

Kyle nodded. "Yeah. I knew I couldn't say that to you back then, but I got it too. My mom always talked about it. How hard it was to go from here to there. The feeling is just different. People are people up here. It's not about how much money you make, who you're married to, or what your affiliation is with a certain group of people. They just look out for each other. It's really something special."

"That's what I always wanted from The Royal Court," I admitted. "I wanted this warmth. I guess I just figured out that it's not something that can be forced."

"I don't know," Kyle said. "Maybe not at first, but we've stayed stuck to each other for four years."

"Yeah, because I'm a piece of shit," I replied. "Not because they wanted to be. I lied to Cherri, I blackmailed Alistair, I bribed Avery and Colette, and Jaxon came with Nikita. Let's face it, most of you are only in it because you didn't know what I'd do if you tried to leave."

"Ah, so *this* is what we're doing, huh? The self-loathing?" Kyle asked, sipping a cup of coffee.

"I'm just joining the club," I replied.

Kyle took a deep, long breath. "Well, okay then. I'm your best friend, so we'll get through it together. I expected something a little angrier, not melodramatic pity, but however you gotta get through it, I get it."

I glared across the table at him. "Is this your version of tough love?"

"Sure," he replied.

"Most of my friends are fabricated, I snapped and raped my ex, my mom is dead, and my dad and brother are missing," I rattled off. "The fully-grown adults at my dad's company keep relying on *me* to make their decisions, and the woman I love won't go all-in with me because I did the *one* thing that she hates most. I think I've earned the right to be a little emotional."

Kyle's eyes softened. "Sorry. You're right. You have. This side of you is new, so forgive me if I don't know how to deal with it."

The anger that had been growing in me dissipated. "Yeah, that's fair."

"I meant what I said, regardless," Kyle said. "The part about being here for you. I'm your best friend. I've stuck by you through everything, and this is no different, so…" He sighed. "Please don't shut me out for two weeks ever again. I've lost sleep."

Guilt didn't describe how I felt at that statement. "Okay. I'm sorry."

"Don't be. Just don't do that again."

A waitress came over, took our order, and brought me some coffee. As I stirred some creamer and sugar in, I looked up at Kyle. "It's not just you, you know. I haven't talked to anyone except for Nikita."

"I know," Kyle replied. "How are things with her? Still not going great?"

"How could they? She doesn't trust me, and I can't blame her," I replied. "We've been…intimate, but there's still this huge wall between us, and I honestly don't know how to break it down."

"It may just take time," Kyle said. "Nikita loves you. That's not some big mystery."

"Yeah, and if I hadn't done what I did to Cherri, there would be no issue, but I did." I stared down into the caramel-colored coffee. "I fucked up, Kyle."

"Yeah, you did," Kyle said. "We have spoken *at*

length about kicking your ass for what you did, but you've been through a lot, and Avery didn't want to make things worse."

"I'd have deserved it." Kyle gave me an exhausted look, and I backed off. "Sorry. Anyway, you've talked to everyone, then?"

"All except Cherri," Kyle replied. "She's not talking to anyone. Everyone's tried, but no luck. It wasn't a great Christmas all around for The Royal Court."

"How bad off is everyone?"

"Well, not to make you feel even more terrible, but it's worse than I thought it would be." Kyle took a sip of his coffee. "Avery's inconsolable, having lost Cherri. Apparently, she bought her a ton of Christmas presents and tried to drop them off for her at her parent's house, but her mom wouldn't even take them. Said she didn't want to waste Avery's money because Cherri wouldn't accept them."

My heart broke. For all the shit that I'd caused, forcing The Royal Court into existence, Cherri and Avery's pure, real friendship was one of the good things that came from it. I hated knowing that I caused that rift. "Damn."

"Alistair has, of course, been with her the entire time, but he doesn't know how to help her. He's been trying non-stop. He's pretty exhausted. Jaxon is Jaxon. You know, he's not much of a talker, but he's been exceptionally quiet. Brayden is who I've talked to the most."

"He called me non-stop during Christmas break."

"Yeah, he wouldn't stop talking about you for a second. Kept saying that we should do something to help you, but I told him you just needed space. He wanted to try and force the Christmas party, but I knew people wouldn't be in a celebratory mood. I hung out with him a lot over Christmas break."

I raised an eyebrow, knowing that Kyle wasn't Brayden's number one fan by any stretch. "Really?"

"Well? No one really likes dealing with him other than you, but you were MIA. I was… I don't know. I was trying to look out for everyone. Him too."

In truth, Kyle would probably make a way better leader of The Royal Court than I had been, but I knew he wouldn't take it if I offered it, so I kept that thought to myself. "Thanks. What about Colette?"

Kyle's face went from indifferent to flat out depressed. "She's, uh…" He let out a sigh. "She's taking it hard. Like, really hard. She's decided to step down as valedictorian and class president."

My stomach twisted into a tight knot. "What? Why?"

"I don't know. She was willing to talk to me, but not about very much, and not for very long. Whenever I would call to check on her, the very first thing she would ask me is if I'd heard from Cherri, and when I said I hadn't, she would clam right up."

"Shit," I grumbled. "She was the one person I thought might be doing okay."

"Yeah, me too. I don't get it. She's really struggling with it," Kyle said. "I've asked what I can do to help, but I honestly don't think she knows."

Our food came, but we both slowly picked at it as the tension of the conversation blanketed over us.

"What's next for us, do you think?" Kyle asked.

"Damned if I know," I said. "I don't even know what's next for *me*. I know that's a horrible thing to say as a leader, but it's true." The food both smelled and tasted amazing, but I was struggling to eat much of anything because of the way the guilt over hurting my friends was eating away at me. "I am gonna make it up to all of you, though. You don't deserve the way I've done things."

Kyle nodded. "We'll just take it one step at a time. Start with just being around again."

"I can do that."

"Speaking of what's next for you…" Kyle cleared his throat. "About your mom."

"I don't want to talk about it," flew out of my mouth without my instruction to do so. I'd said the phrase a dozen times or more to Nikita over the past couple of weeks as well.

"Fair enough," Kyle said, "but I'm inclined to say as a best friend that you have to deal with it. If you don't, it's going to eat you up."

"I've dealt with it," I shot back. "I'm fine."

He and I both knew that it was a lie.

4
———

NATHAN

"I'm honestly surprised you have this much stuff," Kyle commented as I pulled the box of Cherri's stuff out of the trunk of my car.

"You and me both," I responded.

My mind traveled back to the day after everything came to a head with my dad and Deon. After I finally managed to let Nikita go long enough so that she could go home, change her clothes, and pack some things for an extended stay, I walked around both my house and the main mansion that my parents lived in and slowly started to clean everything up.

To my surprise, I had quite a few of Cherri's things—the spare laptop she kept at my place so that she had something to do homework with when she stayed over, more than one article of her clothing, a large supply of makeup, and even shampoo, conditioner, and soap from my bathroom. With all of that, I shoved the fuzzy blanket I'd bought her for snuggling up on the couch on cold days into the bottom of the box, along with all of the snacks I'd bought that she liked to keep around for days when she was over.

For the fact that she was in love with someone else, and so was I, we'd gotten more than a little comfortable together. I imagine, apart from what happened at the very end of our relationship, there was probably something salvageable as a friendship between us. She'd seen more of the tension between my dad and me than anyone else had, and even when she had no obligation to do so, she stayed by my side when I was going through the worst of it, right before I lost my cool altogether. The thought of Cherri leaving gave me horrible flashbacks of when Deon left. Once again, I'd invested in someone who was just going to leave, and that caused something in me to break that I had not realized was so fragile.

"Nathan?" Kyle's voice snuck into my thoughts and pulled me back to reality. "You okay?"

"Yeah," I replied, shutting my trunk, pulling my backpack over my shoulder, and starting for the front of the school. "I guess I just realized how real things had gotten between us."

"You and Cherri?"

"Yeah. I tried to convince myself that our relationship was just a means to an end, but it must not have been. This is going to be difficult."

"Well, you guys were together for damn near four years. I imagine that if you spend that much time in a relationship with someone, whether the relationship was political or not, you're bound to get attached, even if it's not romantic."

"I really do love Nikita so much," I said. "So much so that I was terrified of her seeing all this shit I had, but..." My voice trailed off. There wasn't a clear and concise thing in my life. Everything was complicated. Nothing was clean-cut or black and white. Every single thing, from my ex to my wayward brother, had all these layers that needed sifting through, and I didn't know how to begin. "I'm tired, Kyle."

Kyle put his hand on my back. "I know, man. Just take it one day at a time. That's all you gotta do. Don't think about too much all at once. Just worry about today."

That was the exact opposite philosophy to what my father had chiseled into my brain for the past eighteen years. Everything had to be a step toward the next thing. I always had to be thinking days, weeks, months, or even years into the future. Just thinking about today made me feel like my brain was being lazy.

"Just get through today," I repeated. Why did something so simple seem so difficult? "Well, can you help me get this stuff to Cherri without Nikita seeing? She doesn't know I have this much stuff."

"Would she really be upset? You guys *did* go out for four years. Is it all that shocking that you would have amassed some stuff?"

"It's not so much about that. Discussing Cherri, even briefly, always ends badly for us. I'd rather not bring it up at all."

"You got it, man," Kyle said. "If I see her, just shove the box at me, and I can bring it over to her."

Part of me wanted to let him do that, but I felt like I owed it to Cherri to face her straight-up. I still hadn't gotten the chance to apologize to her. Hopefully, winter break gave her enough time to cool down. Maybe The Royal Court could start fresh and begin repairing.

"If you see her, just let me know," I said. "If you see Nikita, let me know that faster."

"Uh, oh…" Kyle said before pointing forward. "I see Nikita." We were just passing through the doorway of school, and, sure enough, Nikita was a bit down the hallway, standing with Jaxon and Colette. They had gathered in front of Colette's locker, which also happened to be where mine and Kyle's were. Kyle grabbed the edge of the box. "Here, just give it to me. I'll tell her it's some stuff I have to give back to Avery or something."

"She won't believe you. You and Avery broke up over a year ago, and she's with Alistair now." I sighed. "Besides, I don't want to lie to people anymore. You guys have put up with a lot of shit from me, most of which is a whole lot of lying to your fucking faces. I didn't want to bring Cherri up with Nikita, but if she asks about the box, I'll just tell her the truth and take whatever punishment comes my way. It's the least I can do."

Kyle shrugged. "Okay, man. Suit yourself."

With my fate sealed, Kyle and I continued down the hallway until we had made our way to where Nikita, Jaxon, and Colette were standing. My eyes found Nikita first, and I couldn't help but smile. She grinned back at me, but there was hesitation in her gaze, so I didn't try to initiate any sort of intimacy with her. I gave her a little nod as a greeting. She nodded back, and then my gaze shifted to Colette, and the smile quickly faded. Her hair, which was typically perfectly brushed, was unkempt and curling along the back where split ends were fraying outward. Her eyes were sunken in as if she hadn't slept in weeks, and though she was already an absurdly thin person, she looked borderline emaciated with her collar bone jutting out from her neck and her cheeks slightly sunken. When Kyle said she wasn't doing good, I didn't think it was *that* bad.

It shattered me.

"Hey, Colette," I greeted. "I missed you over the break."

She forced a smile that she was no doubt attempting to make seem bright but only looked pained. "Hi! I missed you too. I have a Christmas present for you! You were the only one who I didn't get a chance to give it to over the break." She reached into her open locker, pulled out a small and perfectly wrapped present, and handed it over. "Open it!"

My hands were full with the box, so I shifted it to balance against my hip while I worked on getting the present open. Nikita tried to pull the box from me, but I clung to it, and she furrowed her brow at me. "Sorry," I said quickly. "I got it."

But the damage was done. Nikita was already picking her way through the box's contents, and I had no choice but to continue with my present from Colette and wait for the impending doom. I pulled off the wrapping paper, lifted the lid of the box, and laughed. Inside was a small porcelain nesting doll. My relationships with the members of The Royal Court were strained on a good day, but until the beginning of this year, we did all have *something* like a friendship. During a conversation with Colette, I'd revealed that I hated the concept of nesting dolls because I didn't understand why anyone would feel the need to fit progressively smaller things into larger replicas. My irritation over the concept was amusing to her, and it became something of an inside joke between us.

"A nesting doll." I leaned forward and gave her as best a hug as I could with my arms full. "Thank you." Pulling back, I rubbed the back of my neck. "Um, I kind of completely ignored Christmas this year, so I don't—"

Colette held up a hand. "Nope. Don't worry about reciprocity. I knew you'd like it, so I got it for you."

I grinned. "Thanks."

"Nathan," Nikita's voice was low in my ear, "what's this box of stuff?"

I might have been hoping for more time before she brought it up, or maybe even that she'd wait and do it the next time we were alone, but public embarrassment was just as good. I looked over at her with a frown. "It's a box of Cherri's stuff that I need to give back to her."

"I was at your place every day for two weeks. I didn't see any of this stuff."

"Yeah..." I took a deep breath. Kyle, Jaxon, and Colette all watched us with evident nervousness. "I packed it all up after you went home to change that first day and hid it in my closet."

"You hid it?" she asked. "Why?"

All I could do was shrug. "I don't know. She's a bit of a rough subject for us, and I didn't want to bring it up."

"So instead, you carted a box of her stuff in here right in front of me?"

"Well, truth told, I was hoping to bump into her before you so that I could just hand it over without needing to talk about it," I admitted, and Nikita crossed her arms. "I now realize it was potentially not the right way to do things."

Before Nikita could say anything else, Colette reached forward and snatched the box from my grip with a strength that belied how weak she looked. "Oh! I'll give it back to her."

"Uh, n-no," I said, trying to pull it back. "That's okay. I really want to do it myself."

"Why?" Nikita asked. "Why do you have to do it yourself?"

"I want to apologize to her," I said.

"You've apologized to her already," Nikita said. "Many times."

That sounded so strange, coming from someone who believed no number of apologies could be enough. "I mean, I've said sorry with a bunch of people standing around, and I more or less said it to say it, but I want to, I don't know, make it clear how sorry I am."

"Like in the past?" Nikita asked.

At first, I wasn't certain what she was talking about, but then I thought about all the times I've apologized to Cherri in the past. I had often orchestrated big, extravagant displays to get her to forgive me and resume our relationship. "Of course not. Cherri and I are done. I just want her to know how sorry I am."

Nikita was looking me up and down like she couldn't decide if she believed me or not, but I didn't get the chance to say anything to convince her otherwise. Our conversation was interrupted by a cacophonous murmur of voices bubbling up from the direction of the door. Everyone around us was stopping, pointing, and whispering to their neighbors with looks of shock on their faces. All five of us turned and looked around the growing commotion, and when we saw the point of shock, all of our jaws collectively dropped.

Cherri was walking through the front door, but it wasn't the Cherri we knew.

The sea of students parted as a nearly unrecognizable person entered the building. Her formerly long hair had been cut short, all the way up to her shoulders, and it was straight apart from a crimp here and there rather than wavy like it once was. On top of that, it was no longer blonde. It was now dark brown at the roots and faded to blond at the tips. Her ears were covered in piercings down the cartilage, and two gold studs were in each of her ear lobes, which seemed to match the gold chain choker she was wearing. She was rocking a black leather jacket that I recognized as being one of Deon's, a pair of dark blue jeans with rips and tears all over them, and a pair of knee-high combat boots. Her makeup palette was much darker than the light, pastel colors in the box I'd brought with me. Black mascara encircled her eyes, and her lips were a deep and dark purple color. She walked in with a scowl on her face and a swagger that I'd never seen Cherri move with before.

She'd morphed into a totally new person.

Jaxon was the first to break the silence amongst us. "Well, someone isn't handling PTSD well."

My hand flew out before I could stop myself, slamming into Jaxon's arm. "Watch your fucking mouth."

Jaxon looked shocked. "What the fuck?"

Nikita's eyes widened, and I knew my reaction didn't improve my position with her at all. "Nikita."

She just looked away from me, back toward Cherri, and I did the same.

Behind Cherri, Sicily walked in, the go-to guy at Postings Proper for all your shady needs and Deon's best friend. I can admit that I didn't expect Deon and Sicily to bond the way they did, but it seemed they found a common enemy in The Royal Court and me. When everything went wrong with Deon, my dad and I made everyone drag Cherri away, even if they had to do it with her kicking and screaming, and the only person she would talk to after that was Sicily. It seemed the two were still spending their time together in the wake of Deon's *death*.

"Cherri!" Colette screeched, and it scared everyone within ten feet of her. She went shoving through the crowd and walked boldly up to where Cherri was standing with Sicily just behind her. "Oh, I missed you! I have a Christmas gift for you, and look." Colette shoved the box toward her. "Here's some of your stuff from you-know-who. I want to know how you're doing with everything. Can we go get dinner after school today? Avery can come too!"

My heart was at a total standstill, and the looks on Kyle's, Nikita's, and Jaxon's faces suggested they felt the same. Colette was standing in front of Cherri with the box outstretched, smiling as if nothing was wrong, but Cherri was staring back like Colette was covered in horseshit.

"I'm going over there," Jaxon huffed, already starting to move, but Nikita grabbed his arm. "What?"

"I know. I know you're worried about her, but she has to do this on her own. Maybe once Cherri shoots her down, she can start to get over it."

I'd rarely seen Jaxon without a cool, collected look on his face, but that statement brought a look of anguish to it. "It's gonna kill her."

"Yeah, but we'll be there to catch her," Nikita said, and we all just looked back at the scene.

"Are you gonna take this box or what, girl?" Colette asked with a cheery tone in her voice. "You have so much stuff!"

Cherri rolled her eyes, and I held my breath as she swung her hand out, uppercutting the box, sending it flying out of Colette's hands. The contents of the box went flying everywhere, and the sound of the box clattering to the ground was the pin dropping in a room of total silence.

I wasn't sure what I expected Colette to do, but when she just sputtered out a laugh and dropped to the ground to start picking things up, it truly sunk in how bad off she was. "You're so clumsy. I'll get it. Jeez, Cherri."

Cherri just shook her head and stepped around Colette to continue down the hallway, and it was Kyle who decided to take the next swing. He stepped out from the rest of us and into Cherri's path. She stopped, looked Kyle up and down with an unimpressed expression, and crossed her arms.

"Cherri, please. We just want to make sure you're okay. We only did what we did because we love you. Please return my calls. We can talk about this."

There was no response from Cherri as she took a few steps forward until she was face to face with Kyle. She stood there, sizing him up despite the fact that he was a good half-foot taller than her, and eventually, Kyle relented and stepped to the side, allowing her to pass. She didn't even look in our direction as she passed the rest of us, but Sicily tossed us a quick, sympathetic gaze as he followed her.

When Cherri was finally out of sight, everyone

looked at poor Colette on the ground, trying to collect all the pieces of the spilled box. Nikita released Jaxon, and he walked out to where she was and knelt down next to her with a hand on her back. She didn't acknowledge his presence at first, but when Jaxon reached out to pick up some of the makeup containers, Colette slammed the box against the ground.

"No! Don't touch anything!" she screeched. "I've got it!" Jaxon recoiled hard, his eyes widening. Then he stood up and slunk back to the rest of us. "I've got it," Colette said, quietly and to herself. "I'm going to fix everything, okay? Everything's gonna be fine."

"Holy shit," Kyle muttered to me.

"Yeah," I whispered as my heart broke even more than it had already. "Things are worse than I thought."

5

NIKITA

Words couldn't quite describe how much I wanted the day to be over already. It was stressful, trying to focus on school on top of everything that was going on with The Royal Court, and Cherri's big reveal certainly wasn't helping things. I'd gotten pretty lucky, if it could be called that, to share all of my morning classes with Colette, so I was able to keep an eye on her, but it was painful to watch. After her frustrating interaction with Cherri, she hadn't said much. She only clung to the box of Cherri's things and stared at whichever teacher was leading the class, though it was obvious she wasn't listening. By the time I sat down across from Jaxon at The Royal Court's typical lunch table, I was exhausted beyond measure.

"Okay, that should be the last one," I said to Jaxon as I sent him the last of the four recordings of my morning lectures while we waited for everyone else to arrive. "You sure she's gonna listen to them?"

Jaxon poked at the fries on his tray while he made sure all the recording would play properly. "No, but maybe I can play them when we're driving to and from school or something. I don't know. I'll get the info into her somehow. Colette is going to snap out of this at some point, and she is going to flip her shit when she realizes how much she was slacking in her academics. It was brilliant to record the classes. I'm sure she'll be grateful."

"I also took pictures of the notes. All things considered, I'm glad the teachers are still operating like Connor and Nathan have control. Otherwise, my phone would have ended up in that little lockbox thingy."

"No kidding. It was nice getting preferential treatment before, but with all this shit, we're really gonna need it," Jaxon replied.

Jaxon definitely wasn't wrong about how much we were going to need that special treatment. There were about five months of school left, and all of us were graduating, apart from Brayden. It wasn't like there was ever a *good* time for all this shit to go down, but there was certainly a worst possible time, and we were in it.

Over the next ten minutes, everyone slowly arrived at the table. Nathan and Kyle arrived at about the same time, both with about the same level of exhaustion on their faces as I felt. Colette, who'd gone right to the bathroom and begged me to leave her alone after their last class, showed up a little after that and immediately sat down next to Jaxon, dropped her head against his shoulder, and was asleep not long after that.

Avery and Alistair were next to arrive, though they came in much later. It was likely because Alistair was damn near pulling Avery to keep her moving while also balancing both of their lunch trays on one arm. He put their trays down before helping Avery to sit down at the bench, and then he sat down next to her and gently rubbed her back.

"Baby, how about some of your salad? Just a little? I have an orange soda you can have if you eat a little," Alistair coaxed under the watchful gaze of everyone, even Colette, who had stirred once they sat down.

Avery's normally exuberant cocoa skin was a few shades paler, and though she didn't look as malnourished as Colette did, she was much thinner than she was before all of this put her under so much stress. She had only managed to pull her hair back into a messy bun, and she wasn't wearing any makeup. Avery didn't really *need* makeup since she was one of those annoyingly natural beauties, but she never left the house without a full face. Still, beautiful though she was, she almost looked sickly without a layer of artistry on. To say I felt bad for her would be an under-statement.

Fortunately, in the wake of Alistair's bargaining, which was so practiced that it made me uncomfort-able, Avery finally lifted her fork and stabbed it into her salad. It was almost as if that was what everyone else needed to see before *they* would start eating. Once she put the first forkful of salad in her mouth, everyone else dug into their plates. It did little to brighten the mood, though. As I ate, I noted that Avery scanned the lunchroom for Cherri every few minutes, only to be distracted in some way or another by Alistair.

"I'm sorry, Avery," he said. "It's just going to make it worse."

Avery ducked her head. "I know. I just miss her."

"You know what, Avery?" Colette started in a much brighter and cheery voice than I expected. "I talked to Cherri today."

Avery's head shot up, and she looked over at Colette. "You did?"

"Uh-huh," Colette confirmed. "I had to give her back some of the stuff that she had left at Nathan's. It may take a little while, but trust me, everything is gonna be fine."

A small smile slid across Avery's face, and Alistair let out a sigh of relief. He was the only one. The rest of us were there for what happened, and we knew the interaction wasn't as optimistic as Colette made it seem. I'd been with Colette all day other than when she went to the bathroom before lunch, and the box of stuff was in the locked classroom where she would have her next class. Unless she was some sort of wizard, I was confident that she had not returned the box to Cherri. Whether Colette was lying to make Avery feel better or whether she was that delusional about how their morning interaction went, I wasn't sure, nor was I sure which one would be worse.

Finally, Brayden arrived at the table, dropping down into a spot across from Nathan with a huff, his tray of food skittering across the table.

"Hey, man," Nathan greeted. "You okay?"

"No," he spat back. "You could have fucking died for how many of my calls you returned over the break. If I hadn't talked to Kyle, who talked to

Nikita, who talked to you, I probably would think that you were dead. That's pretty fucking cold."

"Hey," I started, but Nathan put his hand on mine and shook his head.

"You're right," he replied to Brayden. "That was totally out of line. I was worried about myself and didn't stop to think about how it would make you feel." He looked straight into Brayden's eyes. "Forgive me?"

Brayden looked Nathan up and down and then rolled his eyes. "I guess."

"If it makes you feel better, I missed having you around."

Brayden's eyes skipped back to Nathan's. "Really?"

"Yeah. You're one of my best friends. I missed all of you guys." He reached across the table and gently tapped a fist against Brayden's hand. "It killed me not to be able to host the Christmas party. Remember last year, when you dressed up as Santa. I fucking loved that."

Brayden's expression seemed to lighten at that. "Yeah. That shit was hilarious."

"You kept pulling out that mistletoe and holding it over everyone's head, didn't matter who it was, trying to get a kiss."

Brayden laughed. "It didn't work." Nathan

forced out a laugh to match Brayden's, and the tension in Brayden's shoulders released a little bit. "Anyway, don't do that again. I was worried."

"I'm sorry. I really am. As a matter of fact," he started as he looked down at Kyle, then back at Brayden, "what if we go out to dinner tonight, just the three of us?"

Brayden looked down at Kyle. "Yeah?"

Kyle seemed dog tired, but a warm smile slid across his jaw. "Yeah. I'd like that."

"Yes!" Brayden pumped his fist in the air and then dug into his food, and the table returned to its quiet tension for a while.

"Uh, what was that all about?" Jaxon whispered to me.

I shrugged. "Damned if I know."

As if perfectly timed to make everything worse, murmurs started to fill the lunchroom as Cherri walked in and over to Sicily's table, where he used to sit with Deon. She sat down across from him, not even bothering to go get food, but when Sicily slid some of his over to her, she took it. Jaxon and I were probably the nails in the coffin as we both stared in her direction, and eventually, everyone at the table turned to look as well.

"Whoa," Brayden said. "Is that Cherri?"

"Yeah," Kyle quickly replied, throwing a

nervous glance at Avery.

Avery seemed about as bad off as she could be already. I didn't imagine that anything could make it worse at this point, not even her estranged best friend's apparent culture shock.

"Wow," Avery muttered. "She…" She sniffled in and dropped her head to the table, and Alistair put his hand on her back and rubbed.

"Sicily doesn't seem all that surprised," Alistair added.

"He was with her this morning," Jaxon said. "I guess they're bonding over Deon's death."

Nathan and I quickly side-eyed each other, but fortunately, no one saw the look that passed between us.

"Bonding," Brayden said with a snicker. "Sicily is smart as hell. A woman like *that*, all vulnerable from losing her man. He's the best friend going through it too. I wouldn't be surprised if he hit that within forty-eight hours. If we've learned anything, it's that Cherri doesn't have any trouble moving on quick—"

Nathan was over the table in an instant. He had Brayden by the collar and had dragged him clear out of his seat.

"Nathan," I huffed, but he wasn't listening.

"What the fuck?" Brayden hissed.

"Watch how you talk about her," he growled, his nostrils flaring.

"Fuck," Brayden said. "I'm sorry."

One glance around proved that everyone, Cherri and Sicily included, were watching the interaction, so I grabbed Nathan's jacket and pulled. "Everyone's watching."

That seemed to snap Nathan back to attention. He let go of Brayden and took a few deep breaths. "Shit. I'm sorry, man." He smoothed Brayden's shirt out from where his balled fists had left wrinkles. "It's just that she had every right to tell me to fuck off."

"Fine," Brayden said. He slunk back down into his seat, and to my surprise, he turned, and his eyes locked with mine.

There was a moment of silent understanding that I couldn't quite put my finger on. Maybe it was because I generally didn't understand Brayden, or maybe it was because my ears were still ringing with how angry Nathan got. He swore that he didn't have real feelings for Cherri, but the day so far had proved the contrary. Maybe it was easy for him to say that when she wasn't right there, but with her around again, it was harder for him to hide how he felt about her.

The rest of lunch was a silent, tense mess. Jaxon

and Alistair both respectively took Colette and Avery away as soon as they stopped eating, and after a little bit of time, Nathan got up and left as well, leaving just me, Kyle, and Brayden at the table.

Kyle looked over at us and likely found us both staring down into our food. He pounded his hand on the table. "It's complicated with Cherri. You guys know that. You're not dumb."

Brayden didn't stick around after that. He lifted his tray from the table and left without another word. I looked at Kyle and nodded. "Yeah. I know."

With that, I stood up, headed over to dump my tray, and made my way out of the lunchroom, bound for my next class.

"Look, just name your price." I heard Nathan's voice from down the hallway. I snuck my way along the wall until I could peek around the corner, and I saw Nathan and the vice-principal talking to each other in hushed tones. "It's the first day back, and she's been through a lot. Just look past it."

"Cherri has skipped *every single class* so far," he replied. "It's not going to be cheap."

"Like I said," Nathan replied, "name your price."

"Since it is just the first day, I suppose I can let

her off for five hundred dollars."

My heart dropped. Five hundred dollars to cover Cherri's ass for a few hours seemed a steep price to pay.

"Fine," Nathan said. "I'll have it to you by the end of the day, but if she skips any more classes today, just look the other way. Five hundred at least covers the day."

The vice-principal sighed. "Very well, but if anyone else catches her out of class, I won't be able to cover for her."

"Yeah," Nathan said. I watched as the Vice Principal walked down the hallway in the direction opposite of where I was, but Nathan turned around and recoiled when he saw me staring back at him. "Nikita."

"That's a lot of money," I said.

He walked up to me and attempted to grab my hands, but I pulled away. "Please," he begged, "let me explain."

"You don't have to explain. I can see it very clearly. You *do* have feelings for her." Again, Nathan tried to touch me, but I shoved his hand away. "Don't. Just leave me alone."

I gave Nathan a shake of my head before turning to walk away, just as a tear betrayed me and streaked down my cheek.

6

NATHAN

Unlike the more laid-back place that Kyle had taken me to for breakfast, Brayden dragged us to an upscale restaurant in the middle of downtown Postings. Chandeliers hung from the ceiling, and white tablecloths and crystal ware adorned all the tables. It was fancy from top to bottom, and it was packed with people. Everyone in the restaurant was likely catching an early dinner reservation, and they were all dressed formally. The only reason the maître d' looked the other way at three designer-dressed teenagers was that I quickly flashed him a hundred dollar-bill when we walked in. He knew who my dad was, so although at least fifty people were standing around in the lobby who didn't make reservations and were waiting to be seated, the staff immediately brought us to a table in the back near the windows where we could look out over the cityscape of Postings Proper.

"I've always wanted to try this place," Brayden said. "Thanks for getting us in, Nathan." He smiled brightly at me, and I mustered as much of a smile as I could back at him.

"Yeah, man, of course. It's the least I could do. I mean, jeez, as if I wasn't a shitty enough friend for completely ignoring you all break, you guys didn't get the Christmas party or any gifts. Terrible."

At that, Brayden frowned. "I was sad about the Christmas party, but only because I've grown so used to it. It's not about the gifts. I just wanted to hang out with you."

Brayden was like a puppy I'd neglected to feed, and now I had to look at his baleful, round eyes and emaciated stomach and know that I'd caused that. "Yeah. It's just—"

"Hey, listen," Kyle cut in. "Let's not focus on the past so much, huh? The good news is that we're back, right?" He looked at me and then Brayden. "Right? I told you, once the winter break was over, we'd go back to normal."

A small sigh of relief left Brayden's lips before he spoke. "Yeah, you did. You were right." He looked across at me. "Anyway, I'm glad you're okay and that we're back."

"Me too," I said.

My head was pounding against my skull from how exhausting the day had been, and it would have been my preference to go straight home and try to contact Nikita so that I could explain myself. Still, she needed time to cool down, and I owed it to Brayden to spend time with him after worrying him so much. In truth, I wasn't in much of a position to deny *any* of my friends anything they wanted. If Nikita wanted space from me, she'd get it. If Brayden wanted to drag me to every high-brow restaurant in Maine, he'd get that too. After everything I'd put everyone through, not just in the past six months but in the past four years, they certainly deserved it.

"Remember when Brayden joined?" Kyle asked with a smile. "Nathan hadn't let *anyone* outside our grade join before that."

A bright smile of pride crossed Brayden's face, and I side-eyed Kyle with a thankful grin. "I knew he'd be good for The Royal Court," I added.

It wasn't entirely false. During my junior year, my dad bumped into some health issues and started grilling me on how to run his company just in case he got too sick to work or died. I realized that there was no plan in place to keep The Royal Court going if anything ever happened to me. To an extent, I wanted it to follow me, but I also wanted it to outlive me. I had Kyle as a second in case I was ever out of commission, but I knew we'd be graduating at some point, and someone would need to establish a whole new Royal Court. I'd planned to welcome more juniors and younger into the fold to prepare for a new regime, but after adding Brayden, I realized that I didn't really care about The Royal Court existing past me. It was just about my friends and me. Brayden got to stay, but I stopped pressing the issue after that.

"You reminded me a lot of myself," I continued. "I knew that you were the one I wanted to carry on The Court."

"I'll have to pick all new people," Brayden said. "I've got a few people in mind, but I didn't want to make any decisions until I knew for sure."

It all seemed so trivial now. A year ago, no one could have convinced me that The Royal Court wasn't the most important thing in any of our lives. Now, it was really just a title that held us together, one that I was terrified to let go of lest we all fall apart. If leaning back into the idea of The Royal Court continuing on after we graduated was going to keep it from bursting at the seams, I was more than happy to do that.

"You have my official permission to start recruiting," I said.

His eyes widened. "Really?"

"Yeah. No one's in until next year when this group is gone, but yeah. If you have some thoughts in mind, go for it."

He nodded. "Okay. I will!"

Next to me, Kyle shifted uncomfortably, but I ignored him. I honestly didn't care about any reservations he might have. I just wanted to get through dinner so that I could go home.

"By the way, Nathan," Brayden started again. "I'm sorry about that stuff with Cherri earlier. I thought she was kind of free-game to talk trash about because she broke up with you and left The Royal Court."

Cherri and Brayden didn't like each other. It wasn't a secret or a fact which either of them tried to hide. Somewhere along the way, I noticed how little Cherri tried to vie for my attention, and I started hanging out with Brayden more to make her fight for my attention more, but if anything, she was relieved. Nikita did more complaining about how much time I spent with Brayden than Cherri did. Ultimately, my actions hurt all three of them.

Kyle held out a hand. "Look, it's a complicated situation. Nathan and Cherri—"

"It's not," I cut him off. "It's not a complicated situation. There's nothing complex about what happened. Cherri and I didn't give much of a damn about each other, but we took our roles as the king and queen seriously. If Deon had never shown up, we'd probably still be doing that." No one other than Nikita knew much about my true relationship to Deon, and it seemed like Alistair and Avery didn't tell anyone else that he was my brother. Nikita likely told Jaxon since he was her best friend, but Kyle, Brayden, and Colette, at least, were still in the dark. "I raped her."

Brayden winced. "But you—"

"No. Don't make excuses for me. That's what happened. Do you want to know how I did it? Would that make it more real for you?"

"Nathan," Kyle whispered as my voice got louder.

Brayden shook his head. "No."

"She has every right to be angry with me. She has every right to be angry with *us*. You all know what I did to her. Why are you still my friends?" Neither Kyle nor Brayden responded. "It's not complicated. It's really simple. And what we're not about to do is run around bad-mouthing her behind her back after everything I've already put her through. You both have been in relationships before. Imagine someone you truly love *dying*. Now imagine your friends dragging you away from that or someone else you care about hurting you in such an unforgivable way. We are just a bunch of rich kids who are suddenly not getting everything they want, but this is real for Cherri. Why wouldn't she be angry?"

"I get it," Brayden said.

"Do you?" I barked. "Sometimes, I wonder. You're so spoiled and self-centered and oblivious to what's going on around you. Did you expect her to come pal around with us like she did before? Forgive me and get back together with me after all that?" I couldn't pinpoint why I was getting so angry. Was it because I believed that Brayden was spoiled and inconsiderate, or was it because he reminded me of myself?

"No, I—"

"You need to stop. Everything that's happened to us, all this pain and misfortune, it's *my* fault, and I'm not going to let you make it worse for anyone. This is not just immature relationships in high school gone wrong. This is real shit we're dealing with. Do you get that?"

"I do," Brayden said weakly. "I was... I thought

if I just acted normal, things would go back to normal. That's how we were before."

That notion shot through me like a burning arrow. Right. Brayden was emulating me. He wasn't doing anything that he hadn't seen me do already. It was still my fault.

I took a deep breath to calm myself and looked Brayden directly in the eyes. "Look. I'm sorry. I set a precedent for you that I shouldn't have. It's time for you to start thinking for yourself and not follow my lead because I'm obviously no example of how to be." I sighed. "You're going to be king next year. You gotta start acting like it."

A small smile grew on Brayden's face. "Yeah. I will. I promise. I'm sor—"

"No, don't. Don't apologize to me anymore, okay? I'm sorry."

Brayden nodded. "Okay." It was plain to see that he was near tears, so when he stood up and softly said, "I have to use the bathroom," neither Kyle nor I stopped him.

My heart broke as he went, and I was frustrated with myself for getting so angry. "I can't fucking get it together," I huffed. "It's not his fault that shit went crazy. Why am I yelling at him?"

"We're all just a little stressed out right now," Kyle said. "And I know you don't really want to talk about it, but I think you need to…deal with your mom."

Having him mention it again brought a lump to my throat. "I've dealt with it."

"No, you haven't." He put his hands up. "There's a lot you haven't dealt with. Until you do, you're going to keep having these outbursts and not really knowing what to do with yourself. Besides, do you *really* intend for Brayden to run The Royal Court next year?"

I shrugged. "Why shouldn't he?"

"I'm not answering that. You know the responsibilities involved."

"What responsibilities?" I asked. "The Royal Court is nothing but a bunch of rich kids exercising a power they shouldn't have. In the grand scheme of things, it doesn't mean anything, so if he wants to run it, and if it would make him happy to run it, then I'm gonna let him run it."

"So that's what you're doing? You're Santa now because you made a few mistakes?" Kyle asked.

"You say it like there's something wrong with that. I can't give you guys your lives back. I can't un-blackmail Alistair, and I can't take back having yelled at Brayden just now. I can't undo what I've done, and you guys didn't deserve any of it. What's so wrong with doing a little giving?"

Kyle shook his head. "I don't know how to explain it."

"Then don't," I replied.

"But you—"

"Sorry about that," Brayden said as he returned to the table. "Hey, since I'm gonna be king next year, can I run some of my thoughts for new court members by you guys?"

"Sure," I said, and Kyle nodded along.

"Okay. Here's what I'm thinking. You know that girl that is president of my class? Well, I thought she could be one. Maybe the queen? What do you think, Nathan? She's pretty."

Before I could respond, my phone started ringing in my pocket. I pulled it out right away, thinking it could be Nikita, but what I saw was much weirder.

"Who is it?" Kyle asked. "Nikita?"

"No, he looks disturbed," Brayden said. "Is it Cherri?"

My phone was ringing in my hand, and the screen was blank to let me know someone was calling, but there was no name or number on the screen, just the option to answer or decline the call. It made me immediately nervous, thinking it could be my dad, so I planned to let it ring out, but it kept ringing far beyond the time a normal call would.

"It's an unknown number," I said.

"Are you gonna get it?" Kyle asked.

"I have to," I said. "It won't stop ringing." I fished my wallet out of my pocket, but Kyle caught my arm. "Let me pay for it."

"I got it," Kyle said. "You don't even know how much to leave."

"I'll just leave enough to definitely cover it."

Kyle side-eyed me. "Just go." With my phone still ringing in my hand and me not having the time or energy to argue, I relented, and Kyle smiled over at Brayden. "Besides. I want dessert anyway. Their cheesecake is awesome. I know that's why you brought us here."

Brayden snickered with an eye roll. "Nope." He lifted the dessert menu. "But we should get some, just in case."

Confident that Kyle would smooth over my leaving, I pushed my wallet back into my pocket and left the restaurant. My phone continued to ring the entire time it took me to leave the restaurant and get into my car. Once I was safely inside with my doors closed and locked, I finally answered the call.

"Hello?" I said.

"Hey," a familiar voice replied. "It's me."

7

NATHAN

Even though I had been hoping to hear this voice only a few hours ago, it felt like it'd been months.

"Deon." I was unsure of how he'd managed to call me from an unknown number that just kept ringing until answered, but there were so many other questions swirling around in my brain that I didn't think I'd get to that one. "Hey. Uh, how are you?"

He sputtered out a laugh that gave me a little confidence. "I'm fine, Mom. How are you?"

"Shut up. I can ask how you're doing. Last time I saw you, you were bleeding out," I spat.

"Yeah. Well, that's better now, at least," Deon replied, then let out a deep sigh. "How are you?"

"Don't ask if you don't care."

"You fucking piss me off," Deon responded. "How are you? Fuck!"

Despite my best attempts, I let out a chuckle. "I mean, I'm on my feet. All my family is…gone. I have the Court, but we're falling apart at the seams, so…"

"Oh, yeah? Your little gang can't hold it together, or what?"

Part of me wanted to snap at him, but the other part of me knew I deserved the ridicule. "Turns out, we aren't built for heavy pressure."

"No!" Deon gasped. "I never would have guessed that."

"Did you just call to anger me, or did you have something you wanted to say? Shit, I don't hear from you for two fucking months, and all you've got for me is insults?"

That time, the noise that came out of Deon's mouth was sympathetic, almost apologetic. "Sorry. I'm so used to hating you that it's a hard habit to break."

"Why *do* you hate me?" I asked. "What did I do?"

"Is that a joke?" Deon replied. "Ignoring the fact that you tracked down the woman I was in love with and dated her while I was in prison, the very first thing you did was corner me and threaten me if I didn't join your little club."

I didn't respond right away. With everything that had gone on, I'd nearly forgotten that I did that. Yes, I approached Deon when he first came back and told him to join The Royal Court. There wasn't any specific plan when I asked him to do that. If anything, I was just searching for a way to bring him back into the fold of my life. It crushed me when he left, and even though I had a ton of reasons to be angry, he didn't have any to be angry at me.

That's when it hit me like a ten-ton block of bricks—I'd jumped the gun.

"Can I ask you a question?" I asked after a pause. "If I hadn't done that, then when you saw me next, what would you have done?"

"It's difficult to say," Deon responded. "After I went back to North Postings, Cherri and I used to trash The Royal Court. It was nothing personal, but thanks to our dad, her life got totally uprooted when she first moved to Maine, so she wasn't a big fan of his. I wanted to impress her and didn't tell her we were related, obviously. I didn't want her to hate me. If I'm being totally honest, though…" He went quiet for a few seconds before saying, "I probably would have been happy to see you."

That statement drove through my chest like a poison-tipped dagger. "Really?"

"Well, yeah? I mean, you're my brother, and it wasn't like *you* did anything wrong to me. I was angry with Connor, not you. It would have made me nervous, trying to figure out how to explain to Cherri that I was related to the family she disliked so much." He scoffed. "She certainly found a way to get over that, so it would have been easier than I had thought."

"Wow." I kicked the inside of my car in frustration. "I don't even know what to say to that."

"Then, obviously, once I found out you were *with* Cherri, that would have changed some things, but even then, I thought it was just bad luck and mostly on me because I didn't tell Cherri that we were brothers." He started to laugh. "Fuck, yeah. Now that I think about it, if I hadn't learned all that shit about you going for Cherri just to fuck with me, I would have written that shit off as a coincidence. Might have even been happy for you two if you were really in love or whatever. *Might.*"

"I was so…pissed off that you left. That you just packed up your shit and left, not even thinking about me. I couldn't believe it was *that* easy for you to go."

Deon was quiet again for a little bit. "I mean, it

wasn't, really. I…" He let out a growl. "Fuck. Are we really doing this? This sappy shit. Right now?"

I shrugged, though Deon couldn't see it. "We don't have to. You called me."

Deon let out a loud sigh. "I mean I…loved you or whatever. You're my brother. I always wanted a brother."

"Yeah, me too."

"Of course, when I left, I knew it meant leaving you behind, and I hated that, but I was a kid. I fucking missed my mom. I didn't know Connor from a fucking hole in the wall. I'm used to barely being able to breathe in a tiny house, and suddenly, I have my own fucking *wing*. And all that shit your dad tried to force on me all of a sudden. You mean to tell me that if you had somewhere else to go, you wouldn't have gone there with all the shit your dad put you through?"

"I would have."

"I didn't want to leave *you* necessarily, and I always thought about trying to get back to you at some point. I knew, if nothing else, high school would roll around, and we'd reconnect there, but… Well, obviously, I didn't make it that far."

I bit down on the inside of my lip. He didn't make it that far, thanks to me. "Okay, well, so… Shit. Do we just do the brother thing, then? Not fucking fight about every little goddamn thing and put the past behind us? I made mistakes, you made mistakes, and we have a shared common enemy at this point."

"Yeah, I'd like that, and can that include not *ever* having a heart-to-heart again. I don't like this shit at all."

I laughed. "Fine." Of all the weights scattered about my shoulders, one of them fell off. It was comforting, if even just minorly. "Well. What's up? I imagine you called for a reason."

"Yeah. I expect Nikita and Cherri are still okay? No one has come for them?"

"Not so far. I didn't let Nikita out of my sight for all of winter break, and honestly, I upset her today. I really need to call her and figure some things out."

"What about Cherri?"

"She's, uh…"

"What?" Deon's voice got serious. "What? What's wrong with her?"

"Nothing. She's fine—er, she's healthy. She won't even *talk* to us, but she has been hanging around with Sicily."

I could hear Deon's smile. "I should have known my best friend would look out for her."

To say I was offended would be an understatement. "I'm doing what I can. I paid five hundred bucks to cover her ass today."

"For what?"

"She's changed, Deon. Chopped her hair, dyed it, new leathery, badass, combat boot look. She's skipping classes, getting into fights." To my surprise, Deon started to laugh. "Um," I said. "What's so funny?"

"Nothing, it's just, that sounds more like the Cherri I know."

"Really?"

"Yeah," he responded. "Before you came and got her, she was rough and tough. I was *shocked* when I saw her all prim and proper. Don't get me wrong, Cherri is Cherri, and I love her regardless, but trust me when I say, the version of Cherri you all got, The Royal Court version, that is *not* the real Cherri."

That explained why it seemed to come so naturally to her. She wasn't remade. She had reverted back to her old, pre-Court self. "That's all well and good, but she's a senior. If she skips classes and gets into fights, she'll get expelled. She had colleges eating out of the palm of her hand, and now she may not even graduate."

"So figure it out," Deon said. "You promised me that you'd take care of her."

"And I will, but…" I pinched the bridge of my nose. "She's taking losing you really hard."

"She'll be okay. Cherri's a tough cookie. Trust me, one way or another, she'll come around."

Cherri was strong, but Deon had a hold over her that even he seemed to be underestimating. Honestly, with the way things were, I didn't think there was a damn thing I could do about it either. I sighed. "I don't know. I think it's just going to get worse."

"Once she's finished mourning me, she'll be okay. Cherri's not the type to just roll over," Deon replied. "I'm surprised with Nikita's attitude that this Cherri strikes you so odd."

"Nikita is…" I thought about her beautiful face and the slightly frightening smile she got whenever she was allowed to punch someone or whip out a blade. "She's a high-brow gangster. It's different."

"Oh, Cherri's a hood gangster. That freaks you out?" Deon's voice was defensive and short.

"No, I—" I shook my head. "We're not doing this. Nikita has always been that way. Maybe *you* knew this Cherri, but this is new to me."

"I get it. Just don't let anything happen to her, okay?"

"I won't."

"Good."

"Okay, have you ticked all your boxes? You can tell me why you called now? Did you find dad?" I asked.

"I haven't found him yet, but I've enlisted some help. How much access to Connor's company do you have?"

"All of it. They won't fucking leave me alone." It'd been hours since I checked my email, but I shuddered to think of what awaited me there when I did finally check it. "Why?"

"A guy I was locked up with has some people on the outside who are good at tracking, and I'm told that your dad is probably using money from somewhere. An offshore account, a credit card no one knew about, a non-profit foundation, something."

"I'll look into it. They've been begging me to come in and look at the finances. I'll take the opportunity to see what I can find. Where do I call you when I know? No number showed up on my phone."

"Just wait for me to call again. I'm afraid of being tracked, so I ditched my old one."

I didn't like that very much but understood the practicality of it. "Fine, but can it not be months this time?"

"I'll do my best."

"Thanks." The conversation was nearing its

end, but as odd as it seemed, I didn't want it to. "Um, given you *do* track down our father and get rid of him, what are you gonna do after that?"

Deon sighed. "I'm trying not to think that far ahead."

To try and make my next statement lighter, I forced a laugh. "You could rise from the dead. Come home, marry Cherri, and run the family business with me." Then I laughed some more.

Deon didn't say anything for a long thirty seconds, and then he just said, "Don't say stupid shit," and hung up the phone.

I stared down at the ended call in shock. Was it really so stupid an idea to suggest that he'd just hang up on me? That was how our first conversation in months ends? How our first cordial conversation in *years* ends?

"Wow."

What was I supposed to do next? I had to look into my father's company, but that wouldn't be able to happen until tomorrow or maybe even the weekend. There was also no way of knowing how long it would be before Deon called again. I felt like a sitting duck, and I didn't like it.

Before I could stop myself, I'd navigated to Nikita's number and pressed the button to call her. For as long as I could remember, she was the person I called when I felt lost. She often knew the way forward, and even if she didn't, being around her brought a certain clarity that I couldn't get from any other source. More than any of that, I just wanted to see her. I wanted to kiss her and assure her that she was the only person I loved. Even if she didn't believe me, just saying it would make me feel better.

"It's Nikita." Her voicemail was simple and understated, just like she was.

"Hey, I know you're mad at me, but I just heard from Deon and wanted to hear your voice or see you, or… I don't know. Nikki, I need you to know that I love you more than myself. Even just these past few hours of not being with you have sucked. I want to see you, but I get it if you don't want to see me. Just know that I love you and only you. Okay? I don't feel that way about Cherri. I never did, but taking care of her is just something I have to do. Anyway. I'm done. I'm on my way home from dinner now. I'll see you tomorrow, I guess. I love you so much. Bye."

I turned and was surprised to see Brayden and Kyle's cars still sitting in the restaurant parking lot, but I was ready to go. I finally started up my car and made my way home. It would be the first night of many that I'd spend without Nikita in my bed, and I doubted I'd get much sleep, so on the way home, I stopped for a cup of coffee and planned to spend the night digging into what of my dad's company I could access remotely.

I pulled into the driveway of the smaller but still luxurious house that my parents built for me and gave me when I turned fourteen. At first, I didn't notice the presence of any other vehicles, but then I noticed a familiar black car out of the corner of my eye. At lightning speed, I hopped out of my car and rushed through the front door. I ran into the living room, and Nikita was sitting on the couch, flicking through her phone.

I let out a sigh of relief. "Hi, beautiful."

She looked up at me and smiled. "Hey."

8

———

NIKITA

When Nathan stepped down into the living room, laid on the couch, and put his head in my lap, I didn't stop him. His eyes immediately fluttered closed, and I threaded my fingers into his hair to stroke his head and calm him. Not only had he endured a dinner with Kyle and Brayden after the intensity of the day, he said in his voicemail that he also heard from Deon, and god only knew how that conversation went. If he wanted to talk about any of it, I'd be there to listen, but if he didn't, that was fine too.

Of course, I realized that I shouldn't have jumped up and gone running over to Nathan's the second he called, but for as long as I could remember, I was there when he needed me. Yes, things were a little off between us right now because of how things were with Cherri, but that didn't change that Nathan was going through a lot at the time. I was the one person who understood it the most and could keep him from jumping off the deep end.

"Did you eat at dinner?" I asked.

"I did, I promise. You can ask Kyle and Brayden tomorrow. I had a rib eye with aioli sauce and roasted potatoes."

"Good," I replied. Nathan's eyes flicked open and landed on mine, and my heart leaped up into my throat. The way I felt about Nathan was the kind of love from movies. I was powerless to refuse him. "Are you okay?"

"I'm okay. Dinner was interesting. I may or may not have told Brayden that he can be the king of The Royal Court next year."

My eyes widened before I could stop them. "Wow. I'm surprised Kyle didn't freak out."

"He did. Kind of. I told him that The Royal Court isn't really as important as we make it out to be, and if being the king of this thing I've constructed will make Brayden happy, then I want to give that to him."

One of my hands rested on Nathan's stomach while the other came to rest on his forehead. "Just to make him happy? Why is Brayden's happiness suddenly so important?"

He shook his head. "It's not just his happiness. It's all of you guys. You've all suffered so much, and I just want to make good with you. Whatever any of you want, whatever would help you guys and make things right, that's what I want to do."

"That's ridiculous," I replied. "You're just going to turn into a pushover to make people happy?"

"Not a pushover, but I want to make amends. I can't turn back time, and I can't give you guys back the peace of mind you lost while messing around with my corrupt family and me, so the only other thing I've got is giving you guys whatever you want."

The resonance of his words terrified me down to my core. "Is that what I am?" I slid out from under him. "You know I have feelings for you, so is that what you're doing? Just making amends?"

"What?" Nathan sat up. "No! Nikita, I'm in love with you. I have been for as long as I can remember." He scooted over to me and put his hands on either side of my face. "Nikita, you mean more to me than *anything* in this world. Deon's out there, hunting my dad down because he threatened to hurt you, and nothing matters more to me than making sure you're okay."

I stared as deeply into his eyes as I could, searching for the truth. "How do I know for sure? If you're doing everything in your ability—"

"Nikita Jones." He leaned in and set his lips on mine. There was a strong, encapsulating heat that boiled up around us and wrapped us closer to one another. Before I could stop myself, my arms slid up Nathan's sides and pulled. He pulled away, only enough to speak, and said, "You are the only thing in my life that has meaning. If nothing else happened, if Deon never came back, if my dad ran rampant around this world, if Cherri got herself kicked out of school, none of that would matter to me as long as I had you."

The hard edges around me were softening at an expedient pace. "You don't have feelings for Cherri?"

"I never did," Nathan replied. "She was about getting back at Deon, and now it's about trying, probably never succeeding, but at least *trying* to do right by her after the pain I've caused her. I know what you think, that someone who has done what I've done doesn't deserve redemption, but even if I never fight my way back, doesn't *she* deserve for me to try?"

Tears fell down my cheeks before I could stop them. "I don't want to compete with her."

"You don't have to." He kissed me again. "Honestly, there's no competition. You win by a landslide, Nikki."

He pushed himself against me, and I didn't resist. We fell back against the couch, and the next hour or several faded from my memory. Nathan was like a blizzard. It was best to just weather it. I couldn't see more than a few feet ahead of me, but I was too entombed by the snowfall to care. It just felt good to have Nathan around me, holding me, touching me, kissing me, anything that he wanted. I loved him so much that it was dangerous, not just for me but for everyone around me. So much of my life had been passively waiting for my life to come to me, but now that Nathan was mine, I didn't want to let him go for anything.

"Can I be honest with you about something?" Nathan asked. Our plan after our dalliance on the couch was to end up in bed, but we ended up in the large bowl bathtub in his bathroom instead. "I was really nervous about coming home tonight."

"Nervous?" I asked, loving the feeling of his arms wrapped around me. "Why?"

"Well, you've pretty much been with me every night for the past month. It was going to be the first time that you weren't here with me. That's why I stopped and got coffee. I was planning to just stay up tonight."

I frowned. "That's not good for you. Even if I'm not here, you need to sleep and eat and do normal things."

Nathan squeezed me a little closer to him. "I guess you'll just have to always stay near me to make sure I do it."

"Brat," I grumbled, even as a smile found my face.

It killed me to know that I was with someone who had done something I was so against. What Nathan had done to Cherri was unforgivable. How could I love him and be with him, knowing that she'd probably be permanently scarred from what he did to her? How could I justify not persecuting him when that's what he deserved?

"So," I started, looking to change the subject. "You said Deon contacted you?"

"Oh, yeah," he replied. "He called me from an unknown number, and no matter how long it took me to answer my phone, it just kept ringing and ringing."

"Yeah, that's a common telemarketer's tactic because so many people will just let the call ring out. Debt collectors, too, because missed calls read differently than declined calls, so they want customers to either decline or answer."

Nathan pulled a little water up over my chest, and I breathed in the warm feeling of it washing over me. "Wow. I had no idea. How do you know that?"

"That's how my grandma made her millions," I replied. "Her company buys and sells old debts. Those debts that most companies would write off or ignore, her company buys them out and then goes through the painstaking process of entering into litigation against the debtors. Most people think that's too much work unless the debt is over a certain dollar amount, but she knew it could pay off because if the debtors didn't show up for court or respond to the subpoenas, she could collect all of the debt plus interest, whereas most debt collectors settle."

"Wow," Nathan replied. "I knew she was in finance, but I didn't know it was all of that." He went quiet for a minute. "You know a lot about it."

"She taught me a lot about it. I think, ultimately, her plan was to train me to be in the company, but I don't know. It's too many numbers and stuff for me. It's not my field."

"Do you think she'd sell it to me?"

I twisted my head as far as I could to look back at Nathan. "The company?"

"Yeah. My dad's business is similar, but not in debt collection. I think there's an untapped market there, though. We have the manpower for it, plus we have an entire legal department. You could oversee it, but you wouldn't have to be directly involved."

My heart started to beat so fast that I thought it was going to start blending the bathwater. "I-I don't know. I'll have to talk to her about it."

He must have noticed my hesitation. "Oh, yeah, and I know we have a lot going on right now, so don't worry too much about it. Just thinking about the future. When I brought running the company with me up to Deon, he hung up on me."

"That's rude," I said.

"Yeah, but I guess I can't blame him."

"Why, did you say something nasty to him?"

"Not in particular. We, uh," he chuckled, "we ended up reconciling a bit, I guess."

"Reconciling how?"

"Well, we just sort of talked about everything. About how wrong things went with Cherri, about how I felt when he left and went back to North Postings, and about me approaching him when he first came back to school this year. Things got really messed up and crazy between us, and most of it was my dad." The sigh that left his lips after that was warm. "He did it begrudgingly, but he admitted that he loved me as his brother and said he probably would have tried to patch things up if I hadn't gone in so hard at him when he first showed up, so there's me making even more mistakes."

"You couldn't have known that," I replied.

"Yeah, but I also didn't really have any reason to behave so aggressively. I mean, I'd already done what I thought would hurt him the most." He started to laugh. "Although, he told me he probably would have forgiven me for that, too, and been happy for us if he thought we were into each other." I watched his hands ball into fists on either side of me. "I don't get it. How did he end up being so much better of a person than me?"

"He's not that much better than you."

He laughed. "He is! He's charismatic, and people love him. He's so understanding and calm. When he first came to live with us, people gravitated toward us, and when he left, so did everyone else."

"Kyle didn't," I said. "I didn't."

Nathan's fists relaxed back into hands, which he wrapped around me once again. "No. You've always been by my side. Thank you, Nikki. I don't deserve it."

I wanted to tell him he did, but the truth was, I didn't know if he did or not. There wasn't much I understood for the time being except just how much I loved the guy behind me. Instead of continuing that conversation, I leaned my head back against his shoulder. "I'm getting sleepy."

"Yeah, me too. Should we get out and go to bed?"

I nodded. "Yeah."

Nathan and I slowly worked our way out of the bath and dried off before climbing into his bed. It was more comfortable than any bed should be, even more so when I had Nathan's arms wrapped around me, holding me close. He had dozed off within minutes, and I allowed myself one final night of sleeping with him next to me. As much as I knew I should get up and leave, I was hanging onto Nathan for dear life, and I didn't want to let go. With my brain pretending as if there was nothing standing between Nathan and me, my eyes grew heavier than my heart, and I slowly but surely drifted off to sleep.

9

———

NIKITA

"Jesus," Jaxon said in between large yawns as we walked toward the school. "How has it been a month already? I feel like we were just on winter break yesterday."

"I know what you mean," I replied. "Every single day since that first day back is just one big blur in my mind. I feel like it's still Christmas."

Jaxon stopped in place, and his cheeks puffed up in amusement. "Uh, is that why your man is dressed up like Santa?"

"What?" I followed Jaxon's gaze to where he was staring down the hallway, and sure enough, Nathan was about ten feet down the hall, dressed in red jeans and a red jean jacket with a white fur. Atop his brown hair, he was wearing a red

Christmas hat, cocked slightly to the side, and a pair of sleek, black boots. He had a brown sack slung over his shoulder and was smiling and waving at everyone he passed. "Um, what is happening?"

My relationship with Nathan had been weird, to say the least. We were together in the sense that neither of us could resist the urge to be near one another, but I refused to let us put labels on it. The reality was, the second I let Nathan call me his girl-friend or I called him my boyfriend, I'd officially be dating someone who raped someone who I consid-ered something like a friend, and I simply couldn't reason that away in my head. More than once, I considered trying to let it go, but every time I thought about it, it caused me anguish all over again, and I wasn't even the victim. Ultimately, I was trying to wean myself off of him by spending fewer days at his house and trying to distance myself as much as possible.

But then he would do something like walk toward me with a bright smile on his face, wearing a Santa costume, and all the resolve I had would snap like a toothpick.

"Hey." He leaned in and kissed me. "Merry Christmas!"

I tried and failed a few times to respond to what I was looking at, and when I started laughing, it was

Jaxon who stepped up and said, "Uh, you *do* realize it's February, right?"

"I'm aware," he replied, "but we never got our Christmas together. I mean, Nikki and I were together, and I know different arrangements of all of you guys were together, but we typically celebrate Christmas as a group. So I have presents for everyone, Sicily and Cherri included. Hopefully, they won't break them. We're going to enjoy the big, Royal Court Christmas we missed out on over lunch."

Jaxon and I exchanged confused looks, but Jaxon shrugged and said, "I like free shit."

Nathan grinned widely at that. "That's the spirit."

On top of all the gifts he'd apparently secured, he had The Royal Court's lunch table decked out and decorated with a fancy white tablecloth, a silver lace overlay, and a couple of real candles. Ordinarily, Nathan wouldn't give two shits about flaunting The Royal Court's special treatment around the school, but for this Christmas in February extravaganza, everyone got to benefit. He'd ordered enough food to feed a kingdom and invited everyone to enjoy it as a Christmas gift to him. Quickly, before Cherri made it to lunch, Nathan ran his presents for her and Sicily over to a guy and asked him to present Cherri with hers as a gift from him instead of Nathan, then returned to the table, satisfied that his gifts wouldn't be in vain.

"What did you get them?" Kyle asked.

"I got Sicily a laptop. I know he doesn't have a great one because I see him in the library using the school computers a lot, so I figured he could use it."

Alistair shook his head. "Barely know the guy, and you got him a computer. That's next-level."

"What about Cherri?" Avery asked.

"She used to tell me this story all the time about the house she used to live in. There were wild horses in the forest behind it."

"Yeah," Avery cut in. "There was a white one that she fell in love with and always wanted to tame, but her house wasn't big enough to keep a whole horse. She would feed it, though, and it would always come around. She named it Marshmallow."

Nathan nodded. "Yeah. So I got her a porcelain horse."

I kept my hands, which were balled into fists, under the table so that Nathan couldn't see them and tried to convince myself not to get jealous. Whatever was going on in Nathan's head, he had a reason for it, and I was trying to pull myself back anyway.

It didn't matter.

It didn't matter.

It didn't matter.

Once Brayden finally arrived at the table and everyone had their food, Nathan took his crystal goblet of water and held it up. "Guys, I know this isn't the Christmas party we're used to, but it's the best I could come up with. Every single year, you guys get me such thoughtful and wonderful gifts on top of being my friends, and I want to say thank you for these past years. I know all of your experiences have been different, but they have really been the best years of my life."

"I legitimately do not recognize you right now," Alistair quipped.

"That's fair," Nathan said. "Which is why I'm giving you *your* gift first." He reached into the sack and pulled out a set of old-fashioned vinyl records. "I think you may have one of these, but I got you all of them anyway."

Alistair's jaw dropped. "Art Blakely vinyls." He took them and looked down at them with true shock on his face. He looked over at Avery. "Did you tell him?"

Avery shook her head. "No."

He looked back at Nathan. "I didn't know that you knew I liked him."

"Yeah, well, I noticed you would pick him every time we went to that one diner, so then I added a few to the stereo at home, and whenever he came on, you'd stop what you were doing and bop along. I assumed you must be a pretty big fan, and I know you have a record player, so it made sense."

"Wow, Nathan," Alistair said. "I'm astounded, really. This is one of the most amazing gifts I've ever gotten. Thank you."

Nathan smiled. "You're welcome. I'll just go around the table from here." He reached in and pulled out a hardcover book, then handed it over to Avery. "Avery. Merry Christmas."

Avery reached out and took the book, and a similarly shocked look covered her face. "A hardcover copy of *Invisible Man*."

"Yeah. I can't take *total* credit for this one. Back when Cherri and I..." He side-glanced me quickly and then snickered. "Well, Cherri had been looking for a copy for you for a long time, but they were always in short supply or not with the original cover, so I just had one made." He pointed toward the pages. "I *can* take credit for the pages, though."

"The pages?" Avery flipped to about a sixth of the way through the book and gasped. "Whoa! My favorite pages are laminated!" She showed it to Alistair. "Look, baby. I won't rip them anymore."

She looked back up at Nathan. "How did you know?"

He shrugged. "I've seen you reading those pages multiple times. I didn't know the *exact* section, so I had that whole chapter laminated."

"Thanks, Nathan." She flashed a genuine smile that was rare for her as of late.

Kyle got a new set of rings, specially engraved with important dates like his father's Purple Heart receipt date, his birthday, and his late grandmother's birthday. Colette got a special notebook with an electronic pen that, when written in, would automatically convert all the notes to an electronic form that was automatically backed up to the cloud. It also had a dictation mode for whenever she wanted to dictate speeches or anything else, and it even had a photography mode for when she traveled.

Jaxon's gift shocked everyone because he kept his personal tastes so close to the chest, but Nathan got him an art set with every kind of art supply imaginable. I knew Jaxon was into creating his own art, but he'd always kept that secret. Similar to Alistair and Avery, Jaxon looked at me, convinced I'd given Nathan a hint, but I knew better. Nathan admitted that he'd seen some of the doodles in Jaxon's notebooks and in his car. Among the art supplies was a tattoo gun, and Nathan told Jaxon that he would love to get a tattoo as soon as Jaxon was ready to do it. The design was totally up to Jaxon. Jaxon was blown away, and for the fact that he was unemotional, he sat there looking at the art set like he'd just gotten a new car.

Then Nathan got to Brayden. He looked down at the junior with a furrowed brow. "I'll admit, I struggled with you." Everyone looked at Nathan with trepidation, and Brayden seemed to immediately take offense, but then Nathan laughed. "I wanted to buy you everything in the world. I realized while I was doing this that, out of everyone here, I probably know you the best."

Brayden smiled. "It's because I'm loud."

"No," Nathan said. "It's because no matter how shitty I got, you stayed by me, always. I haven't been fair to you. I always credit Nikki and Kyle with being my best friends, but there have been plenty of times when I looked up, and you were the only one there. I can't repay you for that. Thanks, Brayden."

Brayden recoiled a bit, and his lips pursed like he was fighting away emotions. "Yeah. Of course."

"I struggled. I knew I could have gotten you the clothes you like, or concert tickets, or whatever, but that just didn't feel personal enough for everything you've done for me, so..." With that, Nathan started fiddling with the white diamond watch on his wrist. He unlatched it, slid it off, and handed it over. Brayden took it, and Nathan nodded. "Look on the bottom."

Brayden turned the watch upside down so that he could see the bottom, and then the emotions that he'd been fighting back seeped out. "Wow."

Alistair leaned over Brayden's shoulder and looked down at it. "Let no man fear a true king." He looked up at Nathan. "Is that a quote or something?"

Nathan nodded. "Brayden said that to me not long after he joined."

"That's so sweet that you engraved it with one of his own quotes before giving it to him," Colette said.

Nathan shook his head. "Wrong again. I had that quote engraved there two years ago." Brayden's head shot up again, and he locked eyes with Nathan. "You just said it like a passing thing, but it meant so much to me. I made sure to wear that specific watch every single day. Not because of who gave it to me or because it was expensive but because that quote was on it. Because of you."

I looked up at Nathan, and my heart melted. It was beyond thoughtful. Nathan had found a way to give Brayden the one thing he always worried he'd never get—true friendship.

I smiled up at him, and he winked at me, then looked back at Brayden and smiled.

"Th-thanks," Brayden said before sliding the watch on his own wrist and latching it. He just stared down at it like Nathan had managed to capture a piece of the universe and give it to him, and in the wake of that, everyone looked at their own gifts with smiles on their faces. After a few minutes, Brayden looked back up. "Well, there's only one left. What did you get for Nikita?"

I waved my hand through the air. "Oh, Nathan and I were together for Christmas. He got me a bunch of stuff. Too much, one could argue."

Nathan laughed. "That's true, but I do have a gift for you." He reached down and pushed some of my hair aside. "But if it's okay, I'd rather give it to you in private. After lunch, maybe?"

"Okay," I said, powerless to refuse.

With that, Nathan folded up the sack and tucked into his lunch. "I promise, next year, we'll all spend Christmas together. Although," he smiled over at Avery, "Miss Yale will have to come home and spare us a few minutes of her time."

The smile that *had* been on Avery's face instantly faded, and Nathan immediately picked up on it. He looked over at Alistair, who just shook his head. One by one, everyone's joy faded out. It was the sobering reality of our lives crashing into us again after Nathan's beautiful display, and despite his best attempts, our lunch ended just as dour as all of our lunches for a month had ended.

"I don't know what happened," Nathan said to me while we were walking out of the lunchroom after everyone had gone. "Did I do something wrong?"

My hand was laced into his, and I was choosing to remain blissfully unaware of my ever-present conflict. "No, you were wonderful. Something else is wrong," I said. "You don't think she lost her scholarship, do you?"

Nathan's head dropped. "God, I hope not."

"I'll ask Alistair about it next time I get the chance," I said.

Nathan kissed my cheek. "Thank you. Hey, can I give you your gift now?"

My eyes went wide. "You have a gift for me? I thought you were just saying that."

He scoffed. "No, I'd never tell you I had something for you if I didn't." He fished into his pocket and pulled out a silver chain, on the end of which was a translucent, purple crystal. Inside were dozens of white dots that reminded me of stars. "Merry Christmas."

I grabbed it. "It's beautiful. What are the dots inside? Just decoration?"

"Nope. Those are stars." He took the necklace back from me and laced it around my neck. "The stars depict the sky as it was the night we met."

It knocked me totally off-center. I'd never received such a beautiful gift before. "I love it. Thank you."

Nathan leaned forward and kissed me. "I love you. I know you're…struggling with me. I just want you to know that I *am* trying."

"I know," I replied, "but I—"

I was cut off by the sound of a growing commotion and tons of people rushing toward the courtyard doors. Nathan grabbed someone by the arm as he was racing past. "What's going on?"

"Cherri is about to get into a fight with Stacey Raffe!" he said as he pulled himself from Nathan's grip and continued following the crowd outside.

"Stacey Raffe?" Nathan mused, looking over at me. "Why would she fight Cherri?"

Stacey Raffe was one of Posting Proper's rougher brood, someone who had tried on more than one occasion to get me to ditch The Royal Court and join her self-made gang of troublemakers. Being turned down once made her determined, but being turned down twice made her vengeful. She must have been lying low in Deon's presence as someone who was worth fearing, but with him gone again, she was on the prowl once more.

"No idea," I replied, "but whatever it is, it *cannot* be good."

10

NATHAN

"Oh!"

Nikita and I rushed out to the courtyard just in time to see Cherri take a hard punch to the face. Nikita immediately started to advance as if she was going to jump in, but she stopped short when she noticed Cherri duck another swing and then throw her own punch. Watching the ability in her movements and the power behind her flying fist as it socked Stacey across the cheek, I found myself frozen from shock. Cherri looked right at home in the tussle.

Stacey was no slouch, though, and kept her fists up. She made several attempts to catch Cherri's hair in her fist, which Cherri eventually noticed, and Cherri turned the tables. Stacey ducked under, trying to get a hold, so Cherri weaved backward and caught Stacey's black hair in her hand instead. She whipped Stacey downward, bringing her face to smash against the concrete. The crowd surrounding them cheered as Cherri stepped up and started to stomp down on Stacey's back.

"Cee!" Sicily shouted, stepping out from the crowd and attempting to grab Cherri under her arms to pull her back. "That's enough. She's down."

Cherri ripped from his grip and reached down to flip Stacey onto her back. Cherri stood over her and threw a fist down, slashing it across her jaw. It seemed like Cherri had gotten the upper hand, but then Stacey swept a leg under Cherri, bringing her down to the ground. Sicily backed away, so I excused my way through the crowd. Nikita followed right behind me as I went over to where he was standing.

I set my hand on his shoulder. "Sicily."

He turned around and looked at me, then groaned. "Aw, man. Hey."

"What the hell happened?" I asked.

Sicily's expression darkened. "Stacey saw Cherri with that porcelain horse you got for her and started clowning her about it. Cherri told her to fuck off, so Stacey smacked it out of Cherri's hand, and it shattered."

It was bittersweet, knowing that Cherri liked the gift I got her enough to come to blows over it while knowing I'd caused more issues for her. The crowd rumbled again, and we all looked back over in time to see Cherri slam Stacey's head against the ground below.

"I had no idea that Cherri had that in her," Nikita said. She flicked her wrist, and one of her held blades came sliding out. "Should I stop it?"

"Yikes," Sicily yelped. "That seems like it'll just make things worse." We didn't get the chance to decide. The sea of students parted as the eleventh-grade math teacher, Mr. Pochetti, came running through. "Fuck," Sicily hissed.

Mr. Pochetti grabbed Cherri and pulled her off of Stacey, and the students who were still standing around started to disperse. Stacey's friends collected her off the floor and dragged her away as Sicily ran over to take hold of Cherri.

"That's it!" Mr. Pochetti growled. "You've caused enough trouble. I'm reporting you directly to Principal Hix, and you'll be out of here!" Fortunately for all of us, Mr. Pochetti was one of the teachers who I had directly under my umbrella. Nikita slipped her blade back into its sheath as I walked over and stood in front of Cherri and Sicily. "N-Nathan."

"Don't you dare," Cherri hissed behind me. "I don't need your fucking help!"

I ignored her entirely. "Christopher. Long time, no see."

He crossed his arms. "Save your breath, Loche. I know your dad is MIA. You don't have any power over me anymore."

It'd been a while since I'd used my malicious arrogance, but luckily, it came back like riding a bike. "Who do you think is running LCE while he's gone? Your daughter works there, right?"

He scoffed. "You're barely eighteen. Nice bluff, though."

With that, I pulled out my phone and quickly called the head of the board at my dad's company, putting it on speaker. Arden picked up after a single ring. "Good afternoon, Mr. Loche."

"Hello, Arden," I replied. "Tell me, does Brittany Pochetti still work for us?"

"Yes, sir," he replied. "She's up for a promotion to Senior Marketing Manager this month."

"Really?" I replied, holding eye contact with Mr. Pochetti. "Who makes the final call on that?"

"Well, per your instructions, sir, because it

involves a raise, a final approval would be required by you."

Mr. Pochetti held up his hands in surrender. "Okay," he whispered. "I'll look the other way."

I smiled. "Okay. Keep me posted on that. I want to ensure she gets the package she deserves."

"Of course, sir," Arden replied. "Anything else?"

"Nope. Thank you, Arden."

"Yes, sir. See you at the board meeting," he said, and then the line went dead.

Mr. Pochetti glared at me, but he looked over at Cherri and stabbed out a finger. "I expect more out of you. I don't know what's gotten into you, but I suggest you get it together."

Cherri didn't respond, and with that, Mr. Pochetti sneered at each of us and then stormed away, leaving the four of us alone in the courtyard.

"Hey." A forceful hand grabbed my shoulder as Cherri flipped me around to look at her. "I told you already to mind your own fucking business. I don't need your help."

"You would have been expelled," I replied, trying to keep my voice low and calm. "I'm just trying to do the right thing here, Cherri."

She looked me up and down like I was covered

in garbage. "When have you *ever* tried to do the right thing?"

"Shows how grateful you are," Nikita jumped in. She reached out, took Cherri's hand, and ripped it off of my shoulder. "And don't touch him."

Cherri smirked. "Aw, are you picking up my sloppy seconds? How cute."

Nikita closed in on Cherri, who stood her ground, but I slid between them. "No. We're not doing this." I reached out and grabbed Nikita's hand. "Let's just go."

"Yeah," Cherri huffed over me at Nikita. "Be a good little dog and do what your master says."

"Fuck, Cee," Sicily groaned.

Nikita's hands were balled into fists, so I looked at Cherri, bowed my head, and said, "Sorry."

I pulled Nikita out of the courtyard and back into the school. I tried to wrap my arms around Nikita, but she yanked herself out of my hold, shook her head at me, and then stormed off. "Nik-ki," I called, but it was useless.

For all the effort I'd put into trying to make that day better than some of our most recent, it felt as if it was just another shitty one for the books. To my credit, the other members of The Royal Court seemed at least slightly warmed to me, apart from

Alistair, who watched me like I was a jigsaw puzzle for most of our remaining classes that day. I considered approaching him or texting to ask what it was about, but I didn't need to when he walked up to me as I was getting in my car to leave school at the end of the day.

"Hey," he said.

I smiled. "Hey."

"Uh." A hand went up to push some of his long, light brown hair out of his face. "Can we go somewhere and talk?"

"You want to hang out? Alone?" I asked.

"Yeah." He turned around and started toward his car. "Just follow me."

Alistair was the member of The Royal Court with whom I had the worst relationship, so I was in no position to turn down a request to get together one-on-one. I started my car and waited for him to pull out, then followed after him as he led me to a small cafe on the edge of downtown Postings. The ground was still covered in snow, so street parking was sparse, but we found a couple of spots not far from the front of the place and walked the half-block it took to get there. Alistair didn't say anything as he walked, just looked ahead, and when we got to the door, I rushed up to hold it open for him. He looked at me with the same troubled expression as he walked in, and I followed closely behind.

The inside bolstered my confidence in the Christmas gift I'd gotten him. The place was a half-record store, half-coffee bar, and different old-fashioned record players lined the wall, one with a glass frame for seeing the inner workings spinning old 60s music. Everyone in the cafe turned and looked at me as I entered. The attention was not shocking since I was still dressed like Santa Claus, but enough events had embarrassed me and made my life harder in the past six months that their gazes rolled off my skin like oil on water.

"Uh," I said to Alistair. "I'll buy your coffee. What do you want?"

Surprisingly, Alistair nodded in agreement. "Just a plain black."

I wrinkled up my nose. "Are you fifty?"

He raised an eyebrow at me. "What? I don't get much sleep these days, and I can't afford to dilute any of the precious caffeine with creamer. Is it a problem?"

"No," I said and scuttled off as Alistair grabbed a table.

In solidarity, I also got a plain black coffee and joined Alistair at the spot he picked out. It was only a couple of sips for me before I was dumping in as much of the table's provided sugar as I could, but Alistair drank the mud like it was a soda.

"So, um…" I cleared my throat. "How's it going?"

"Yeah, we're not doing that," Alistair said. "I need your help with Avery."

"Is she still struggling?" I asked. "Alistair, I'm—"

He held up a hand. "Like I said, we're not doing that. I don't want to talk about any of the shit in our past or anything other than if you can help me help Avery."

So much for finding a moment to try and redeem myself. "I'll do whatever I can."

"She's in trouble with Yale," he said. "Her grades are significantly slipping, and they've started to notice. They haven't sent her any revocations yet, but she's getting warning emails. I'm doing everything I can. I'm literally doing her homework *and* mine to try and keep her in a better spot, but I can't do it all by myself. Do you have a connection or something?" He groaned. "I hate that I even have to ask."

"Yeah. My dad's an alumnus. We vacationed last summer with the dean of students."

Alistair's jaw dropped. "Seriously?"

"Yeah. I can absolutely make the call. It won't be an issue."

Alistair let out a sigh of relief. "Thanks, Nathan."

"Yeah." We were silent for a few minutes, and then I decided to take another stab at something more. "So, listen, I know you said you don't want to do this…"

"I don't," Alistair said. "I have enough going on."

"I get it, but please just let me say my piece. Just this once. You don't have to respond. Shit, if you don't want to listen, you don't have to, but just let me say the words in your direction." Alistair didn't respond one way or the other, so I chose to take the fact that he didn't just get up and leave as an acceptance and proceeded. "There's not a person in The Royal Court who I haven't hurt in some form or fashion. Even Nikki and Kyle. I just… I let this whole idea that this construct means something take me so far outside myself that I didn't even know who I was looking at when I looked into a mirror."

"Yeah," Alistair said.

"You and Monty, you guys were those cool neighborhood kids that I always wanted to hang around with, but I could tell you hated me. I honestly thought that if I could get Monty *in* The Royal Court, things would be different. I could prove to him that I was an okay guy, and then maybe you'd come along too."

"Monty wasn't that kind of guy. He was rich, but he was the kind of guy who would have given up all his money to live inside a fucking bus or something."

"Yeah," I replied. "So I learned." I looked down at what was left of my coffee. "It's not an excuse, but when I told my dad that Monty turned me down, he lost it. He said that no one turns down an offer from the Loches and that if he wasn't going to come willingly, I had to make him. My dad terrified me, man. It wasn't…" I stopped. "No, I'm not going to make an excuse. I could have stopped myself. I didn't have to fight with him, and if I hadn't done it, he wouldn't have hit his head. He'd…he'd still be here." I looked back up at Alistair. "I honestly don't think I would have framed you for that, but that was my dad in me again, telling me not to waste an opportunity. There's not much I can give you to make you feel better about me, so let me just say this clearly. If you want to leave The Royal Court, you can. I won't stop you. Nothing will ever come up about Monty, and you'll never hear from me again."

Alistair tapped the table a couple of times before speaking. "I'm not going anywhere."

"You're not?"

"No." I started to smile, but Alistair held up a hand. "It isn't because of you. I'm staying for Avery, and I'm staying for Cherri. I believe she'll come around, and I want to be there to support her when she does. I promised Deon that I'd look out for her, and that's what I intend to do."

"This is going to sound particularly ridiculous coming from me, but just make sure you aren't taking on too much all on your own. If not me, you do have the rest of The Royal Court. They all have your back, even Brayden. And, of course, if you can see it in your heart to forgive me, there isn't a thing I wouldn't do to help you."

A small snicker huffed out of Alistair's nose. "It's weird. The guy you've been this past couple of months"—he looked directly into my eyes—"is a good guy. That's how bad it was with your dad, huh?"

"I don't know exactly where to stand between blaming him and taking responsibility for my actions, but my dad is *not* a normal man."

"I'm sorry about all of that, but I don't think I can forgive you. Not just for Avery, but for what you did to Cherri."

"Yeah," I cut him off. "I don't expect forgiveness for that. Not from any of you."

"Although I can tell that version of you wasn't really you. Even if *we* can never forgive you for that, I think you gotta try to find a way to forgive yourself."

It was me who snickered then, taking a sip of my coffee with a smile. "Yeah, don't hold your breath."

11

NIKITA

I woke up to the sound of my phone notifying me that I'd received a voicemail during the night. The necklace that Nathan had given me shifted as I sat up as if to let me know he had called me.

"Hey, gorgeous," his gruff voice called out. I laid back down on my pillow and closed my eyes with the sound of him in my ear. "I know we had kind of a rough week, but I'd love to see you today if you're not up to anything else. I don't have many plans except to kick around the house and respond to some work emails. I guess I probably should eat something, but I don't really want to. Anyway, just let me know either way. I love you so much. Bye."

My heart ached in the wake of the message.

Just *hearing* Nathan's voice sent chills running over my body, and despite the fact that I was trying to put space between us, my inclination was to get up and go over to him. My arms were already throwing back the covers, and my legs were dragging me out of bed without my brain telling them to do so. I sighed, knowing that as long as I had access to Nathan, getting to a point where I could stay away from him was fairly unlikely. All I could do was repeat to myself that Nathan probably wasn't good for me, but I was still getting dressed, still loading into my car, and still headed to his house as if my body were acting all on its own.

I flipped through the keys on my keyring from memory, found the one that belonged in Nathan's door, and let myself in. There was quiet, relaxing music coming from his living room, so I stepped over the mess of his shoes, jacket, and backpack in the front entryway and made my way down the hall. When I turned the corner, Nathan looked up, and a bright smile crossed his face. He closed his laptop and stood up in an instant, coming over to me, lacing his arms around my waist, and dragging me into a kiss.

There wasn't a shred of me that was powerful enough to stop him.

With no hesitation, my arms slid around his

bare chest and laced around his neck so I could lean even further into him. All the times I had to sit and endure watching Cherri being able to do what I'd wanted so desperately skated across my mind. No longer did I have to hold back when I had access to Nathan, but Cherri was still a large, looming ghost between us. She was gone, but she still stood in our way.

Not that it was her fault at all.

"Hi," Nathan said when he finally pulled back. "I didn't think you'd come."

I chuckled. "I didn't either." His eyes were heavy with bags beneath them, and wrinkles that belied his age were pulling at the corners. "Didn't get much sleep?"

"Is it that obvious?" he asked. "I'm still getting used to not having you here with me."

"It hasn't been that long since we started…" I didn't know what to call our relationship. Dating? Hooking up? What *were* we? "You should be more used to it."

He leaned forward and set his forehead against mine. "What do you want from me? Now that I have you, I don't ever want you far from me."

That was a feeling I understood from my core. "Well, you need some sleep, so now that I'm here, go get some rest."

"It's not the same if you're not right next to me," he replied. "Come to bed with me."

I knew what that meant, and so did Nathan.

"Okay, how about this? You said you haven't eaten, right?" I looked around. "And this place is a mess. If we're going to go upstairs *together*, then you need to do some basic health stuff first."

Nathan frowned. "How did you go from wanting me to get rest to wanting me to clean?"

"Once we're up there, we're not coming down, and you know that, so take your pick."

Nathan bobbled his head back and forth with his nose scrunched up, so I grabbed my jacket and pulled it off. I tossed it over to the couch and then lifted an eyebrow. "I'm wearing a t-shirt, jeans, a bra, and underwear. I will take each one of them off for everything you do. Eating, cleaning, finishing your homework, and responding to work emails. When I'm naked, we go up."

That struck Nathan's attention much more. "Oh, I *do* like that plan."

"Fine," I said with a chuckle. "I'll go make you something to eat while you pick up."

With that, Nathan pulled me against him again, taking another kiss before saying, "I love you," and then he released me and started gathering things from the front hallway.

While he was getting things cleaned up, I walked into the kitchen and was disappointed with the selection of ingredients I found in the fridge. Somehow, I was going to have to inspire him to do more regular grocery shopping, or at least pay someone to do it.

There was, however, a carton containing a few more eggs left from the last time I'd been there, some summer sausage that could be sliced and fried, and some bread for toast. I pulled out everything I needed and got to work. After about ten minutes, Nathan came wandering into the kitchen and grabbed the base of my shirt. Even though I was cooking breakfast for us, his hands snuck under the fabric, and he left hot trails on my skin where his fingers touched. He moved his hands further up until they were at the clasp of my bra. He undid it, and fortunately, it was strapless, so I didn't have to be involved in removing it from my chest. He dropped the bra on the ground and squeezed each of my breasts with both hands.

"I'm cooking," I complained.

"Yeah," he said, pushing himself against me and feathering his lips against my neck briefly, "but I finished cleaning."

He returned to the spot to abuse it a little more, and a moan slipped out before I could stop it.

Nathan snickered, and I could feel him getting excited against me below, so I used my hand that wasn't stirring eggs to whack him on the head.

"Ow! Why?"

"Because I'm handling a pan over an open fire," I said. He frowned, looking like a child who'd just been denied candy. I craned my neck to the side so that I could kiss him, and then I waved him away. "Go do homework and answer emails. I'll be done here in about ten minutes."

"Fine," Nathan grumbled, and as he walked away, he swatted a hand back and whacked my ass before continuing out of the room.

There was a bright smile on my face that took me several minutes to realize was there, and even once I did, I couldn't pull it away. It wasn't my fault that I loved Nathan so much. I just *did*.

I loaded a couple of plates with the eggs, sausage, and toast I'd prepared and carried them into the living room. Nathan was sitting on the sunken couch with his eyes narrowed in concentration. It didn't help my situation that he was so gorgeous. An ass though he was, Connor Loche was a good-looking man, and he'd picked a former model, Alicia, to procreate with. The resulting Nathan had his father's natural jagged jaw and sharp eyes, but he also had his mother's soft, slender face and slim nose. Nathan probably could have been a model if he was interested in the field, but he, of course, wanted to go into his family's business.

Stepping down into the sunken living room, I set the plates of breakfast food down on the coffee table and then looked down at the paper stacked there. Not surprisingly, it was a pile of Nathan's homework, which he'd either started much before I got there, blazed through in the last ten minutes, or a combination of both. On top of being attractive, he was also as close to a genius as I'd ever met.

"All your homework?" I said.

He pointed down at his computer. "I'm working on my final for sociology, but I got distracted by emails."

"How far are you into the emails?"

"Uh. Considering the fact that there's no way I'm going to get through them all today, I'm about three-fourths through what I'm planning to address today. Nothing's burning down."

"Close enough."

I grabbed the base of my shirt, clawed it over my head, and threw it aside, and then unbuttoned my jeans and kicked them off. Nathan looked up, slack-jawed at the sight of me in nothing but my underwear, but I didn't make eye contact. Instead, I grabbed my plate, sat down, and started to eat.

"Uh," Nathan said. "You expect me to eat with you sitting there like that?"

"Yep," I replied, taking a bite of my sausage. "The quicker you eat, the quicker we can…go to sleep."

That was all the motivation Nathan needed. He started clicking away at the keyboard of his computer at an alarming speed. Then he slammed the laptop closed and put it to the side so that he could grab his plate. He was briefly distracted by the food, taking a while to savor the simple breakfast compared to the extravagant meals he used to eat, and then when he finished, he stared at me, waiting for me to finish.

"You're taking long on purpose," he growled.

"No," I replied. "You just scarfed your food down."

He sat bouncing up and down in his spot until I finally took the last bite of my toast. He stood from the couch in a flash, snagged the plate from my hand, and lifted me up and over his shoulder. I giggled as he carried me out of the living room and up the stairs.

"Impatient."

"You can't just sit there in your panties and expect me *not* to be impatient."

He dropped me on the bed and crawled over me, balancing himself up by his arms on either side of me. I curled my hands around his arms and relished in the feeling of his impressive fitness. He ducked his head to me and kissed me as a hand slid up my stomach. The searing heat where he touched me never ceased to amaze me. I'd heard through the grapevine that Cherri thought Nathan was bad in bed, but whatever she was experiencing had not made its way anywhere near me. His lips moved with expert direction away from my mouth and down my neck. He nibbled at my collarbone as he took one of my breasts in his hand, and I squeaked out a moan as he latched over the other to suck.

My hands laced into his hair, and I dug my fingers down in a spot that I knew always drove him wild. He shoved his hips against me, rubbing me with his hard, waiting self, and I responded by driving a hand between us to massage it through the fabric of his sweatpants. In a moment of telepathy passing between us, he leaned away from me exactly as I sat up, and he turned to sit on the bed so that I could drop down onto the floor in front of him. I took the waistband of his pants and pulled them down. I was happy about his choice to go commando on a lazy day at home.

Taking the leaking shaft into my hand, I leaned in and set my tongue to the tip. Nathan shuddered as a huff came out, and I smiled at how instantly he seemed to feel good from my actions. We were two nodes of energy, reacting to one another from just the smallest bit of pressure, growing and growing until we'd forced everything out of our bodies and brains except one another. I closed my mouth over him, and Nathan's hand found the back of my head. He didn't push, never did, but he caressed my head as if to inspire me to do more, which I did.

As if he wasn't perfect enough, he boasted an impressive size, and I wasn't yet able to take it all the way in. Instead, I worked my way as far down as I could and held him there, enveloping him with my tongue until his grunts and groans got louder and shorter. What I couldn't service with my mouth, I wrapped my hand around and twisted and pulled. Whatever sensation I was creating must have been good because Nathan started to very gently thrust into my mouth, and it drove me insane.

Finally, he tapped the back of my head before applying just enough pressure to push me away. I looked up at him, and he shook his head. "Honestly. You keep doing all that, and we aren't going to make it very far." He slid his hand down over my shoulder and hooked under my arm. "Come here."

I stood up, and Nathan scooted himself back on the bed just enough to give me room to straddle him. His thumb flicked along my most sensitive spot as I situated myself over him. He used his other hand to pull the fabric of my underwear aside, then grabbed himself and guided himself to my entrance. Slowly enough to set us both on fire, I lowered myself, closing my eyes and breathing in the feeling of him sliding into me.

"Nathan," I whined out.

Once he was fully seated inside, his hands wrapped around my torso and dragged me as close to him as he could. He buried his face in my chest, and for a moment, we just sat there and existed in deep connection. My fingers curled back into his hair and rubbed, and his hands dug more into my skin. In another moment of reading one another's minds, we both started to move. He thrust himself up and down, stroking the inside of me and making my brain go numb, and I rocked my hips back and forth to further stir myself up.

"Sh-shit," Nathan grunted. "That feels good."

I slid one of my hands out of his hair and down to cup his chin. I tilted his head back to look up at me, and he did the rest of the work, craning his neck up to bring our lips together. His tongue slipped in briefly before I took his bottom lip between my teeth and sucked.

With his impressive strength, he stood up and turned, bringing me to my back on the bed. We stayed twisted into one another, but his pace quickened, causing my soft moans to come out closer to screams. My arms clamped around his back, and my fingers dug in so deeply that I knew there would be marks there later.

Finally, Nathan buried his face near my neck and huffed, "I'm close, Nikki," into my ear.

"Yeah, me too," I hummed back.

He uncurled from me so that he could sit back on his knees. Then his arms circled around my legs, and he started to slam into me. All sound turned to silence, and then my vision blurred. My lips parted as if I wanted to say something, but no noise came out as my entire body started to shake and shudder. Nathan repeatedly drove home on a spot that made my ears ring and brought sweat to my brow, and just when I thought I was coming down, he continued to push in, sending me clamoring over a second time almost immediately.

"Fuck." Nathan dragged himself out of me just in time, stroking himself and painting the base of my stomach with his seed. I lost all energy in an instant and went limp on the bed, and Nathan blanketed himself over me, laying his head on my chest. "God, I needed that so bad, Nikki."

"Yeah, me too." I stoked along his back with my fingertips, something that typically helped him fall asleep right away. His eyes started to drift shut, but he fought to keep them open. "What are you doing? You need to rest."

"I..." His consciousness was fading fast. "You're always gone when I wake up."

My throat tightened. "I'm not going anywhere."

"Still," he said, "I'll stay awake a little longer, just in case."

I didn't press the issue. After the tense week we'd had, I didn't want to leave him any more than he wanted me to leave, but it was better not to say that out loud. Instead, I slowed the stroking of my fingers over his back to help him maintain consciousness if that was what he really wanted.

We laid there in peaceful silence for a while until Nathan finally said, "I'm thinking about making Kyle the king."

"What?" I asked. "Why?"

"He's better suited to it. It's just temporary, not that I really know what that means right now.

There are only a few weeks left of school, and then, I don't know."

It was clear that Nathan truly believed the only reason anyone hung around him was because of The Royal Court. I couldn't blame him for the conclusion he'd come to, but I also knew that if that were the case, everyone would have left immediately after what happened between him and Cherri. If they all hated Nathan, none of them would have stuck around. Whether or not they were willing to admit it, they all cared about Nathan. I was the wispy thin thread that held The Royal Court together. If Nathan had nothing to do with it, it wouldn't exist.

"I think it could be a good idea," I said finally, "but not because you're not suited to it. I think you need to start focusing on yourself a little bit more."

"Kyle said something like that too."

"You know, I really do think you should consider going to see my therapist." It was something I'd brought up to Nathan before, but he always shut the idea down. This time, however, he remained quiet. "She's really good, and she got me through everything after my foster mom stepped down."

Nathan lifted his head and looked at me. "Okay. I'll go."

"Really?"

"Yeah, you're right. I need to work on dealing with myself. I'll hand the reins over to Kyle for the time being, and I'll start seeing a therapist."

My heart soared as the words left his mouth. "I'm really proud of you."

He smiled up at me. "Thanks, Nikki. For always being by my side long after I deserved it."

No words felt right to respond to that, so I settled for setting my lips gently against his. When we parted, his head went back down to my chest, and it wasn't long before I heard him snoring. I rubbed his back in careful circles until the repeating cycle made my eyes heavy as well, and eventually, I faded out.

12

NATHAN

I had counted well over fifty or sixty deep breaths that I'd taken as I sat in my car outside of my father's company. There were so many more reasons than I could count on one hand why I didn't want to go inside, but delaying the inevitable was getting me nowhere.

"It's gonna be okay," Nikita said, and her voice calmed me in an instant. "Whether or not it was right or fair, you gave up your childhood to prepare for this. You're probably gonna be more comfortable in there than you are in the halls of our high school."

I nodded. The tie around my neck felt like it was strangling me, so I hooked my finger in it and loosened it a little, but the feeling didn't subside.

Nikita handed me the briefcase I'd taken from my dad's office and then put her hand on my face.

"You spent all night last night putting your plans together," she said. "You know this business like the back of your hand. You got this."

Only because Nikita was there with me, I felt like I could manage what was coming up. I took my final deep breath, leaned in and kissed her, and then got out of the car. Nikita climbed out the other side, and we both looked at the front of the hundred-floor skyscraper in the center of downtown Postings.

"I don't remember this building being this big," I said. *Loche Corporation Building* was emblazoned on the front in bright gold letters. "I was younger the last time I saw it, but it feels bigger."

"It's because you're nervous, but you'll be fine." Nikita pointed across the bustling downtown street toward a smaller but still imposing, green steel building. "That's where my therapist is. My appointment is in about twenty minutes, and then I'll meet you there after yours."

"Okay." I leaned in and gave her one more kiss, and then with a tap on my back for good luck, Nikita shoved me toward the building, and I walked through the sliding glass doors.

It was a Sunday, so at least the building was

totally empty apart from the few people who came to work while the place was secluded. The entire building belonged to my family, but only the top twenty floors were designated for our specific company, Loche Corporation Enterprises. On top of these floors, the 101st floor was a penthouse office that belonged to my father. He was the only one who could get into the office, and unless he was present, no one could go in or out. I, of course, knew where his keys were, including the electronic fob that would open the elevator on the 101st floor. He often held board meetings in his office since it was the only place that he felt he could be safe and secure with such matters.

I got off the first elevator I had to take, which only went up to floor eighty so that no one could get into the company without passing through reception. All the board members were waiting in the lobby, and several of them glared at me as I approached, but Arden stood up and thrust out his hand.

"Mr. Loche, thank you for finally meeting with us."

I took his hand and shook it. "Of course, but I still think you could have done more without me. As evidenced by the way several of your cohorts are glaring at me," I started, and everyone who was looking at me at the time looked away, "it shouldn't be down to an eighteen-year-old to make your decisions for you."

Arden let out a long, deep sigh. "I assure you that if we had any other choice, we would have taken it. Please, let us get to a private area, and we can discuss this further. I assume you can't get into your father's office, so we can head to a conference room."

Though there was no reason for me to be snarky, I still rolled my eyes as I held up my keys. "I can get in. Let's go."

Another elevator set against the back wall after passing through reception gave LCE employees access to the company-specific floors. We climbed in, I used the electric fob to activate the button for the 101st floor, and then we rode it up. When the doors parted, we started to climb off, but we all froze in place.

Hanging from the windows in the wall directly opposite the elevator was a large banner reading *Congratulations*. My stomach twisted in anger. Even when he was nowhere to be found, my father was playing with me like I was a chess piece, not his son.

"What's this?" Arden asked.

"I don't know," I replied.

I stepped into the room, which had a huge

board table in the center and my father's imposing obsidian desk on the other side between the table and the windows. Only after taking a minute to walk over and rip the banner down off the wall did I go over to the table and take a seat where my father normally sat. Arden walked over to a cabinet and pulled out a handful of placards, then turned and looked at me.

"What?" I asked.

"These are the name cards for all the members of the board," he said.

I shrugged. "Okay?"

"There's one here for you, but I'm getting the sense this will either surprise or alarm you, so I just wanted to bring your attention to it."

"Why would it surprise me?" Arden sifted through the placards, pulled one out, and handed it to me. It had my name chiseled into a gold plate that was sitting in an easel for display. Under my name were the words *Vice President of Loche Corporation Enterprises*. "What is this?"

Arden handed out the rest of the placards, putting two seemingly unused ones on the table, and then took his seat, setting his name up in front of himself, along with a small gavel. "Well, I think that needs to be the first topic of discussion today, but first." He pressed the button on a tape recorder and then folded his hands together. "I'm calling this meeting to order at eleven o'clock." He read the members of the meeting and then said, "Due to extenuating circumstances, no agenda has been presented for today's meeting. We will handle items as needed and vote to approve them per item. All those in favor?" Everyone affirmed, so Arden moved on. "The first order of business to discuss is Loche Corporation Enterprises' current hierarchy."

One of the other board members, a woman with long black hair and dark brown skin named Christine, raised her hand. "I move to approve the first agenda item."

Another, a man with peach skin, a buzz cut, and glasses who was named Portland, raised his hand as well. "Seconded."

"So moved," Arden said. "We'll proceed." He looked across at me. "Sir, your placard indicates that you are a Vice President of LCE because, quite simply, you are."

"When did that happen?" I asked.

"For as long as the company has been incorporated," Christine said. "It's also the reason we haven't voted on or made any major decisions without your approval. Our bylaws clearly state that we aren't allowed to."

I looked at Arden. "Why didn't you just say that?"

"We aren't allowed to do that either," Arden said. "Your father is…neurotic. He wanted it to be a rule that no official business could be discussed over the phone. As it is, we've operated slightly outside of this rule with the things we've discussed already."

That concept made my head hurt. "Still, there has to be a rule in place that allows the board to make decisions in lieu of any officer."

"There is a rule that says we may do it if we cannot get in touch with either the President, Vice President, or CEO for one hundred and twenty days. You kept answering your phone, so…"

"Well, who is the CEO? If there's a rule that you can default to them, why didn't you?" I asked.

Arden exchanged glances with a few of the board members and then looked back at me. "Uh, we don't know who that is at all, or rather, we didn't know until recently." He lifted one of the unused placards from next to him and slid it over to me. I looked down at it, and my heart sank. "Nathan, why is Deon Keane of all people the CEO of your father's company?"

That question posed more than one complication for me. Not only did I now have to decide if I was going to explain our familial relationship to the board of directors, on a recording that would be supplied to the public no less, but I was operating as if Deon was dead. Nikita knew he was alive, and I knew he was alive. That was it.

"Deon Keane," I started quietly, "is my half-brother." The entire board started to murmur to one another. "I had no idea that my father had put any of the company in his name. I'm flabbergasted to see that this is the case."

"Do you know how we can get in touch with him?" Christine asked. "It's too complicated to go into now, but things would be a lot easier if we had access to you both."

I imagined trying to put Deon in front of a board of directors, and it brought a chuckle out of me. "I don't. He, like my father, is missing."

"Brilliant," Portland grumbled.

"Look. I'm here now. I'm the Vice President. What do I have to approve so that you all can function without me here? Isn't there an emergency shareholder vote?"

"Well," Arden said. "Most of the shares are in your and…your brother's names."

Either my father thought he was going to live forever, or he truly believed he'd be successful in whatever master plan he was working on to bring

Deon and me together under his wing. "Okay, just… *Fuck.*"

"Sir," Arden said and pointed at the recorder.

"Sorry. Um, who is next in line that isn't a high schooler?" I asked.

"That'd be Hunter Quixpin, the Chief Financial Officer," Arden replied.

"Fine. Get Hunter in here and do whatever you have to do to put a majority of decision-making in his hands for the time being. Final sign-offs still come through me, but everything else should go through him."

"You have to make a motion," Arden said.

I closed my eyes and took a deep breath to keep from exploding before I opened my eyes again. "I move to give decision-making power with the exception of sign-offs on major financial decisions to Hunter Quixpin until such time that Connor Loche returns or until another officer steps in full-time."

"All in favor," Arden said.

There was some indecision amongst the board members, but eventually, everyone affirmed. After that, a few additional topics were discussed. Finally, after a painful amount of time, the meeting came to a close. I might have preferred to go bolting out of the room before anyone else, but I had to lock up, so I made my way over to my father's desk and woke up his computer. There was no password on it, something my father would never do unless he believed I'd be coming by. I set it with a password, downloaded a remote desktop app that would allow me to access it from home, and then packed my briefcase full of any important paperwork I could find.

Someone cleared their throat, so I looked up and noticed that Christine was still standing in the middle of the room. "Can I help you?" I asked.

"Just a suggestion," she said. "You're a kid. This isn't your world. You should sell your shares to the company, convince your brother to do the same, and leave the company in our hands."

Crossing my arms, I sat back in my chair and narrowed my eyes in Christine's direction. "Has my father done something with the company you don't approve of?"

Christine shook her head. "No. Your father has continuously led this company with vigor, but he's always played his cards close to the chest. It's unheard of for a board of directors to have as little power as we do."

"You're upset that you don't have more power?" I asked.

"No." Christine appeared to be getting flustered. "I just think there's a…warmer way to run the operations here, and none of that is a decision for a child. You'd be appointed to the board as a member as opposed to an officer and would maintain all your voting power."

"Understand this," I said. "There aren't many people in this world who hate my father more than I do, but he knew how to run this company and has made half this city rich doing it. You say I'm a child, but while your children were playing for your local soccer team and going to bake sales, I was studying economics and Latin. You need not worry about me."

Christine's eyes widened. "I see. I apologize for overstepping."

"If Connor isn't found, when I graduate, I'll be stepping into my rightful place. If you have some sort of issue with that, you can step down."

"No, sir. I understand completely." She didn't say anything else, rather bowed her head and immediately left.

That three hours passed was obscene, but fortunately, Nikita had the frame of mind to set my therapy appointment late enough to compensate, just in case. Exactly as she'd said she would be, she was still sitting in the lobby when I walked in, but I didn't even get a word out to her before the receptionist called my name and motioned me back. I left my briefcase with Nikita and followed the receptionist into the recesses of the office, where I was led into a comfortable enough room with couches surrounding a fireplace, a coffee table with finger sandwiches and coffee atop it, and book-shelves lining both walls.

On one of the couches, a woman sat. She was a blonde with her hair pinned up and, surprisingly, sporting a comfortable pair of jeans and a zip-up sweatshirt.

"Good afternoon, Mr. Loche. I'm Nicole Favor," she greeted, standing up and walking over to me with her hand outstretched. "You are dressed much nicer than I am. So you know, I don't require such formalities. Just wear what you're comfortable with in the future."

"Well, I just came from a board of directors meeting at my company," I responded.

She laughed and then noticed the seriousness on my face, and her smile dropped. "Oh, you aren't joking."

"No."

"Well, Nikita has told me a little bit about you. Don't worry, nothing personal, but she told me you're in quite unique circumstances." She motioned to the couch opposite the one she'd been sitting on. "Why don't you have a seat? Help yourself to any of the sandwiches and coffee. I have bottled water if you'd prefer."

"No, the coffee is much needed," I said.

We walked over to the couches, and she sat with a saddened look on her face. "My, you've been forced to the age of about thirty, haven't you?"

I looked over at her. "Um. I suppose."

"Well, I'll start with the disclaimers. You know, everything you say will stay here. Both legally and morally, it has to. Second of all, I know that you know Nikita, but she hasn't told me much about you personally, apart from your relationship. You should feel comfortable discussing yourself as much or as little as you'd like and know that I don't have any pre-existing beliefs about you."

I nodded. "Okay. Thanks."

"Lastly, if, at any point, I come to a subject that is too uncomfortable to discuss, you may tell me to stop. I believe that discussing everything, even the hard parts, is the road to recovery, but you're not under any expectations to do that all in one session with me or even with me at all. I'm here to help, not hurt." She smiled, and it gave me a warm feeling.

"Thank you."

"We'll start simple. Why don't you tell me a little bit about yourself?"

It was a difficult question for me to answer because I didn't talk about myself often. "Um. I don't know. I'm Nathan. I'm eighteen."

"When's your birthday?" she asked.

"October 8th," I replied.

"Did you celebrate this year?"

"Yeah," I said. "Every year, I hold a big party at the end of homecoming week at school. Instead of going to homecoming, I have anti-homecoming. Everyone from my school is invited."

"Wow, that sounds amazing. Did you have a good time?"

The night flashed through my mind in a few quick scenes. My father, furious that I didn't mention that Deon had come back to school. Not being able to find Cherri and seeing her sitting with Deon in the gazebo outside. Getting into a fight with Cherri and then with my father about letting Cherri leave instead of forcing her to stay.

"No," I said. "Normally, it's fine, but this was a tough year."

"How come?"

"My brother…" I stopped.

Nicole held up a hand. "Don't worry if you don't want to talk about it."

"It's okay. It's just one of the first times I've described him that way, so it caught me by surprise."

"You don't normally call him your brother?"

"Well, no. He's my half-brother. We share a father. My dad brought him to live with our family for about a year when we were kids, and then he left suddenly. Right before high school, he went to prison, but he got out this year."

"Were you frightened?"

"No," I said. "More…frustrated. I was dating his ex, so…"

"Ah, that's a tough spot. Did you know they'd dated?"

"Yeah. My dad helped bring her to me, but I wasn't really into her. I was just doing it to get back at my brother."

"Why?"

"For leaving, I guess? I don't know so much anymore. When it was happening, it made so much sense, but now when I think back on it, I feel kind of dumb."

Nicole smiled at me. "That's common. We often make emotional impulse decisions that, when those emotions fade, we regret. I can't tell you the number of times I've done it."

Dating Cherri wasn't the first of those decisions I'd made by any stretch, but I kept that information to myself. "Anyway. She was still crazy about him, so it stirred up a bunch of trouble."

"I'll admit, I have heard just a sliver of this story from Nikita. I can't tell you about what she and I talked about, but she did talk about some of the weird relationship dynamics there."

"Yeah. I was really happy to break up with Cherri and start focusing on Nikita, but things between us have been less than ideal." Despite the fact that Nikita was out in the lobby waiting for me, I knew that she and I weren't good. She still had reservations about me and had every right to have them. I didn't just hurt one person when I attacked Cherri. I hurt two. "She doesn't trust me. At least, I don't think she does."

"Do you think that she should?"

"No," I responded. "I don't think Loches are meant to be trusted. We lie our way through our lives. My father and brother are no exception."

"It's a survival tactic, though it's not one I would recommend. People think lying makes them bad people, but nothing could be further from the truth. Whether you're defending yourself against others or yourself, sometimes lying feels like the only way out."

I took a long drink of my coffee to let that concept marinate. "Yeah."

"Tell me about your parents," Nicole said. "You've brought up your father a few times. Are you close?"

I scoffed. "No. He is the worst kind of person."

"I see. So not close with dad, what about mom?" My throat closed a little bit, and my nose burned. Again, Nicole held up her hand. "I'm sorry. Maybe talking about parents is too sore a subject."

"She's dead. Killed."

"I'm very sorry, Nathan," she said. "For how long?"

"Is it...February?" I asked, and Nicole quickly scribbled a note on her paper. "Three months."

"Oh, it's new. Let's leave that one alone for now, then."

For the next forty-five minutes, Nicole asked me questions that didn't seem specific to me, but they all seemed to lead to discussing deeper subjects. I kept clamming up on things that made me the most uncomfortable, like Cherri, The Royal Court, and my family, but Nicole still seemed to be getting to the grit of who I was. When the clock on her mantle rang, I jumped, not realizing the whole hour had passed.

"Well, Nathan, thank you so much for talking to me today. It may not feel like it to you, but we got a lot of good work done today. I hope you continue therapy, whether with me or someone else. I really think it could be good for you."

"Yeah," I said. "I feel a little better."

She smiled at that. "Good. There is something I have to tell you, though, and I think this could be hard to hear."

"Okay?"

She crossed her legs and set her notebook flat on top of them. "I believe you may be suffering from post-traumatic stress disorder."

13

NATHAN

"This is perfectly normal," I said aloud to myself. "Lots of people use these. It's perfectly normal."

Somehow, I'd left the therapist with prescriptions for not one but two medications, one for PTSD and one for depression. My father used to tell me all the time that taking meds was a sign of weakness, but I had seen my mom taking some on a few occasions. I hadn't managed to make my way back into the main house on our property since I went in there to have my mom cleaned up and carried out, but maybe once I did, I could see if hers matched either of the ones I'd been prescribed.

No, I was not ashamed of the medication I had,

but I was well aware of the associated stereotype. The very last thing I needed was a rumor buzzing around school that I was on meds now, so because I had to collect them on my way to school that morning, I was sitting in my car, taking them without the risk of prying eyes.

I dumped the allotted number of each pill into my hand and then tossed them into my mouth and swallowed them dry. Just as I was about to twist the top back on the second pill bottle, there was a knock on my car window that made me jump so hard that the pills flew out and scattered all over my car.

"Fuck!" I hissed and looked over. Jaxon was standing outside my window, and fortunately, he had his back to the window and hadn't looked in, so I quickly rolled down my window. "What do you want?"

"Jeez," Jaxon said, barely glancing back over his shoulder at me. "Is nice Nathan gone now?"

I cracked my neck and took a deep breath. "No, but you scared the hell out of me."

"I have to talk to you about something. It's important. About Cherri."

The car was covered in the small white pills that would need to be picked up, but Jaxon wasn't one to classify something as important if it wasn't. "Get in the car."

As Jaxon walked around to the other side of my car, I started to collect the spilled pills, but I didn't have them all gathered by the time he was opening the door. He stuck a foot in, then noticed the chaos and stopped. "Uh."

"I'll explain. Just get in. Pick some up on your way."

Jaxon did as I asked, picking up the pills he could get to and then handed them over to me, and after making sure they were free of any hair or debris—I was grateful that I regularly had my car detailed—I dropped the pills back into the bottle and put it and the other bottle in my backpack.

"You're taking meds?" Jaxon asked. "For what?"

"Nikki convinced me to go see her therapist this weekend," I said. "She diagnosed me with depression and PTSD. Now I take pills for them. It's not a big deal."

"You're right. It's not," Jaxon said. "Avery and Colette have been taking antidepressants, and, well, I'm sure you know Nikki takes them for anxiety. So do I. I'm confident Brayden should be taking *something*, but damned if I know what."

"I had no idea," I replied. "I really don't know enough about you guys."

He shrugged. "So you learn stuff. Maybe bring it up. You'd be surprised what being able to relate to someone can do for your closeness."

Given that Jaxon was such an unemotional person, it was shocking how often he had really sound advice. Though I might not have had many attributes to brag about at the moment, I had to admit that I knew how to surround myself with good people. Obviously, it would have been better if I hadn't destroyed my relationships with them all, but if I could fix them, if even a little, we could be a legitimate force to be reckoned with.

"I may do that, but just don't say anything for now."

"It's not my business. I only brought up Avery and Colette because they don't hide that information." He looked over at me with his upper lip hiked. "Do I have to ask if you're okay and have a sentimental talk with you about it?"

"No, god, please don't."

He nodded. "Cool."

"So, what did you learn about Cherri?" I asked, and my pockets were already burning with whatever I'd have to pay to get her out of it.

"It's not about Cherri, directly, but it involves her. It's about Sicily."

I tilted my head. "What about him?"

"A few of my flies have told me that he's looking for Deon," Jaxon said and then side-eyed me. Jaxon was Nikita's best friend, so I automatically assumed that anything I told her made its way back to him, but he was looking at me with genuine shock. "You know, your half-brother who's supposed to be dead."

"Yes, okay? He's alive, but Sicily shouldn't know that unless… Is Deon contacting him?" The last time Deon called me, he seemed shocked to learn that Cherri had been hanging around with Sicily. Maybe that made him curious, but if he *had* called Sicily, he would have sworn him to the same promise of secrecy regarding Cherri that I swore to, wouldn't he have? "Do you know why Sicily is looking for him?"

"Nah, just a few people have overheard him talking about it with Cherri."

"Shit. We gotta find them." I scooped up my backpack and climbed out of my car, and Jaxon got out right after me.

We rushed through the throngs of students clamoring into school to start the day and went down to Sicily's locker. Fortunately, he and Cherri were there, and though I'd seen several interactions with Cherri go badly as of late, I threw caution to the wind and stormed right up to her.

"Cherri," I said.

She turned and looked at me, sniveled at me, and then turned her back to me. Jaxon shrugged and started to walk away, but I walked around her and slid between her and Sicily so that she was facing me.

"What do you want?" she hissed.

"Is it true you're looking for Deon?" I asked.

Her eyes widened. "Yeah, not that it's any of your business."

"Cherri, don't go chasing ghosts. Nothing good can come of it," I said. "I'm sad he's gone, too, but—"

"Are you?" she said. "I couldn't tell. You're just moving on. He's supposed to be your brother, and you haven't even acted sad that he's gone."

"You don't think I'm sad that he's gone? I had a brother one day, and then I fucking didn't. Then he came back, and I had him again. Then I didn't," I said. "You should let this go. He's dead, and you know it."

"What I know," Cherri said, "is that I over-heard you talking to Nikita about it."

I'd been careful never to talk about Deon while

I was in school where Cherri could overhear. Nikita was the only one who knew until Jaxon learned a few minutes prior. There was no way that was true. "I don't know what you thought you heard, but you didn't overhear me talking about anything."

"That day that we all came to get you," she said. "You told me he was dead, and I left, but I forgot my phone. I came back to get it, and I heard you telling Nikita that he was still alive."

My stomach turned inside out. We *had* discussed it after I thought everyone was gone. I should have been more careful. Still, Deon made me promise not to tell her, and after everything we'd been through, I intended to make good on it.

"Cherri, you probably just heard what you wanted to hear. I saw it. I saw my father kill him." Her shoulders fell a little, but I wasn't sure whether or not she believed me. "He's dead." Her hands balled into fists at her side, and I braced myself to be hit, but instead, she just turned around and stomped off down the hallway, shoving kids as she went. I turned and looked at Sicily. "What are you doing? Why are you helping her with this? She's only going to get more hurt."

"I know he's out there," Sicily said. "Deon ain't so weak that some suit and tie was gonna take him out with a gun. Cherri was right about what she heard. You know Deon's alive, and soon, I'm gonna know it too."

"You're going to lead her down a road of pain," I begged.

For the fact that Sicily had tried to remain more neutral between Cherri and me, when I said that, he snarled. "You are the *last* person who can say that to me."

It was like a slap across the face, and he was right, so I didn't respond. When I didn't say anything, Sicily nodded, grabbed his materials from his locker, and then walked off after Cherri. Jaxon tapped me on my back and led me away from the spot, off toward our first class.

When lunch finally came, relief rocked through me. Seeing my friends was the only thing that got me through the day, and though I had scattered classes with each of them throughout, the time to talk was never there. Lunch was the only break I got from the monotony of getting through schoolwork that was way too easy just to get a degree when my position at a Fortune 500 company was already secured.

I munched on my lunch while I waited for everyone to arrive, the last of whom was Brayden since the juniors always got released a little behind the seniors in order to stagger the lunches.

Once everyone was there, and with Nikita rubbing my back to comfort me, I cleared my throat.

"Hey, guys. I'm not gonna take up our entire lunch with a bunch of nonsense, but I have an announcement to make." I looked over at Kyle, nodded, and then addressed the table. "Yesterday, I went to therapy for the first time." I was almost shocked when the words came out of my mouth. It hadn't been my plan to mention it, but it just felt like the right thing to do. "I was diagnosed with PTSD."

"Well, sure," Avery said. "After everything you've been through, that makes sense."

"I'm still working on making it up to you guys, I promise, but I also have to start taking care of myself a little bit more." I took a deep breath. "I'm stepping down. Early, I guess." Across from me, Brayden sat up a little straighter. In an instant, I felt bad, and I probably should have talked to him about it first, but it was too late for that now. "Kyle is going to be our new king."

Kyle nodded and smiled. I'd taken some time on Sunday night to let him know that it was my plan. "Thanks, Nathan. I think it's awesome that you're taking the time you need to help yourself. This is gonna be good for us all in the long run."

"Uh," Brayden said. "So, who's the prince in line now?"

"Well," I said, and Kyle and I exchanged looks. I opened my mouth to continue, but Kyle held up his hand.

"I've asked Nathan to retain the prince in line position," Kyle said. "Just in case he wants to step back in."

Brayden and Kyle stared at one another long enough for me to get borderline uncomfortable, and then Brayden threw me a heartbreaking look of disappointment and stood up from the table. He walked away, and I started to stand to go after him, but Kyle put a hand on my shoulder and pushed me back down and went after him instead.

"Should I have made Brayden king?" I asked. It was mostly a question for Nikita, but it was Alistair, surprisingly, who answered.

"No. Kyle is a good center for us. He'll deal with Brayden. It's fine."

"Yeah. You're working on you now. That's so great," Colette said.

"Thanks, Colette." I waved my hand. "Enough about me. How are you guys?" I looked at Avery. "How's Yale? You should be getting welcome materials, right?"

"Yeah," Avery replied. "I just got my roommate

info for dorms."

Internally, I was relieved. She wouldn't be getting that information if her scholarship was at risk of being revoked. The call I made must have worked. I looked at Alistair, and he gave me a subtle nod. I smiled. "That's so exciting. We're gonna miss you next year."

Avery's expression didn't get any happier, though. "Yeah, me too."

Suddenly, Colette slammed both hands on the table. "Avery!"

Avery looked over at her with her eyes wide. "What?"

"You're still missing Cherri, right?"

"Yeah," Avery said. "She's my best friend."

"I'm gonna get her back for you!" Colette said, standing up. "I'm going to go and talk to her until she listens."

Colette rushed off from the table, and Jaxon was up and off right behind her.

I looked over at Nikita and shook my head. "I can't. I can't watch that again."

"I got it," Nikita said, and she stood up and rushed off after them.

"God," Alistair grumbled. "This fucking sucks."

I slammed my head down on the table. "Tell me about it."

14

NIKITA

"Angel, wait."

When the words left Jaxon's mouth, it tripped me up a little. For as long as I'd known Jaxon, I'd never known him to use any terms of affection, let alone such a cliche one. I wanted to stop and ask about it, but stopping Colette was priority number one.

"I have to talk to Cherri," Colette said. "She needs to hear how hard Avery is taking losing her. If I can just tell her, I'm sure Cherri will come back. I'll tell her she doesn't even have to be the queen if she'll just be friends with Avery again. She'll listen to me. I'll talk to her until she listens. Cherri's a good person."

"Colette, she's changed, or maybe she's back to her old self. I don't know, but I know that Cherri isn't the same person she was when she was in The Royal Court," I explained. "I saw her fight. She's different now."

"No," Colette yelped. "Cherri is Cherri! That she's a little rougher around the edges than we all thought doesn't matter."

Neither Jaxon nor I responded to that. It was a sweet enough sentiment, but it was directed toward someone who had decided to cut off all of her friends from the past four years without a second thought. Sure, The Royal Court was mostly vapid, but what Cherri had with Avery and even what she had with Alistair was deeper than that. Clearly, Colette had found something real with her.

If we could all stick together after everything we'd been through, why couldn't she? None of us were asking her to forgive Nathan, but we didn't kill Deon or create the issues that lived in the Loche family. Why was she blaming us for wanting to see her safe? If I'd been snatched away from Nathan in that situation, it would have made me mad, but I hope I'd have enough discernment to see that my friends were just trying to help.

Colette burst through the door that led out to

the courtyard, a place where Cherri and Sicily were known to hang out during lunch. There were a few other students hanging around, but the second Colette walked out with Jaxon and me behind her, a bunch of them filtered out. Apparently, Cherri and Colette's experience from the first day back after the winter break was still fresh in people's minds, and they were expectant of round two.

"Cherri," Colette said with a whimper as she approached her.

Cherri was sitting on the edge of the fountain in the center of the courtyard and flicking through her phone when Colette called out to her. She looked up, rolled her eyes, and looked right back down at her phone. Sicily was next to her, clicking away at the computer Nathan had gotten him, but he stopped and looked up when Colette approached. Sicily gave her the same exhausted look that Nathan had given me. Whether or not he was willing to admit it, he must be growing tired of seeing the different members of The Royal Court get into it with Cherri.

Colette was not sick of it, apparently. She plopped herself down next to Cherri like they were still best buds. "Whatcha looking at?"

Cherri locked her phone and looked over at Colette. "*What* do you want?"

"Did you know that Avery finally got her full ride to Yale?" she replied. "Aren't you excited for her? She worked so hard for it! I'm sure we'll all take a big trip to visit her. You'll come, right? You're her favorite, and she misses you so much."

"Leave me alone, Colette," Cherri said simply and stood up to walk away.

She didn't get far, though. Colette jumped up and ran into Cherri's path. "Do you remember when we all took that trip to Cabo during our spring break and hung out with all those college students?" Despite the fact that she was forcing a smile, tears were streaming down her face. "You and Avery ditched us for, like, half of the time. Your friendship is so sweet. You miss her, right? You should tell her."

"Colette, if you don't get out of my fucking face, I'm gonna punch you in yours."

Jaxon stepped forward, but Colette threw her hand out. "No! Don't!" she said to him, and then she looked at Cherri. "Do you want to punch me? You should do that! Punch me! Punch me as much as you want until you feel better."

"If I punch you, it's gonna be until your body hits the concrete," Cherri said.

"That's fine!" Colette said. "Hit me until you

knock me out. If I let you, will you talk to Avery again?"

"Colette," I said. "It's not worth it."

"She's going through grief!" Colette yelped. "It's okay, Cherri. I understand. When Deon died—"

That was all she got out of her mouth. I honestly didn't think Cherri would do it, but the second Deon's name left Colette's mouth, Cherri lifted her fist and punched Colette square in the nose. Jaxon got behind her just in time to catch her body as it started toward the ground.

Colette ripped out of his grip. "Jaxon, stop!"

"I'm not gonna stand here while you get your ass kicked!" Jaxon shouted back.

"Then leave!" she screamed.

"Fine!" Jaxon threw his hands up in the air and stormed away without looking back.

Colette walked back up to Cherri and stood in front of her again. "Hit me again."

For a quick moment, I saw the sadness in Cherri's eyes. It flashed there briefly and then disappeared. "Move."

"No! Keep hitting me!" Colette replied. "Deon's dead!"

Again, Cherri socked Colette right in the face. That time, she flew back and collapsed on the floor, a splatter of blood splashing across the concrete.

"Colette, stop it," I said.

She ignored me entirely as she stood up off the ground again and got back in Cherri's face. More and more people left the sad scene behind as each time Colette got back up, Cherri knocked her back down. Eventually, it was just Colette, Cherri, Sicily, and me in the courtyard. On the last of a series of hits, either because she was growing angrier or because she was ready for the interaction to be over, Cherri cocked her fist back as far as she could, and when it slammed into Colette's face, her entire body rigidified, and her eyes rolled into the back of her head. As quickly as I could, I slid behind Colette's body as she fell backward, sending us both toppling to the ground.

Sicily jumped up to grab Cherri's arm and pulled her back. "All right, Cherri. That's enough."

"That's what she wanted," Cherri snapped back. She looked down at me, and all I could do was glare up at her with Colette's limp body collapsed against mine. "Keep her away from me."

"I knew Deon before you," I said. "He'd appreciate that you are tough, but he wouldn't like knowing you're evil."

Cherri pulled back. "What'd you just say?"

"You heard me," I growled back. "He wouldn't accept this."

For a long time, Cherri just looked back at me, but her pupils were shifting in all directions, and I could tell she was considering what I'd said. Finally, though, they settled back into their same steel, and she wrinkled up her nose at me. "Just stay away from me. All of you."

With that, Cherri stepped over Colette and me as we slumped on the floor and walked back into school.

"Jeez," Sicily said, rubbing the back of his head. "What do you need me to do?"

"If you're gonna support her, then nothing," I spat back. "She'll listen to you if you even *try* to talk some sense into her. That's not Cherri, and you know it."

Sicily nodded. "Yeah, I know, but I can't blame her. Can you?" It was clear on Sicily's face that he, either from being insightful or from knowing more than he was letting on, could tell I related to Cherri's plight as much as I was against it. He didn't rush an answer out of me, but when it was clear that I wasn't going to answer him, he nodded. "Yeah. Exactly." He stepped over Colette and me too. "See ya, Nikita."

The bell rang to signify classes restarting as

Sicily walked into the school and out of sight, but I didn't even try to move. Instead, I settled back, repositioning Colette in my arms, and just waited. I'd been in more than my fair share of scraps in my day and knew that she wasn't concussed or suffering from any serious injuries. It was just a matter of waiting until she regained consciousness. Still, both her eyes were totally swollen and already turning black and blue, and her lower lip was also cut and bleeding. I used the edge of my jacket to dab as much of the blood away as I could, but she'd need a formal cleaning up once she came to. She would probably be wearing the battle scars from that fight for several weeks.

After almost an entire class period, Colette shifted in my lap, let out a groan, and then opened her eyes as much as she could with the swelling. It broke my heart how little she could open her eyes, even more so when tears started to slide out of them that I knew weren't from the physical pain.

"Is Cherri still here?" she asked.

"No," I replied. "She left."

"Did she say she'd forgive Avery?" I let out a sigh before I could stop it from coming out, and Colette started to cry a little harder. "I'm not stupid, you know, Nikita? I'm one of the smartest ones in our whole group."

"I know that," I replied. "That's why I don't get it. Why do so much? Why keep giving Cherri the time? Doesn't it upset you how she's acting?"

"She's my friend," Colette replied, "and I want Avery to feel better again. I know that they were closer to each other than they were to me. I even knew that they probably didn't like me a whole lot. I'm vain and kind of stuck up and full of myself, but at the end of the day, you guys are my friends. I'm that way because you guys just accepted me like I was. Cherri did too. I want her to know that, even if this is how she's going to be from now on, I'll accept her, and I know Avery would as well."

"Neither you nor Avery deserves that." My arms were half wrapped around her, so I squeezed a bit in a sort of half-hug. "You're a good person. No one deserves to be treated this way."

"You saw it too," Colette said. "That look in her eyes. She didn't *want* to hit me. Not at first." I had seen that look. It was brief and fleeting, but it was there. "Somewhere between the Cherri we knew and this version of Cherri is the genuine article. I want her to know that we'll be with her while she tries to figure herself out and while she tries to get over Deon. She's angry right now. I can't blame her."

"No offense, Colette, but I did *not* expect you to be the most forgiving and humble out of all of us."

Colette laughed a little, wincing in pain as she did it. "Yeah. That's fair."

"I don't think anything we have to say to Cherri is going to change her right now," I said. "She needs to go on whatever journey she thinks she's on, and then, maybe, once it's all over, there could be a place for us in her life again." I wiped some of the tears from Colette's face. "We're all starting over from square one. I now realize just how much I love all of you guys, and I can't just stand back while she continues to hurt you. Whatever she needs to go through, I get it, but I'm *not* going to let her take out her anger on us. We don't deserve that any more than she deserved what happened to her."

Colette nodded. "Maybe you're right." She smiled a little. "Jaxon was pretty upset, wasn't he?"

"Yeah, he's..." I shook my head. "I've never seen him like this before, Colette. You've got him right where you want him."

She let out a squawk that was either meant to be a giggle or a cheer. I wasn't sure which. "Sooner or later, they *all* come after me."

I laughed. "I love you."

Colette looked up at me. "Really?"

"Yeah," I said.

She squeezed my arms. "I love you too, Nikki. I'm glad we're friends."

"Me too."

Every time I thought the year had brought the last of its surprises, it threw me another curveball. The respect I'd developed for Colette was beyond measure. So too was the despise that I was quickly developing for Cherri.

15

NATHAN

The expensive blue and gold Versace bathing suit seemed so pretentious as I stared down at it. I still remembered when I first purchased it. Kyle, Brayden, and I were out shopping, and I thought it was astounding that a pair of swim trunks could cost damn near six hundred dollars, and then I immediately wanted to flex my wealth by purchasing them. Brayden and I spent a vast majority of that day making fun of Kyle for buying a twenty-dollar pair from Target. Little did we know, he was just sensible.

"What are you doing?" Nikita asked from behind me.

I motioned to the swim trunks. "These look like

the fucking Sistine Chapel or something. I can't wear these to Kyle's house."

"Listen, for as much money as you paid for them, you'd better wear them," Nikita responded. "You can't look more ridiculous than me in jeans and a leather jacket at a spring break party."

Turning around and looking at her on the edge of my bed, I smiled. "You'd look good in anything, but why aren't you swimming?"

"I don't swim."

"Yeah, but *why*?" I asked. "Is it a fear of water or something? It's the one thing about you I've never known."

"Well, it started out as a thing with my dad," she said, and I sat down next to her on the bed and wrapped my arm around her. "We had a pool growing up, and it was one of the places he'd…you know."

"Yeah."

"My foster mom helped me get through that, but I don't know. I never developed an enjoyment for it after that. It's probably residual issues from that experience, but I just don't like swimming. It's not fun for me."

"I get that. Consider me shutting up, then." I kissed her on the cheek. "And because I'm an ass,

I'll wear the expensive, royal swim trunks so that you can at least enjoy that."

Nikita laughed. "Thank you for your consideration."

I swapped my boxers for the swim trunks, then grabbed a pair of equally expensive sunglasses and slid them on as well. I looked back at Nikita. "Okay. You ready to go?"

She nodded. "Yeah, let's go."

It was one of the last few days of the spring break, and Kyle had opted to flex his new position as king to host a pool party and invite all the members of The Royal Court. Colette hadn't been out much since her big confrontation with Cherri, but it had been about a month, so with her injuries mostly healed, she agreed to step out again. Kyle invited us all, telling us not to worry about bringing anything but our suits and selves. Nikita and I seemed to be the last two to arrive if the cars in the parking lot were any indicator, but it didn't bother either of us. We had a little more stability in our relationship since I'd started going to therapy, so we locked hands after getting out of my car and enjoyed a slow walk from the circular driveway in the front of Kyle's house to his enclosed, heated pool house in the back.

Kyle greeted us when we walked in with an enthusiastic, "Hey!"

He was wearing his twenty-dollar Target bathing suit and a tank top, but he wore them with his own pair of Prada sunglasses and had a drink balanced in his hand. The entire pool house had been decorated with different cliche and tacky paraphernalia, and the Olympic-sized pool had been topped with a variety of brightly colored floats, noodles, rings, and blow-up sea creatures.

"Wow, this looks amazing," I said.

Kyle laughed. "Yeah? I wanted it to be as tacky as possible. If it didn't look like a staged photo for a Wal-Mart catalog, I wasn't happy."

"Why?" Nikita asked with a giggle.

"Because I feel like we all spend too much time trying to look fancy and sleek. We all need a good, long break from all of the airs we try to put on." He motioned to the decorations. "Therefore, Wal-Mart catalog."

Nikita nodded. "Got it. I approve."

"Come over here!" he said, turning around and waving for Nikita and me to follow him. "Guys! Come over to the bar!"

Alistair, Avery, Jaxon, Colette, and Brayden got up from their varying spots around the pool and walked over to the curved bar that was situated along the back wall of the pool house. Nikita and I spent a few minutes greeting all of them, and then Kyle walked behind the bar, so the rest of us sat down on the stools.

"Okay," he said with his eyes wide and excited. "I've been working on this with Kaylee all week." Kaylee was Kyle's older sister, and she was a professional bartender at one of Posting Proper's highest-end rooftop bars. "She helped me design drinks for all of you."

He started to pour different liquors and flavored syrups into a tumbler and mixed them together as we all watched, stunned and silent. A playlist of popular music was playing quietly and was a perfect soundtrack to Kyle's mixing. He poured the contents of his first drink into a glass—something light blue and somewhat ethereal-looking—and slid it over to Colette.

Colette took a drink of it, and her eyes lit up. "Oh, wow! It's amazing."

Kyle smiled. "You're bright and mysterious. I told Kaylee that you have a sweet tooth, so there's a little bit of white chocolate in there."

Alistair got a darker drink that looked like a regular brown liquor until he lifted the glass to drink, and I saw shimmering particles swirling throughout it. "It's bitter, like you," Kyle said, and we all laughed. "But I know you're a classic guy, so it's a bitter twist on a tried and true."

"It's awesome," Alistair said.

Avery got a cocktail with aged wine because of how old-school and intelligent she was. Jaxon got something sour because he was sharp, both mentally and physically. Nikita got her widely known favorite drink, an Amaretto Sour, with a black cherry twist and coloring that made it a little darker but a little sweeter.

I got an amalgamation of expensive liquors and flavors. When Kyle slid it to me, he said, "I call this a top-top shelf Long Island iced tea because it's pretentious, but you forgive it because it's good."

The smile that rose to my face was so large that it made my cheeks hurt. "Thanks, man."

After that, Kyle started mixing a drink. It was easily the most complicated of all the drinks he'd put together and required several mixes, liquors, syrups, and a carbonated soda. When he finished, it had a shining gold hue to it. He stuck a straw in it and slid it across the bar to Brayden.

"Uh." Kyle let out an awkward chuckle. "Not to pull a Nathan, but I think I spent the most time putting this one together. It hits your tongue with a little bit of sour, but then it's really sweet going down. When it hits your stomach, it makes you kind of warm all over." He shrugged. "Like you."

Brayden gave Kyle a wide-eyed look first and then looked down at his drink. "Wow."

"Kyle, this is amazing. Thank you," I said.

"Did you make one for yourself?" Avery asked.

Kyle lifted the cocktail he was already working on when Nikita and I arrived. "Yeah. Kaylee made it for me. It's a light liquor with a sour tinge to it because Kaylee says I'm a brat, but after the first sip, you don't wanna stop."

Avery let out a bright, loud laugh. "Oh my god! That's so true!"

"It is!" Colette tacked on. "When I first met you, I was like, who *is* this guy? Then after, like, a week, I was like, where's Kyle? Let's hang out with Kyle."

"It's perfect for you," I said.

"You okay, man?" Alistair asked, looking at Brayden. Brayden was still just staring down at his drink, looking dumbfounded.

"I'm okay," he murmured in response. "Thank you, guys. I feel selfish."

"Why do you say that?" Kyle asked.

"Because I know how hard these last few months have been for all of you, but for me, it's been amazing. I get to spend time with you guys, and I feel like we're friends. I never really thought of myself as being part of this group, more like I was just someone forced on all of you by Nathan." He looked up at Kyle. "I don't know what to say?"

"Don't say anything," Kyle replied. "Just drink."

"I remember when Brayden first came," Colette said.

Jaxon nodded. "Yeah. That was funny."

"What happened?" Brayden asked.

"Well, Nathan was all up in arms about wanting to enlist a bunch of younger members so that The Royal Court could go on after we'd all graduated. A hundred kids must have come to Nathan, all wanting him to bring them in, but when Nathan asked if anyone stuck out to us, at the exact same time, we all said—"

"Brayden," Kyle, Colette, Jaxon, Nikita, Alistair, and Avery all said in unison.

"He was just *so* much like Nathan," Nikita said. "I was like, it *has* to be him."

"Then he started," Avery continued, "and it was like, huh. This kid really changes our dynamic."

Alistair nodded. "Yeah! We didn't really laugh. We didn't really do a *ton* of stuff as a group. Just the Christmas party and Nathan's birthday, but then this little twerp comes along and wants to do everything together, so what do we do? We fucking do everything together."

"Cherri," Avery started, and everyone went quiet. "Cherri could not stand you." She laughed. "But I remember one day, she comes up to me, and she just lets out this exhausted sigh and says, 'Ugh, thank god for Brayden.' It was so confusing to me because she didn't like you, but I guess you'd been there and prevented her and Nathan from getting into a huge fight, and you didn't even mean to."

"Yeah," I said. "I remember that. Vividly. It was right before we broke up at the end of junior year. We'd been fighting more and more. It was mostly because of Ms. Abrams. We were in each other's faces, and tension was rising, and then Brayden just waltzed in the room with Cocoa in his arms. He was elated that he *finally* had a puppy, and he didn't even want to show me. He wanted to show Cherri. It wasn't like we could fight with Cocoa and Brayden sitting on the floor all...cute." I sputtered out a burst of laughter. "The rest of the night was really good."

"Maybe you didn't see it," Kyle said, "but you're one of us."

Kyle and Brayden looked at each other for a little bit, then Brayden got up from his stool. He rushed off toward the door and bolted through it, and a few minutes later, we heard his car starting in the distance and driving away.

"What the heck?" Kyle queried. "Did I do something wrong?"

"No." Colette reached across and put a hand on Kyle's. "This is *wonderful*."

I pulled out my phone and tried to call Brayden to tell him to come back, but he didn't answer his phone. As soon as his voicemail came on, I hung up and called again, but that time, his phone went straight to voicemail. Everyone was looking at me, so I shook my head and said, "Nothing."

"He's been telling me this stuff lately," Kyle said. "He said that he doesn't feel included, so I *really* tried to make him feel like he's one of us."

"I thought you did that really well," Avery said. "I think it may be something else."

"Me too. He's been acting weird lately. I can't explain it. He's just not himself," Alistair said.

It killed me that I hadn't seen it. I made a quiet promise to talk to Brayden the next time I saw him at school.

"You know what I was thinking about? Nathan's always been praised for bringing together the best students of our school for The Royal

Court," Avery said. "I think he just found the other people who are as fucked as he is."

I started to laugh. "You know, that came up in therapy recently. My life was so fucking hard, and I think I could see that all of your lives were hard too. Kyle, you had all that shit with your parents. Nikki had shit going on with her family. Alistair had Monty. Hell, I saw Avery sitting outside all by herself while her parents all fawned over her brothers. Jaxon was a thirteen-year-old who smoked and drank, and Colette was writing novels instead of playing at the playground. I don't think I did it on purpose, but I just sort of gravitated toward you guys. I think, deep down, I knew."

Colette took a sip of her drink. "We're supposed to be elite, but we're really just rich enough to make our problems not look like problems."

Kyle laughed. "Damn. I need to start mixing up another round of these cocktails."

I held out my drink. "To The Royally Fucked-Up Court!"

Everyone held their own drinks up, and we toasted. Kyle cranked up the music, and we got the party going in full swing. It was the first time I had truly let myself go and had a good time without worrying about what people thought. My friends weren't going to judge me, so I was just myself. It was the first time that I could remember being so free and feeling so accepted in my entire life.

"Maybe we're the most screwed up kids that Postings has to offer, but at least we found each other," I said to Kyle as I looked at my friends, who were all laughing and enjoying one another.

"That pairs really well with my cliche decorations," he responded.

I chuckled. "Yeah. It does."

16

NIKITA

Nathan came running into the lunchroom so fast that everyone who had already arrived for lunch for the day stopped eating to stare at him. He didn't even get in the line to go get food. Instead, he ran directly up to our table.

"Has anyone seen him?" he asked. Jaxon, Colette, Alistair, Avery, and I all looked up at him with our own varying sad expressions, and he just sank down into the seat next to me. "Nothing?"

"I went and talked to a bunch of the junior teachers before coming here," Colette said, "but all of them say that he hasn't been in any classes at all. He's not here."

April was well underway, and none of us had seen Brayden since he left Kyle's house during our spring break. It was the Friday of the first week back after the break, and as far as any of us knew, not only had we not seen Brayden, but no one else had either. Wherever he was, he wasn't at school. Nathan had even gone by his house a couple of times, but no one would even answer the door. All attempts to contact him had been fruitless, and we were officially starting to get worried.

Nathan slammed his head down on the table. "This is my fault."

"How?" I asked. "You didn't do anything wrong. None of us did. He was doing fine, and all of a sudden, he wasn't. I really think something else is wrong."

"Kyle's not here yet," Colette said with hopefulness in her voice. "Maybe he knows something more."

"Maybe not," Jaxon said, and at first, Colette seemed frustrated with him, but then he nodded his head in the direction of the entrance. Kyle was trudging into the lunchroom, looking just as dejected as Nathan.

It was a little odd to me that Kyle seemed to take Brayden's sudden and inexplicable absence as hard as he was, but then again, I thought the same thing about Colette. I was beginning to understand that there was a lot more going on behind the scenes with this group than I realized at first.

"Nothing?" Nathan asked as Kyle reached the table.

Kyle shook his head. "Nothing. I've been calling him and texting him. I've asked a few of his other acquaintances. No one has seen him."

"Nathan, have you asked the office if his parents have called in his absences?" Alistair asked. "Maybe he's just sick."

"I checked," Nathan replied. "It's strange. Not only will they not tell me, but even the administrators who I usually exercise some level of control over wouldn't tell me anything."

"That *is* strange," Colette said. "Have you ever experienced that before?"

"Never. Whether through intimidation or bribery, I usually have some kind of sway over them, but none of my tactics seemed to work. I even threatened to let it get out that Principal Hix kept Miss Abrams on staff after she and I had our little thing, but he seemed confident that it wouldn't be an issue. Either that or he was more afraid of someone else."

The table went silent, and I had a feeling that everyone was thinking the same thing I was. The only person in Postings with more power than

Nathan was his father, Connor. Nathan had mentioned that after he saw that Connor had been in the office before the board meeting, he felt like Connor was sticking closer to Postings than he first thought, but what would any of that have to do with Brayden?

"You guys, I'm sorry," Kyle said.

"Wait," Colette said. "*You're* blaming yourself now?"

"I agree," Alistair said. "The whole self-blame thing is getting really old."

"Yeah, especially when I don't think anyone is to blame here," Avery said. "There's an outside factor at play here, and none of us know what it is. All we can do is be patient and hope that everything works itself out. We should also probably employ some sort of buddy system. No one is alone, ever."

As if we all sensed it telepathically, our eyes drifted over to Kyle, who just rolled his eyes. It was unspoken. By default or by whatever bond the two had developed as of late, Brayden *was* Kyle's partner in the eight of us. Nathan and I nor Colette and Jaxon were official couples, but we all understood the dynamic.

"I like groups better," Alistair said, recovering Avery's dropped ball. "Three other friends as much as you can, but at least one other person if nothing else. Doesn't matter who."

"Yeah," Kyle said. "Thanks." He looked across the table at Jaxon. "I want you to do some digging, though. I've been trying not to rely too much on our old roles, but we don't have any better options. Look for anything suspicious at all. Just find him."

Jaxon nodded in agreement and immediately left the table, despite our previously decided rule to stay in pairs, not that Jaxon needed backup.

"Good luck," Kyle said after him, sounding broken, and I wondered if he and I were close enough that I could ask about it.

"Hey," I said, tucking that thought away for the time being. "Can I do some hunting too?"

Kyle raised his eyebrows. "Sure. I know you're not his number one fan, though."

"Things have changed with us." I caught Colette's gaze. "All of us. Besides, if it really is that he just didn't feel like he was one of us, we all had a part to play in that. I'm not blaming myself or anyone, though. I just want to do my part in bringing him home."

"Yeah, I get it," Kyle said. "Do what you think is best."

I nodded. "Thanks."

Lunch was a silent, tense affair, and all the

conversations that Colette or Alistair attempted to start fell on mostly deaf ears. We'd provide a one-word answer here or there, but it was evident that the healing wound Cherri's leaving the group had made ripped wide open again when Brayden went missing.

Eventually, everyone wandered away. Kyle, Nathan, and Colette left as a group, and after I'd assured Alistair and Avery that I'd be okay, they left together. With them all gone, I got up and went out to the courtyard. As expected, Cherri and Sicily were there. I had no interest in getting much closer to Cherri, but I was interested in helping to assure that my friends didn't suffer any more losses. Sicily often saw what other people didn't, and I was hopeful that he might have seen Brayden off on his own or talking to someone suspicious and could point me in the right direction. He was a tracker, through and through, and if he had even an inkling of a lead, it'd be better than the nothing we had.

With a deep breath to keep calm, I walked up to where they were sitting. I was sure to approach on Sicily's side and made sure to only look at him, but it didn't stop Cherri from looking up at me with a scowl and growling, "What do *you* want?"

My gut reaction had me locking eyes with her,

but then I turned my attention to Sicily. "Hey. Can I talk to you? I need a favor."

Cherri stood up. "You have a lot of nerve, coming over here at all."

"I don't want to start up with you," I replied. "I didn't come over here for you. You asked me to leave you alone, and I am." Then I turned to Sicily. "A moment, please?"

Sicily stood up, preparing to come with me, but Cherri grabbed his arm and shoved him back down into his spot. "What the fuck, Cherri?" Sicily barked.

"They've got more than enough money and power to get whatever they need. They were perfectly fine to *punk* you at the beginning of the year, or don't you remember that?" She glared at me. "See yourself off."

It'd been a while since I'd been in a fight of any kind, and I was really trying to exercise patience with Cherri. I really was trying, but she was starting to piss me off so much my skin was buzzing. "And what if I don't?"

"Cherri." Sicily stood up and slid between us. "I can do what I want. Just because you have a problem with 'em doesn't mean I do. Just stay here. I'll be back." He turned around and looked at me. "Hey, c'mon. It's not worth it. Let's go chat."

"Sicily, move," Cherri hissed. "I don't want you to get hit."

With that, I started to laugh. "Ah, you're cute. You think a few months of being big and bad makes me afraid of you? I've fought demons that would make you piss your pants."

"Oh, sure, your fake bad-girl. You've lived in South Postings all your life," Cherri said. "You always ran around with that unearned sense of toughness." She started to crack her knuckles. "I've been waiting for a chance to show you that you aren't all that bad."

Sicily said something to us, but I couldn't hear it. "You think you can beat me, Cherri?"

"Believe me. I've wanted to fuck your face up more than once. I certainly know how to do it."

"Run along, little girl," I replied. "You're gonna get yourself hurt."

No other words passed between us. Cherri shoved Sicily aside and threw a punch right at my face, and I ducked my head to the side. Her fist passed by me, and I threw my fist up into her gut. She crumpled around my arm with a heave and dropped to the ground. Staring down at her where she lay on the ground, I cracked my fists and twisted my head to loosen my neck, just in case she got up again.

I knew I should have walked away. It wouldn't have been difficult to find a different time to talk to Sicily or even take him with me and let Cherri calm down on her own, but my anger was exploding past its limit. I tried to do the right thing. I tried to leave her alone and just talk to Sicily, but she insisted on starting something with me, and once she did, everything came flowing out all at once. Her relationship with Nathan, his possible feelings for her, the way she'd beat Colette black and blue, the grudge she was holding against The Royal Court—it all bubbled up and had me reeling my leg back and kicking my black boot hard into Cherri's side. She fell even further back, sputtering out blood as she went.

"What's wrong, Cherri? I thought you were tough?" I laughed. "You were gonna fuck up my face, remember?" I rubbed my hands over my skin. "Funny. It doesn't *feel* fucked up. Did you forget all that stuff you just said?"

"Stop it, you two," Sicily said, looking around. "You're attracting a crowd." He put a hand on my shoulder. "Just walk away." I glared first at Sicily's hand on my shoulder and then up at him, and he pulled his hand back. "Come on. This is dumb."

Cherri rolled over and brought herself to stand

up. She balled her hands into fists, posed in my direction, and stepped forward.

"Cherri," Sicily whined.

"Come on, *your highness*," I said. "Show me all this badassery you've been hiding."

Cherri started toward me with her hands up, and I didn't even raise my fists. I believed Cherri when she said there was a dark side to her that no one had seen until now. Colette had said that somewhere between the delinquent she'd been the past few months and the prissy queen she was in The Royal Court was the real Cherri. That was a concept that I received and promoted. I *hoped* that Cherri figured out who she truly was and would one day feel comfortable enough to show the world that person. If she thought she'd been through enough to handle me, though, she was going to have to learn the hard way that she was wrong.

Cherri threw a fake punch with her left hand and then a real one with her right. It was a good move, and if I were someone less knowledgeable, it would have been good enough. I caught her right arm at the wrist and dragged her toward me before slamming my head against hers in a painful headbutt. It hurt me, but it sent her stumbling backward, and a stream of blood immediately slid down her forehead.

She charged at me after that, ducking and trying to get me around the waist. The jeers from the students who had gathered around us grew louder with her charge. She did, to her credit, get circled around me, but she didn't have nearly enough strength to topple me over. I dug my feet into the concrete to maintain my stance, but then she got her first lick in. She threw her head upward, slamming into my chin, rattling my teeth.

I wedged my arm between us and shoved her back, punching her as she went. A majority of the students in the school had gathered around us by that point, and my stomach turned in frustration as I saw The Royal Court shoving their way through. Nathan was leading the pack. I didn't want them to see me fighting Cherri after everything we'd been through, so I tried to back off and hold my hands up, but Cherri took advantage of the moment and cut a punch right across my nose.

"Fuck!" I barked.

Cherri tried to back away after socking me, but I got my hand out to take hold of her shirt in just enough time. I pulled her closer to me and used my dominant hand to punch her once, twice, three times in the face, letting her go on the last so she'd fall back and down to the ground.

"Nikita, stop it!" Avery yelped.

"She fucking started it!" I screamed, shocked that Avery would defend Cherri over me. "I tried to stop, and she sucker punched me!"

Cherri's entire left eye was swelling to the point that she could barely hold it open, but that didn't stop her from getting to her feet and trying to come at me again. I cocked my shoulder back, prepared to keep fighting, but Nathan shoved out of the fray and stood between us.

"Stop!" he yelled at Cherri. He looked over at me. "Stop it." But Cherri continued to push. Nathan tried to batten down and keep her from getting to me, but when she tried to shove him aside, I got so angry that I charged toward her. "Nikki, stop!" Nathan begged.

"All right! That's enough!"

Multiple teachers came through the sea of students, some of them working to disperse the crowd while others ran in and worked together to restrain Cherri and me. The school's safety officer rushed over to me. He wrestled me into a full nelson and dragged me backward. Jaxon jumped out from the crowd and ran over to me.

"Let her go!" he bellowed.

"Nathan." Principal Hix stepped out to where he was standing between Cherri and me. "Shit! I feel like all I hear lately is all the trouble you and your little group are getting into."

"I'm sorry," Nathan said immediately. "It's done."

"No, I'm sorry, kid, but I can't just keep looking the other way." He looked at Cherri and then over at me. "One of them is coming with me. I don't care if it's who started it or who was losing. Someone has to get slammed for this. I'd lose my license. Who's it gonna be?"

That Nathan didn't immediately defend me was painful enough on its own, but then he started to exchange looks between Cherri and me. His eyes finally locked with mine, and I knew what was coming before the words even left his mouth.

He turned away from me just as he said, "Nikita wouldn't let it go."

My jaw dropped. Next to me, in the crowd, Colette whispered, "Nathan, no…"

"Fuck," Jaxon whispered.

Principal Hix looked over at me. "Fine. Nikita, my office. Now."

The SRO released his hold on me, and Jaxon quickly flinched in his direction before wrapping an arm behind my back and leading me through the onlooking students, including all of my friends, and down to Principal Hix's office.

"It would have been easier to suspend Cherri with all the problems she's been causing," Principal Hix said as he walked into his office about thirty minutes later. He sat down at his desk and pinched the bridge of his nose between his fingers. "I'll be happy when you kids fucking graduate. This has been the worst four years of my entire career."

"You're not the only one," I grumbled back.

He turned and faced me. "Look, Nikita. I know your reputation around here. I also know that you're either really good at hiding it or rich enough to pay off my staff. Either way, you don't have a blemish on your record, and with your grades and how close it is to graduation, I'd be insane to suspend you."

I let out a sigh of relief. "Thank you."

"What's her deal? Cherri? Weren't you all friends at one point?" he asked.

"Yeah," I responded. "Turns out, she doesn't know the meaning of the word."

"This can't go without some consequence, though, you understand. This isn't just *a* warning. It's your *last* warning. You don't get three. You get this one. I can't have you out there, beating someone's face off."

"I tried to stop," I replied.

"Well, try harder next time," he said and then

waved his hand. "Go, get out of my office, and don't say I never did anything for you."

"Thanks, Hix." So as not to waste the second chance I'd been given or let my misery-induced nausea get the best of me in the principal's, I stood and left the office as quickly as my feet would carry me.

The entire Royal Court, apart from Brayden, was waiting outside the office, Nathan included. Even though I wanted to hold a grudge for the fact that Avery seemed to take Cherri's side, the fact that she jumped up and rushed over to hug me was apology enough, so I accepted it. I wasn't about to repeat the cycle.

"Are you okay?" Kyle asked.

"I'm fine." I rubbed my chin. "She didn't get many hits in."

"I'll say," Alistair said. "From where I was standing, you were whooping her ass."

It might have given me pride if I didn't feel so empty inside.

"Nikki." The Royal Court stood aside, and Nathan was standing there, staring back at me. "I can explain."

Jaxon walked over and stood between Nathan and me, facing me. "Are you listening to him?"

I looked over Jaxon's shoulder at Nathan, biting

the inside of my cheek to hold back the lump of emotions gathering in my throat. "No. I'm not."

Nathan took a step forward. "Nikki, please."

In a swift movement, Jaxon whipped out his switchblade and flipped it in Nathan's direction. No one in The Royal Court even jumped at the movement, and Alistair quietly grumbled, "Same."

Jaxon braced a hand on my back and motioned me forward, and I passed Nathan by with Jaxon keeping him at bay. I didn't even look in his direction. Once I was far enough ahead, Jaxon followed after me, and we stayed side-by-side as we walked out of the school. I managed to keep my cool until we were standing next to my car, but then, everything clamored over all at once.

I collapsed against Jaxon's chest, sobbing harder than I had since I was a child, and Jaxon held me close and rubbed my back. It felt like someone was physically chiseling pieces of my heart away.

"I can't believe it," I whimpered. "I can't believe he chose her."

17

NATHAN

If I were the Hulk, the pounding on my door would have turned me green and brought out the worst of my muscles. Hell, if I wasn't only a pasty eighteen-year-old with relatively good fitness, if not enough to take anyone or anything out, I might try to fight whoever was on the other side of my door. Instead, I laid in bed with my eyes closed and thanked any god that was listening for locks on bedroom doors.

"Nathan!" Kyle's voice called through the closed door. "Come on, man. I know you haven't eaten in two days."

"I had pop tarts yesterday!" I shouted back.

"That's not enough. Get up. I'm taking you to breakfast."

"No, that's okay," I replied. "I'd rather just lay here in self-loathing if it's all the same to you."

"That's not an option." He pounded again. "Get up!"

I sat up straight, anger bubbling through me. "Stop hitting my door!"

As opposed to listening, Kyle opted to start slamming his fist against my door in a continuous stream without ceasing. He alternated between his fist and an open hand smacking against the door, and eventually, it was enough to drag me out of bed. I stormed over to the door, unlocked it, and threw it open, leering at Kyle.

"Well, good morning, sunshine," Kyle said.

If he wasn't my best friend and the only thing holding our group together, I would have punched him. "Go away."

"No," he said, pushing his way into my room. "Get dressed. We're going to breakfast."

"I don't want to."

"It wasn't a request." He walked into my walk-in closet and started opening and closing the drawers. "Can I be honest with you about something? I really hate your wardrobe. You aren't this douchey."

I threw myself down on my bed in protest. "I'm pretty douchey."

"You're not." Drawers opened and closed a few more times, and then Kyle walked back into the room with some folded clothes in his hand. "You do smell, though." He held out the clothes with one hand and used the other to usher me toward the bathroom. "Please, do us *all* a favor and clean up. Then we'll go get delicious breakfast food at a hole-in-the-wall in North Postings."

"We're gonna go to Gerald's?" I asked.

"If you hurry. He's only open until eleven," Kyle said. That was enough to get me up. The endearingly caring man I'd met back when school first resumed was topped only by how delicious his food was. "I also have someone else meeting us there, so please, get going."

"Who?" I asked.

"I will tell you if you take a shower." Then he looked me straight in the eyes. "Seriously. You're offensive."

I snatched my clothes from him. "No one told you to storm your way in here." I much preferred Nikita's kind, gentle way of coaxing me into taking care of myself, but she hadn't spoken to me since I saw her at school on Friday. "Just wait downstairs," I said as I entered the bathroom and shut the door behind me.

As annoyed as I was that Kyle had burst his way

into my room, I was glad for the shower. It was definitely needed. I moved fast, but I made sure to spend a little extra time really scrubbing myself. I'd come home Friday night and quickly fell into a slump that didn't end until Kyle arrived early that Sunday morning. When I was done, I got dressed in the outfit he picked out, an understated but effective set of navy slacks and a long-sleeved light blue t-shirt. I grabbed a pair of light blue Vans and made my way downstairs.

"See?" Kyle asked, holding his hands out to me. "You look *much* better like that. Less is better."

"Sure," I said.

After a short drive to North Postings, we parked in front of the small restaurant and climbed out. The snow had mostly melted from the winter, and though the grass was still brown and muddy, I could tell in the height of spring, the place had a great view on top of the amazing food. Gerald wasn't outside with his friends, so we walked into the restaurant, and to my surprise, Jaxon was already sitting at one of the tables.

"Hey," I said as I walked up.

Jaxon glanced up at me and then looked at Kyle. "You didn't tell me you were bringing him."

"Yeah," Kyle said as he loaded into the table on

the other side of Jaxon. "Because you wouldn't have come if I did."

"You're right," he said. "I've spent the last forty-eight hours consoling my heartbroken best friend." He glared up at me. "So, yeah, if I'd know he was coming, I would have skipped."

"Exactly." Kyle slapped the chair next to him, and I sat down at it. "We're gonna talk it all out. It's gonna be fine."

"There's not much to talk about," Jaxon said.

"Jaxon, I swear to god, I do *not* have feelings for Cherri," I said. "Cherri's just been in so much trouble already. Nikita has a clean record. I knew Hix would let her off with a warning, and I was right!"

Jaxon was looking at me as if none of my words were getting through. "You've done a lot of supporting Cherri and not very much supporting Nikki."

That hurt to hear. He wasn't wrong. My main reasoning for everything that I'd done was ultimately for Nikita, but I couldn't blame her for the way it looked from her perspective. "I didn't know what else to do." My stomach sunk as I imagined the answer to the next question, but I forced myself to do it anyway. "Did I mess everything up?"

"You might have," he snapped back.

"Jaxon, have you ever had the food here? It's amazing!" Kyle said, and we both looked at him like he was insane. He looked up at us and rolled his eyes. "Fine. Fuck me for trying to break the tension."

"Sorry," both Jaxon and I grumbled out.

"What do I do?" I asked Jaxon.

"I wouldn't ask me," he replied. "I'd tell you to stay the fuck away from her. You've hurt her enough."

He was right. I shouldn't have asked him. Nikita was my whole world. I couldn't just give up on her that quickly.

"Let's change the subject for now," Kyle said, looking across at Jaxon. "Have you had any luck tracking down Brayden?"

That seemed to disturb Jaxon more than I was expecting. "No."

Kyle deflated. "Nothing?"

"Well, I didn't find him, but I did find *something* interesting. I think we're being watched."

I looked up at him. "What?"

"Couple of guys I've been seeing around. I saw them for the first time over spring break. Nikki, Avery, Alistair, and I went out to lunch, and there were some guys in the next booth over, watching us really closely. I thought maybe they just thought

Nikki and Avery were hot since they are, so that made sense. I was prepared to beat the shit out of them if they even tried it, but they never did. Not long after they noticed me watching them back, they paid and left. I figured I scared 'em off. I didn't think anything else of it, but then Friday after school, I saw them right outside the school grounds. Same two guys."

"What did they look like?" Kyle asked.

"One of 'em was a typical bodyguard type guy. You know, tall, built, the whole thing. He was wearing a zip-up hoodie and jeans, but it barely fit on him. The other guy was smaller, but he was still pretty tall. Similar clothes. The bodyguard guy had short black hair and a goatee, and the other guy had brown hair, also pretty short, and was cleanly shaven."

"Blending in," I said.

"Pretty much," Jaxon replied.

"Do they sound familiar, Nathan?" Kyle asked.

"I mean, not specifically familiar. My dad kept a handful of guys around to clean up messes, and they were all similar. Black or brown hair and a couple of blonds. Close goatees or no facial hair at all. Muscular enough to be useful, but not so much to stand out. My dad knew what he was doing. I'd have to see them to be sure."

Jaxon pulled out his phone, flipped through it a bit, and then slid it over to me. "They didn't notice me at first, and I was able to get that."

I looked down at the picture. "Neither of them looks like any of the guys my dad kept around."

"Still, similar MO. Could be that he hired them," Kyle said.

"It's possible, but I don't know what the point of that would be," I replied. "Is that the only other time you've seen them?"

"Nope," he said and looked straight at me. "Yesterday, when I was leaving Nikki's house, they were there."

I sat up straight. "They were watching her house?"

"They were down the road a bit, and they weren't looking in my direction when I noticed them. It was almost like they were there just to be there, not necessarily to keep an eye on her, but then I pulled my gun on them and told them to fuck off, and they did."

"So at this point, they definitely know you're onto them," Kyle said.

"Yep. I figure now we'll see if we get different guys or if they stay the same."

"If my dad's responsible for it, they'll stay the same," I said. "He's an intimidator down to his core. He's probably fucking giddy, thinking we're bothered by them." I slammed my hand on the table, rattling it. "Where's Nikki now?"

"Nikita can take care of herself," Jaxon responded.

"I know that," I replied. "Where is she?"

There was a beat of tense silence between us, and then he shrugged. "I asked her to sit with Colette while I was here."

"Good. Thank you."

Though it was quiet and kind of uncomfortable, we received and ate our breakfast, and both Jaxon and I appreciated what Kyle was trying to do enough to humor him whenever he tried to start different topics of conversation. Jaxon and I ended on as good of terms as possible for the circumstances. After seeing Jaxon off, Kyle and I got back in his car to drive back to my place.

"I knew you'd be worried about her," Kyle said once we were driving. "I figured the best way to assure you that she was doing okay, if hurt, was by inviting Jaxon so that you could talk about it."

"I fucked up, Kyle," I said. "I mean, I *really* fucked up."

"We were all shocked when you picked Cherri," he said. "Jaxon's right. I get that you're trying to make peace with Cherri, but she's obviously not being very receptive to that right now, and in the meantime, you're fucking things up with Nikita. I miss Cherri too, but we all need to *stop* trying to get through to her right now. We need to have each other's backs right now. When Cherri's ready, she'll come back."

"Yeah. I just feel like I *deserve* that. Every single day of the rest of my life should be an apology to her."

"You can't live like that," Kyle said. "I get it. Trust me, I do. I consider Cherri to be a friend, and I was just as frustrated as everyone else was when I heard what you did, but I don't think it's just the end. There's a difference between retribution and damnation." He shrugged. "I don't know. This shit is so hard to navigate. You know what you did was wrong, and it was borne of your own mental insta-bility. You're in therapy, you're on meds, you've apologized, you're never gonna do it again, and you know it was wrong. Pay your dues, then make peace. There's a future for you. I refuse to believe there isn't."

"Thanks, man," was all I could say. I wasn't sure if I bought into that or not, but it sure sounded more promising than what I'd been living up to.

"Thank me by figuring it out," he said. "Give Nikki some time to cool off. Then tell her how you feel. Put Cherri in your past where she belongs, and—"

He was cut off by the sound of my phone ringing in my pocket. I quickly fished it out, hoping it might be Nikita, but when I saw who it was, I was equally happy and frustrated. The call read as unknown, no numbers on the screen, and it rang no matter how long I stared at it. It was Deon, but I couldn't answer it in front of Kyle. He thought Deon was dead, just like everyone else.

"What the heck?" Kyle said. "I've never heard a phone ring that long."

In the few times I'd spoken with Deon during the past few months, the call never stopped ringing. Even if that was an option, I didn't want to wait long enough to find out if it would stop. I *needed* to talk to Deon.

I tossed my options back and forth before finally grunting, "Fuck." I hit the answer button and put the phone to my ear. "Hello?"

"Hey." An odd sensation of relief flooded through me as I heard Deon's voice speak back to me. "Sorry that it's been so long since I called. I think I'm being tailed."

"Us too," I replied.

Kyle tilted his head. "Who is that?"

"Uh," I said and then let out a sigh. "Shit."

"What's wrong? You guys are being tailed too?" Deon asked.

"Hang on a sec," I said, and then I looked over at Kyle. "You should pull over."

Kyle recoiled a bit, but he didn't question it as he switched lanes so that he could take the next exit.

"What's going on?" Deon asked. "You're with someone?"

"Yeah, Kyle," I replied.

Kyle's interest was piqued by the mention of his name, but he pulled off the highway without asking any additional questions until he turned into a gas station and parked his car. He looked over at me. "Who is that?"

"Okay," I said back to him. "I'll explain everything later. Also, I'm sorry."

Kyle looked confused. "Okay?"

I pulled the phone away from my ear and put it on speaker. "Dee?"

"Yeah?" Deon replied. "What the fuck is going on?"

"You're on speaker. Kyle is here."

Kyle's eyes went wide. "Wait. Deon?"

Deon chuckled. "Yeah, hey. Long time. We never got to chat after I came back."

Kyle touched a hand to his head. "Am I drunk or something?"

"No," I said. "Deon's alive."

"Holy shit," Kyle said. "Holy shit!"

"Yeah, your emotions are valid right now, and I *am* going to deal with that, but we don't get many chances to talk. Hey, Deon. Are you okay?"

"Yeah. It doesn't really matter where I go. I keep seeing the same couple of guys. They haven't made any move. It just seems like they're keeping their eyes on me. You think Connor sent 'em?"

"That's my inclination," I replied. "We've got some on us too. Jaxon started seeing them last week."

"Is Cherri okay?" he asked.

"Holy shit!" Kyle asked. "Cherri thinks he's dead!"

"Yeah, and we're keeping it that way," Deon said. Kyle and I locked eyes, and I hoped he understood the position I was in. "Answer my question."

"Yeah, she's fine apart from getting her ass kicked by Nikita on Friday," I replied.

"What?" Deon said. "Why did she do that?"

"Cherri started it with her," Kyle said, and not even I knew that. "I spoke to Sicily, and he told me that Nikita was trying to ask him something, and Cherri got in her face."

"That doesn't sound like her," Deon said.

I rolled my eyes. "It's like I told you, she's in a place right now. It's because she thinks you're still alive."

"Wait. What?" Deon asked. "Why?"

"I'm not sure," I lied. "She and Sicily are trying to track you down, but they've been coming up empty. With you so off the grid, I imagine they'll keep coming up empty."

"Why don't you tell her?" Kyle asked. "That would fix everything!"

"No, it wouldn't," Deon and I said in unison.

"I don't even know that I'm gonna survive," Deon said. "Even if I do, I'm probably headed back to prison for the rest of my life. Trust me. It's better if she believes I'm dead."

Kyle looked at me and shook his head. "I'm sorry. I just don't think that's true."

"Kyle, I swear to god, if you tell her—" Deon started.

"I won't, but let the record show I do *not* agree with this," Kyle said and looked across at me. "This is a *terrible* idea."

I didn't respond. It wasn't like I had much choice, and I *did* see the logic behind Deon's reasoning. If Cherri was already this bad from losing Deon once, I was terrified of how she would be after losing him twice. "Hey, here's a question for you," I said. "You know my friend Brayden?"

"That mini-me jackass?" Deon said.

Kyle immediately opened his mouth as if he was going to yell at Deon, but I got my hand up just in time to stop him. "Yeah." Kyle glared at me. I'd have to chisel out some time to ask him what his newfound protectiveness was all about. "Have you seen him by any chance?"

"Seen him?" Deon said. "No. Why?"

"We haven't seen him all week. I don't know that his absence has anything to do with Dad, but I just wanted to make sure. Can you keep an eye out? Let me know if you *do* happen to see him."

"Yeah, of course."

"Thanks." I crossed my arms and leaned back in my seat, leaning my head against the rest. It was pounding, but I wanted to make sure I got all my questions for Deon out since I didn't know when I'd hear from him again. "Uh, any leads on Dad, by the way?"

"I think I'm getting closer ever since you sent me that information, but——"

The call dropped.

"What happened?" Kyle asked.

I shook my head. "I don't know. He's never done that before."

"Call him back."

"I can't. He calls from an unknown number so that he can't be traced." I picked up my phone from where I'd put it on the dashboard and stared at the screen, waiting for it to ring again, but nothing happened. "Shit."

"Do you think something happened to him?" Kyle asked.

The truth was, I had no idea. "Maybe he just thought the guys tailing him were getting close or something, so he had to go."

"Is that really what you think happened?" he asked.

My stomach was already twisting into knots considering the alternative. "I have to hope so."

18

___

NATHAN

It could have been that after staying up all night, Deon never called back, or it could have been that after hoping all weekend, Nikita never called, but when I woke up Monday morning, I felt like deep-fried garbage. My brain was slamming in my skull, my sinuses felt congested, I had chills all over, and my stomach was queasy. If that weren't bad enough, when I walked into school at the beginning of the day, I saw a huge crowd of people all gathered around the front office. At first, I was terrified that maybe Cherri had gotten into another fight or something worse, but then I saw that everyone was huddled around a long piece of paper hanging on the wall, and it hit me like a collapsing building—final track grades.

Whether Postings Proper believed in peer pressure to make students perform well or liked humiliating the bottom of the pack, I wasn't sure, but every year, they posted a huge list of all the senior students' current grades and GPAs, dubbing these grades the *final track*. They were posted about a month before finals and gave all the seniors an idea of if they and their peers were on track to graduate from high school in a month's time. Not surprisingly, I didn't see any members of The Royal Court looking at the paper. Typically, they were in good standing with their grades, but because the last couple of months had brought us each our fair share of challenges, they were probably as afraid as I was about how that may have affected their grades.

Still, if anyone was going to be the brave one, it was going to be me, but not because I was the brave one. I was the one who most deserved to have to suck it up. I excused my way through the crowds of students until I was facing the paper, and naturally, my eyes skimmed the sheet for my own name first.

"How is it you have a GPA *above* 4.0?" one kid asked me just as my eyes landed on my 4.12 GPA.

Though I was certain many people thought I bought the extra points, nothing could be further from the truth. Not only did I always do all of my homework, score perfect or near-perfect on all of my tests, and actively participate in all of my classes, but I was also the kid who always took any extra credit opportunities when they were presented. I didn't need the extra points that the assignments were designed to provide, but Connor Loche didn't like it when I *didn't* have homework. He used to tell me that a hardworking man was *always* working, and he taught me that I should never turn down an opportunity to gain favor.

None of that was worth explaining to this kid whose name I didn't even know. I ignored his question and scanned the list for each of The Royal Court members, one-by-one. I was most concerned about Colette and Avery, followed closely by Kyle and Alistair. Both Kyle and Alistair had taken on some extra weight that they didn't deserve in this second half of the year as they tried to keep Avery and Colette afloat after things went to shit.

To my surprise and total delight, as I scanned the list, I saw that everyone's grades were above average, either near or at 4.0. Somehow, Colette and Avery had managed to claw out of their depression enough to get their GPAs back to perfect, and Kyle's was at 4.0 as well. Alistair, Nikita, and Jaxon were all sitting nicely between 3.5 and 4.0 and were all on track not only to graduate but graduate with honors like those at the top of the pack.

As I looked the list over, a few other names jumped out at me. The first was Deon Keane. He had a dismal but still surprising 1.1 next to his name. It wasn't a GPA worthy of graduation, not that it mattered, but it was indicative of the fact that before he went on the run to find my dad, he was doing pretty good in school. If my father and I hadn't interfered with his life the way we had, he might have been that rare story of a reformed convict who recovers and does something with their lives.

Add yet another person to the list of lives I'd ruined.

Sicily was doing pretty good with a 3.4. He probably wouldn't eke out honors, but he'd graduate even though he had to hold up Deon for the first half of his senior year and Cherri the second half. In the back of my mind, I was prepared to exercise my resources to bump him up if he needed it. He unintentionally ended up being the cleaner for The Royal Court's mess and was certainly worthy of some gratitude.

The last name that called out to me on the list was the one that also made whatever illness I was battling double in severity. My stomach flipped as I moved down the list to Cherri's name. Next to her name was a horrendous 1.8 GPA, which was only slightly above her boyfriend's GPA, a guy who hadn't been at school since October. I knew she was skipping and generally ignoring school, but Cherri had to have had a very similar grade point average to mine before Deon *died*. She must not have done *anything* in the time between then and now, given just how far she had fallen.

That wasn't good.

I thought about Nikita and all the advice I'd been getting to stop worrying about Cherri so much, but I also had a brother who was expecting me to take care of her. Despite everything that we'd been through these past few months, I couldn't just let her fall like that, not after all that I'd put her through.

As quietly as I could, I slipped from the middle of the group of students and slid into the front office. The receptionist looked up and prepared to greet whoever was there, but then he saw it was me and looked back down. I couldn't blame him. I very rarely came into the office for anything that wasn't untoward. Having some deniability just in case only made him a smart man. I slunk along the wall to the right and down to the last office on the left. The door was open, so I knocked a couple of times and then entered, closing the door behind me.

"Nathan. Congratulations on getting top of your class. That's very exciting."

D.J. Motley was our school guidance counselor and the only person who had unimpeded access to each students' grades and progress reports. Though she saw students from all four grades, her specific job was to aid seniors in reaching graduation, so her next few weeks would be packed with helping anyone who was falling below the mark.

"Thanks," I replied. "The Royal Court is all looking pretty good. All except one."

D.J. reached over and snagged the very first file on the top of a pile to her left. She flashed it at me, and I could see Cherri's name in bold on the tab. "Your queen isn't looking so hot."

"She's had a tough year," I said. "That's why I'm here. I'm hoping you can help."

"Will it be blackmail or bribery?" she asked plainly. "I heard you tried to get Hix with his affair with Jessica. I was shocked to hear that he didn't go for it."

"You and me both," I said. "But no, I won't be using blackmail. I don't want to use bribery either." I sat down in one of the chairs that faced her desk. "It's fucking April. I'm out of here in a little over a month, and I'm just trying to get everyone to the finish line. Almost everyone has done what I needed them to. It's just this one little hiccup."

"So bribery, then?" she said.

I nodded. "There's gotta be something."

D.J. flipped open the file and looked down at it. "It's not an easy thing, Nathan. I'll be putting my whole career on the line. She hasn't gone to a single class or done a single homework assignment, nothing since last semester. There will be squirrels suspicious of me if she walks in June."

"So she won't walk," I said. "Just change the grade and mail her the degree. Trust me when I say she's not showing up for graduation anyway."

"What happened?" she asked. "I tried to do my job the right way and get her in here to talk, but she wouldn't give me the time of day. I tried cornering her, and she looked like she was going to kick my ass."

"She probably would have," I said. "I can't really go into it, though. It involves all that shit that happened with Jessica and Deon. Believe me when I say that hearing the details would not be a good use of your time. Just know that she's been through the wringer, and I've put in a lot of work this past couple of months just trying to keep her in good standing. I've sacrificed a lot, and I don't want it to all be for nothing. Come on. You know Cherri's a good person, and she worked her ass off up until all this shit happened. You honestly want someone like her to fail?"

D.J. leaned back in her seat. "No, I suppose that would be unfortunate." She ran a hand through her brown hair.

"Be honest. If I wanted to buy her graduation, what would it cost me?"

"First of all, you'd have to pay off all the other teachers to go along with it. Hix is gonna have to sign that diploma, and if he sees hers come across his desk, he's gonna come straight to me."

"I can do that," I said.

"*Paid*," D.J. said. "No threatening people's kids or jobs or anything."

"It's like I said. I'm over that. I'm just trying to get out of here."

"As for me," she looked up to the ceiling as she thought, then her eyes came back to me. "I'm in the process of buying a house. It'd be nice to use the money I currently have earmarked for the down payment for my renovations."

"So you want me to pay the down payment for your new house?" I asked.

"Is it too much?"

"How much is it?"

"About fifty grand."

It was like a punch to the gut. Fifty grand was no small amount of money to take out, especially not without raising some questions, but it was my family's money at the end of the day, and it was for Cherri. If that was what I'd have to do, then that's what I'd do.

"Done."

Her eyebrows went up. "Really?"

"Really. I'll get her teachers all paid off, and I'll need the name of your loan company so that I can send the money over," I said. "Can you get it to me by the end of the day?"

A smile rose to her face. "I'll have it for you by the end of the hour."

After that, I went home. I was sure to send a group text to all the members of The Royal Court so that no one panicked or thought I'd disappeared, and then I went straight home to sleep. I probably would have slept through the night if my alarm hadn't gone off to remind me of my therapy session that evening. I needed it more than ever, so as much as I hated it, I dragged myself out of bed and went.

Ever since I admitted to Nicole that my favorite sweet treat was oatmeal raisin cookies, she'd always had a plate ready when I arrived at therapy. I helped myself to a few before we even started speaking, and she accusingly raised her eyebrow at me.

"What?" I asked.

She crossed her arms like a disapproving mother. "Have you been eating?"

"I ate yesterday," I said back.

"You should be eating every day, Nathan," she replied. "You also seem sick."

"I don't feel great today. I had a rough weekend."

"Do you want to talk about it?" she asked.

"Nikita is mad at me. I heard from my brother, but we got cut off, and he never called back," I said.

"What happened with you and Nikita?"

"More Cherri stuff," I replied. "They got into a fight, a bad one, and when the principal asked me to take sides, I took Cherri's."

"Why?" she asked.

"Honestly, I don't really know. It was dumb. My reasoning at the time was that I thought Cherri would get in more trouble than Nikita did, which turned out to be true, but I don't really think that was why I did it."

She hummed. "More guilt?"

"If I'd taken Nikita's side, Cherri would have

gotten expelled for sure. I couldn't be the reason she got expelled."

Nicole sighed. "You know, Nathan, being in a position to prevent someone from suffering the consequences of their actions does not make when they see those consequences your fault."

I tried to blame it on the sentence's complicated phrasing when I said, "I don't understand," but it was more that I didn't understand how Cherri getting in trouble at that time *wouldn't* have been my fault. If I could have prevented it and didn't, that made it my fault.

"There's a difference between robbing a store and harboring the fugitive."

"Both are wrong," I said.

"Correct, but one is self-inflicted, and the other is self-imposed."

"Aren't those the same thing?" I asked.

She laughed. "You and I both know that *you* know they aren't."

"Well, all I've got right now is giving until I figure out the next step of forgiveness. Is that such a bad thing?" I asked.

"No, but what you'll find is that people will always accept gifts. Even though Cherri claims to be angry at you and has even said not to help her, she's always accepted your help. She could have easily turned herself in or asked the teacher who accepted your bribe not to look the other way, but she did anyway. People will *always* accept gifts. Until they're ready to truly accept you, nothing will make a difference."

"Is it bad to give them gifts until then?" I asked. "As long as I know that's not what's affecting whether or not they're choosing to forgive me?"

"No, but you have to be careful," Nicole said. "If you've passed the point of no return, then you're beating a very expensive dead horse."

19

NIKITA

Fortunately, I quickly pulled out two blades as someone snatched me while I was getting into my car. Unfortunately, it didn't matter because whoever had their arms around me seemed to know I'd be armed. They wrapped around my arms and held me until I was too coiled to move. Then they dragged me backward until we were slipping into the shadows on the side of my garage. A hand cupped my mouth so that I couldn't scream, but I knew what to do. I relaxed a bit to make my captor think that I was going to comply with what they had planned, and as soon as I felt that slight bit of release on the hand around my mouth, I craned my mouth and bit down on the hand.

The body behind me grunted, but they seemed to be trying to keep their voice down. The hand cupped further around my mouth despite the bite. Eventually, they tried to switch their arms, briefly releasing my arms and hoping that the hold they had on my mouth was enough to keep me still. That miscalculation cost them. I rolled out of their hold, bringing up my blades, and flipped around to bring them up to my captor's neck.

Jaxon backed against the garage wall, wincing at my blades held to his throat. I opened my mouth to ask him what the fuck he was doing, but he slapped his hand over my mouth, and I could taste the blood from my bite where it trickled out. He tilted his head toward the street, and I looked around just in time to see a gray minivan sliding down the street at a slow pace. I leaned further into the shadow and kept my eyes on it as it pulled slightly up the street and parked in front of a house a few down from mine.

"That's them," Jaxon hissed to me. "Sorry for the snatch and grab, but I saw them park down from your house and get out, and I was terrified that they were gonna try to get you. I think they're looking for you now."

"I nearly cut you in half," I groaned and then hugged him. "Thank you." I slipped my blades back into the hidden holsters in my jacket sleeves and then peered around the corner of the house. The car was slowly inching its way forward, and I could see the driver looking back in our direction. "They're definitely looking for me."

"They're gonna turn around and come back," Jaxon said. "I gave them the slip the other day, and that's what they did."

Sure enough, the car inched a little more forward until it was out of the view of my house, then drove back out onto the street and out of sight.

"Come on. Get in my car. We're going after them."

"What?" Jaxon asked.

"What if they have Brayden? Or what if they try to snatch someone else?" I asked.

Jaxon shook his head. "I get the strange feeling that they're *only* after you and Cherri." I looked at him, and he nodded. "Yeah, I've had a busy week-end. They keep tabs on all of us so that they know when we're not together, but they've only gotten out of their cars when they could potentially nab one of the two of you."

That had my heart racing, but it also made me angry. "Then we're definitely going after them. If these guys think they're gonna snatch me up, they have another thing coming."

I bolted out from the shadows on the side of my garage and raced over to my car. I hopped in, and my heart jumped with relief when Jaxon got in next to me. After bracing my hand on the gear to shift as soon as I got in, I stared through my rearview mirror. Jaxon did the same, and we sat in total silence while we waited to see if the van would come back. Around ten minutes passed, and I was beginning to think they weren't coming back, but then the van appeared, creeping down the street. Jaxon and I both slid down so that our heads didn't appear above the seats. As soon as the van was past my driveway, I threw my car into reverse and backed out of the driveway.

The van didn't immediately pull away, but I boldly pulled up behind it, and then it took off, flying down the road at top speed. I followed after it, not letting it get too far from me but also not speeding so much that I inspired a call to the police. Once they'd pulled out of my neighborhood and onto the main roads, I opened up my car's speed and started to close the distance. They may have been going fast, but they were in a minivan. Not in a million years were they going to stay ahead of my sports car.

They must have figured this was the case because as I started to close the distance, they began to weave in and out of traffic, using the other cars on the road to keep us separated. At one point, I managed to get alongside them. Whether they were going to use it or not, the guy in the passenger's seat pulled up a gun and pointed it out the window. I let my foot off the gas so that my car would fall behind with my heart pounding in my chest.

"What's the plan here, Nikki?" Jaxon asked. "I mean, say we drive around until we both run out of gas. Then what?"

"I'd be lying if I said I had a plan," I responded. "I don't necessarily want to catch them. I just want to know where they're going."

"Uh, then a subtler approach may have been better," he replied.

"You're not wrong, but I'm kind of just figuring it out as we go."

"Do you honestly think they'll go back to their home base or their boss or whatever with us following them?" he asked. "We have to make them think we aren't following them anymore."

Again, he wasn't wrong. They probably weren't about to let my car fall out of their field of view, but I didn't trust myself to get out of their sight without losing them. So, yes, following them until we both ran out of gas was the current plan.

I did slow down, though, and tried to keep a few car lengths between us. They eventually made their way to the highway and got on, so I let a few cars go first and got on behind them. They changed lanes as if they still saw me following, but I didn't mimic the action. As long as I stayed in the far-right lane and didn't let them get too far in front of me, they wouldn't be able to get off the freeway without my knowing.

Whether because they didn't want to attract the attention of the police or because they thought I'd left them alone, their van slowed to a normal pace and started going with the flow of traffic. They passed by all of the exits out of South Postings headed northbound, which was an odd thing, considering all of their targets were in the southside of town, or so we thought.

"Are they headed to North Postings or just trying to run us out?" Jaxon asked.

"I don't know. I'm sure they know I'm still back here," I replied.

But then they carried past a lot of the South Postings exits as if they were headed straight out of the city. It wasn't the worst thing. If they were leaving town, then the rest of The Royal Court was safe for the time being. Once cars tapered out as we left the city behind, I'd have a harder time staying hidden, but I planned to cross that bridge when I came to it.

"Oh, shit," Jaxon said suddenly. "Left exit."

"What?"

Jaxon pointed frantically. "That's their plan. 28th is a left exit!"

Just as he said it, I glanced up at the signs overhead and noticed one under the 28th Street Exit that had the words *Left Lane Only* in big, bold letters. I was all the way on the right of four lanes of traffic, and I immediately started to panic. Getting into a wreck while trying to follow these guys was *not* a good outcome, but I didn't want to lose them. If I put on my blinker, I'd tip them off, so I waited for a good opportunity and slipped one lane over.

"Nikki, you gotta move faster. The exit's in a quarter mile!"

"Shut up!" I barked.

Once again, I waited for an opportunity and moved my car over to the next lane. The far-left lane was the one designated for the exit, and it was bumper to bumper with cars getting off, but ahead of me, the van hadn't changed over yet either.

"What are you doing?" Jaxon said.

"I think they're baiting us," I quipped. "They're

hoping we go."

Jaxon didn't respond but kept glancing ahead to the exit. "This is our last chance."

I didn't know what to do. If I hopped over, they'd no doubt stay in the current lane and remain on the highway, but if I stayed, they could pull a last-minute switch and hop off. I kept my hands braced on the wheel as the exit got closer and closer, preparing to react as soon as I knew what was going to happen. Right at the last second, the van hopped into the left lane, just barely cutting a car off to take the exit.

"Fuck!" I barked and then cut my car to the left. A car blared at me as I nearly hit it, sliding to the side and onto the shoulder to avoid an accident. "Sorry!" I screamed as if they could hear me.

"Shit, Nikki," Jaxon hissed, then pointed ahead. "Look! They're turning toward North Postings."

Trying my best not to do a whole lot more that would definitely result in my license plate being sent to the sheriff, I changed lanes, used my blinker, and tried to keep up, but a red light threatened to foil me. The van got just ahead of the light and turned left, and I had to slam my brake as cars immediately started to file out, cutting off my turn.

"Damn it!" I screeched.

Both Jaxon and I craned our heads, trying to

see where the car was going, but Jaxon gasped. "They aren't getting back on the highway," he said. I was sure they would, but the van carried on straight into South Postings. "Is there any possibility they didn't see us get off the highway after them?"

It was doubtful, but when my light finally turned green, I made my way around the corner and down the street as the van turned into one of the neighborhoods up ahead. We followed, turning right. The van was traveling even slower, and I just caught a glimpse of it turning right again, heading even further into the neighborhood. I turned to the right, and this time, the van was just reaching the light at the end of the street. It turned red, and the van stopped to obey the light.

"I don't think they see us," I murmured.

There was another car on the road, so I let it go ahead of us and started to creep my way down. The light turned green, and I started to pick up my speed until Jaxon reached over and took my hand.

"Back up!" he yelled, staring out his window.

"What? Why? We've almost got them!"

Jaxon looked over at me with the most serious look he'd ever given me before. "Nikki. Back up the car."

Frustrated and watching as the van carried off down the street, I threw my car into reverse, made sure there were no cars behind me, and then started to back up. I kept going, waiting for Jaxon's sign to stop when he smacked my leg and pointed. "Look! Isn't that Brayden?"

I looked around him and out the window and saw someone down the street who was walking down the road with no real sense of direction. I craned my eyes, and sure enough, the person was none other than our missing friend, Brayden. "Oh my god."

As quickly and safely as I could, I turned my car down the street and parked, and Jaxon and I jumped out. We raced down the street, and I walked in front of Brayden. His eyes were sunken and empty, but they widened a bit when he saw me. "Nikita?"

"Oh my god!" I couldn't stop myself from pulling him into a huge hug. "Where the hell have you been? You've been missing for two weeks!"

"No," he murmured, much more muted than his typical self. "I just needed to take a break."

Jaxon dropped his jaw. "Just needed to take a break? You didn't think we'd be worried?"

"Did Kyle do something wrong?" I asked.

A little life fluttered into Brayden's eyes at the mention of Kyle. "Kyle? No, he's..." His voice trailed off. "No, he didn't do anything wrong."

I exchanged a look with Jaxon and then hooked an arm around Brayden's shoulders. I was relieved when he allowed me to lead him back toward the car. Jaxon helped me dump him into the backseat, and then we walked around to our respective doors. Before we got in, Jaxon looked across the roof at me.

"That's not true, right?" he asked. "It had to have something to do with those guys. Do you think they dumped him?"

"No. If they had taken him, he would have gotten out of the van," I said.

"Maybe he couldn't," Jaxon offered.

"Well, it wasn't like they were traveling around with him in the van for two weeks. I don't think he was with them just now, but the fact that he popped up right here while we were chasing them is a little too coincidental for me. Whether he was dropped by them or someone else, it was done to distract us."

"It worked," Jaxon replied. "I'm sure that van is long gone."

"Yeah. That's probably good. I really didn't have a plan."

Jaxon gasped. "No! I couldn't tell!"

"Shut up. Let's just get him home," I said.

Jaxon nodded. We both climbed in, and I

started the car. Before driving away, I pulled out my phone and sent a text message to our group message.

It's a long story, and we'll explain tomorrow, but Jaxon and I just found Brayden.

Alistair: *Thank god. I'll wake Avery and tell her.*
Kyle: *Is he okay? Where is he?*
Kyle: *What's he doing? What happened?*

Kyle, relax, we're bringing him home.

Kyle: *I'll meet you there.*
Nathan: *$50,000. Make the check out to Postings Free National Bank and put D.J. Motley in the memo.*

All of the responses to the text were to be expected apart from the last one. "Whoa, why is Nathan giving fifty grand to the school counselor?" Jaxon asked, but I didn't answer. I'd seen Cherri's failing grade on the grade list, and D.J. Motley was the one person who could change that.

Alistair: *Uh, I'm guessing that message was for someone else?*

No fucking kidding.

20

NIKITA

I fought and failed many times to find the words I needed to say. Nathan was sitting on his couch, not pressing or pushing, just waiting for me to make the first move. I'd driven straight back to my house and left Jaxon to get Brayden back home to try to get more information out of him. I had to talk to Nathan.

His taking Cherri's side in the fight had been bad, and his paying off teachers left and right to cover for her had been bad. But fifty grand? That was a *lot* of money. I simply refused to believe that it wasn't related to some form of feelings anymore. Nathan hadn't spent that amount of money on anything in his life before. The only thing he owned that cost that much was his car, and his parents had given him that.

"Nathan." I finally started. "Fifty *thousand* dollars? For what?"

"She's not going to graduate," Nathan replied. There were tears already bunching in the corners of his eyes. "After four years of hard work. After everything she's done, she's not going to graduate unless I help."

"That's a *lot* of help!"

"It's not just her!" Nathan said. "I had to help Avery too. I was going to help anyone who needed it, even Sicily."

"But none of them did," I responded. "Just her. Why does it keep falling to you to look after her? And why do you keep doing it? She's made it *very* clear how she feels about you."

"Can you blame her?" Nathan asked. "You said so yourself that you understand the position she's in more than anyone."

It wasn't fair. No, I didn't blame Cherri for the way she felt about Nathan after everything that had happened. No, I didn't fail to understand the position she was in after thinking that Deon died. But I had people that I loved too. I loved Nathan, and I loved The Royal Court. For the past few months, she'd done nothing but embark on a course to hurt and harm them continuously. Why wouldn't they give up on her? Was there something I was missing? I'd been hurt by my father too. I had to watch my mother turn her back on me too. Did that mean that I'd earned the right to run around with callous disregard for everyone else? I had to hoist myself up and figure out how to deal with it.

Why didn't she?

"What about me?" I asked. "Would you have paid that amount of money for me?"

"Nikita." Nathan stood up and walked over until he was able to reach out and put his hands on my arms. "Fifty thousand dollars is the *least* I would pay for you. I'd do whatever I had to for you but, *fuck*." He laughed. "You don't need me. You take care of yourself just fine." He reached out and lifted the pendant of the necklace he'd given me and turned it over in his fingers. "I'd love to take care of you for once, but all this time, you've been the one taking care of me."

"If I asked you to stop taking care of Cherri, would you stop?" I asked.

Nathan looked up at me. "Are you going to ask me to do that?"

"If I did, what would you do?" The tears bunched in his eyes started to slide down his cheeks.

Emotions turned to a knot in my throat. "Is it *that* bad? Thinking of just letting her go?"

"Nikki." He caught me off guard, leaning forward and pecking my lips. It had been a while, and it felt so good to have his lips on mine again, so much so that I leaned toward him as he pulled away, keeping us tethered a bit longer. "Nikki, do you think your dad should pay for the pain he caused you?"

"It's…different," I responded, but even as the words left my lips, I realized it wasn't different. Well, it was different because Nathan wasn't even a portion of the monster my father was. "I get that you're trying to do what's right, but I think you're fighting a losing battle. There is nothing that my dad could do as payment for his actions. He could give me millions and millions of dollars, and nothing would make it right."

Tears gathered a little more in the corners of Nathan's eyes. "So you're saying he's unredeemable?"

"Maybe?" I replied.

"But…" Nathan wrapped his arms tighter around me and pulled me into him. His head landed on my shoulder, and he started to cry outright. "If he's unredeemable, doesn't that mean I am? I don't want to be a man who brings you pain. I want to be someone who you can look at and be happy to see and not feel conflicted by." He pulled away and looked into my eyes. "Doing all of this for Cherri, it's about doing right by her, but it's also about doing right by you. I want to be a good man that you deserve." My heart started to beat even faster as I was overwhelmed by that sentiment. Was he doing all of that to try and earn my second-hand forgiveness? "If you thought I was like that, like your dad, you wouldn't want to be with me, right?"

"Yes," I said, "but you're not like him. I don't know how it all works, but you aren't like my dad. Don't do it for me. You're different. I don't know why, but you are."

Nathan pulled me toward him and pressed his lips against mine again. I was powerless to resist him. After the time we'd spent apart after the fight, I didn't want to spend any more time apart from him. I didn't understand anything. Was there some invisible line that all rapists fall on? I'd always assumed that it was one size fits all, but Nathan wasn't the same as my dad. Some people *could* be redeemed. I believed that. It was all so complicated, but did I have to figure it all out right now?

Did I have to question myself when Nathan's hands felt so good sliding up my spine? His lips traveled away from mine to trail down my jaw and eventually over my throat. He nibbled a little bit there, and I fell back onto the couch, taking Nathan with me. He slid his hands up my torso, taking my shirt up with them, and he peeled it over. My hands went to his stomach, dragging his shirt up as well, and he leaned back just enough to pull it the rest of the way over and tossed it to the side.

He started to climb back over me, but I put my hands on his chest and pushed him back to sit on the couch. I dropped to my knees in front of him, my body already growing hot all over.

"You don't have to," Nathan said.

But my hands were already on his jeans, unbuttoning them. "I want to. I like doing it."

Nathan rolled his eyes. "If *that* were true, then it would mean you're even more than perfect."

I shrugged. "I guess I'm just that perfect."

Nathan didn't complain. His hands combed into my hair and gently held the back of my head as I pulled his growing arousal from his jeans and leaned in to lick it. He let out a deep sigh, and I closed my lips over him, sliding my tongue down until I hit his base. I slid my way back up and spent some time on the tip before slipping down again. I closed my hand over Nathan's shaft and worked it down as I pulled my mouth back up and moved into a rhythm. Each time he let out a groan, my skin prickled with excitement. My other hand moved between my legs, with the plan to service myself, but Nathan noticed and grabbed it.

I looked up at him, and his eyes were wide and dark with lust. "No, you don't have to do it for yourself."

He pulled me up, effectively pulling me off of him, and he kissed me before positioning me over the back of the couch, leaning over until my hands were almost on the floor. He reached his hands around me to undo the button of my jeans and pull them off of my body.

He threw them aside before leaning in and letting his tongue slick across my heated center. I let out a moan as one of Nathan's hands wrapped around my thigh and started to rub the sensitive bundle of nerves there. Between the movements of his mouth and fingers, my mind started to go hazy. It felt like the room was getting hotter by the second, and I closed my eyes and let myself breathe in the intense feeling of pleasure that was washing over me.

"Nathan," I whimpered, but I didn't get any additional words out before a powerful orgasm washed over me. He continued to lick and rub me through the feeling, and once it had finally subsided, he stood up and positioned himself behind me.

With his hands situated on my hips, he pressed his tip to my opening and blanketed himself over me. As he did so, his hot breath caressed my skin, leaving a collection of goosebumps in its wake. Then he bit onto my ear as he started to push his way into me. The feeling of him filling me, closing around me, grumbling through his bite into my ear—it created a euphoria I couldn't control. My arms clawed into the carpet, and without much work on Nathan's behalf, another powerful orgasm went rocketing through me again.

"Fuck, Nikki," Nathan grumbled. "If you keep doing that, I'm not gonna make it."

"It's your fault."

I drove myself back into Nathan's thrust, and he responded by wrapping his arm around my stomach and pulling us both up to our knees. His lips clamped down on the crook of my neck and drove into me. I let out a loud scream, and Nathan pushed into me again and stuttered, and I could tell he was releasing inside me.

It was a good thing that I made the decision to start birth control once he and I started hooking up more frequently. It started to drip out of me, and I moaned at the feeling of it, collapsing forward onto the floor in front of me.

He gently rubbed the skin of my ass. "Sorry. I couldn't get out in time."

"That's okay. We should be good," I responded, still mentally planning on going to get some emergency contraceptive just in case after I left.

Nathan pulled himself out of me, and after cleaning ourselves, we decided to go and sit outside in the hot tub. I curled myself against Nathan and set my head on his shoulder. After not talking to him for a couple of weeks, it felt good to be in his arms again.

"So…" He chuckled. "I will probably kick myself for asking this question, but where are we? We've kind of been doing *this* for a while, and there's nothing wrong with *this*, but I want more. I don't want to apply pressure if we're not ready, though."

It wasn't as if people didn't know that Nathan and I were a thing. We kissed and had sex from time to time. We didn't really go out on dates or anything like that, but we saw each other at school every day.

But school was ending soon.

Apart from Avery, no one had really mentioned college, and I hadn't thought much about it because the idea of leaving Nathan behind scared me. He'd be staying back to run his dad's company, but I didn't want to give myself that level of permanence by stating that I'd be staying with him. He'd mentioned having me head an expansion of his business into my family's business, but I needed to figure my relationship with Nathan out first because I couldn't go work with him if we weren't going to be together.

"I don't know," I answered. "It's not even about pressure. I just really and truly don't know." I turned my head to look at him. "Is it okay if I take a little bit longer to figure it out?"

He kissed my forehead. "You can take all the time you need. I'm not going anywhere, Nikki. You're my soulmate."

That statement and its resonance sent a chill through my body, one that emanated even in spite of the hot water around us.

"Thank you," I said. "I promise to figure it out soon."

21

NIKITA

Despite the fact that Nathan ended our last interaction on somewhat uncertain terms, I felt better about where we were than I had in days past. Maybe it was because of that, maybe it was because we finally tracked down Brayden, or maybe it was because school was finally coming to a close, but I felt anxious in a good way. I still had more questions than answers about the men that Jaxon and I were following, what had happened to Brayden, and how to sort things out with Cherri, but I was getting an unearned sense of ease. I wasn't sure where it was coming from. Maybe it was just a sense of confidence that came from losing so much that the only direction to go was up, but I was hoping to ride it out, at least for a day.

"You seem to be in a better mood," Jaxon said as he sat down at the lunch table. Colette was at his side, and she sat down next to him. I noticed the hickey on her neck, but I didn't mention it.

"Yeah. I kind of feel like it's fake confidence, but whatever. It's the best I've felt in months." I took a few bites of my chicken wrap and smiled at Jaxon and Colette's evident infatuation with one another. "How was your night last night?"

Colette looked up with her jaw dropped and a very Colette-like gasp. "*That* is inappropriate, Nikki."

I giggled as Jaxon shot her a look of annoyance. "You realize that if you hadn't reacted that way, she wouldn't have known, right?"

Colette folded her lips into an adorable look of guilt. "Sorry."

It made me happy that she seemed more like herself again. Her last interaction with Cherri and the subsequent conversation we had seemed to have left a lasting impression on her, which was good. Maybe they were all willing to give Cherri more leeway than I was willing to, but I would appreciate just one week where my friends and I didn't have to get hurt.

Slowly, everyone came to the table, including the recently recovered Brayden. In spite of the fact

that Nathan and I still failed to define our relationship, he wrapped his arm behind my back and set a
soft kiss on my forehead as he sat. My heart jumped
a little, and I couldn't keep from smiling at him.

"Hi," I greeted.

He smiled back at me. "Hey."

Kyle sat down on Nathan's other side, and
Brayden sat across from him, looking like he had a
little more life but still less than normal. Kyle
opened his mouth to speak, but Brayden's hand was
up, stopping him before he could get any words
out. He lifted the hot dog off his tray and took an
aggressive bite, then dropped it back on his tray.

"Happy?" he said with a full mouth.

"Yes," Kyle responded. "Thank you."

Brayden rolled his eyes, but a small smirk found
his face. "Fucking mom."

"Whatever," Kyle snapped back. "It's working."

Avery seemed a little perkier when she sat down
at the table, as well, and by extension, Alistair
seemed to be in a better mood. They both looked
more rested and seemed a little more flirtatious
with one another. Alistair kept sneaking kisses
against Avery's head until she turned and took one
on the lips.

Maybe everyone just had the spring love bug?
Maybe it was something totally different, but for

the first time since the year began, The Royal Court felt totally at peace, *almost* like we were back to normal.

"Hey, Nathan," Avery started. She looked across at him with a grin, then opened her phone, navigated through it a bit, and slid it across the table toward him. "Got my room placement."

Nathan slid the phone over so that he could look down at it, and I looked over his shoulder. Along with a ton of other admissions information was Avery's dorm assignment, a single-occupant room in Loche Hall, aptly named after the hall's benefactors, the Loches.

"Oh, hey! You're inside of me!" Then he frowned as everyone looked at him with varying expressions of disgust. "Holy shit, that came out so wrong." He looked at Alistair. "Please don't hit me." Then he turned to me. "Please don't hit me." We both just rolled our eyes and chuckled, and Nathan went back to scrolling through Avery's room information. "You're not taking a roommate?"

"Nah. I'm not very good at sharing." Both Kyle and Alistair scoffed, and Avery gave them each a glare. "Okay, I didn't ask for comments from the peanut gallery."

"It went okay with Cherri," Colette said and

then looked up with shock, realizing what she'd said. "Oh my god. I'm so sorry."

Avery reached around Jaxon, who she was sitting next to, to set a hand on Colette's hand. "It's *okay*. I'm feeling a little bit better, and she's bound to come up from time to time, so we should just get used to talking about her now." She pulled her hand back. "And you're right. I did get pretty used to sharing things with Cherri, and she would sometimes stay over for days at a time, and it was never an issue, but I don't know how common that is. Besides, I'll only stay in the dorms for a year before moving off-campus with Ali, so I'd rather not get all attached to someone if I'm moving anyway."

"You're moving to Connecticut too?" Kyle asked. "I guess that makes sense. I just didn't really think much about it."

"I don't think any of us have thought much about it," Nathan said with sadness in his voice. "I know I'm not your favorite person in the world, but I'm gonna miss you guys."

Avery looked at Alistair, and then Alistair looked at Nathan with a smile. "We spent about twenty minutes last night talking about how much we're gonna miss you. You've been a huge part of our lives, even if an annoying one."

Avery swatted Alistair's arm. "You said you were going to leave that out."

Nathan laughed and held up a hand. "Avery, he just admitted he's gonna miss me. He can insult me all he wants."

Everyone at the table laughed a little bit, and it drew the attention of some of the people around us. I noticed someone at a nearby table let out a full-blown sigh of relief, and then the tension at their table loosened a bit. The Royal Court's fractures had been stressing out the people outside of it, apparently. The Royal Court, and Nathan, specifically, sort of ruled over the school, so it stood to reason that our *subjects* would take on some of our emotions.

"Do you think you'll come back?" Kyle asked, dragging my attention back to our table.

Again, Avery and Alistair exchanged a look, but that time, they were referring to one another for the answer. "I don't really know," Avery said, and then she looked back at everyone else. "If I'm totally honest, during Christmas break, we were out of here, and we weren't looking back. We started looking into places in New Haven, and Ali started looking for jobs there. The whole nine yards. But with everything that has happened in the past few months, I guess it changed some things for us. Now we have to figure out what we really wanna do."

"I don't say this out of self-blame or desire to pay you back or anything like that, but you guys know if you need *anything* as we move onto our next state, I've got you covered, right? We may not all stay here, but we've still gotta stick together," Nathan said.

No one responded, but everyone gave their own forms of affirmation, and then the table went a little silent as we all ate our food in quiet bliss. It wasn't until Alistair finished that anyone said anything, and when he cleared his throat and looked around the table with a wince, we knew it wasn't going to be good.

"Okay, listen. I love this"—he waved around the table—"a lot, but are we just going to *ignore* what happened to Brayden?" He looked down at the guy. "I mean, you were missing for, like, two weeks."

"I wasn't missing. I just took a break for a couple of weeks," Brayden responded.

"You took a break right after the spring break?" Colette asked.

Brayden held up his hands in frustration. "Yeah? You honestly don't think my parents would have filed a missing person's or something?"

Jaxon and I locked eyes for a moment. We hadn't had a chance to explain what happened with the people we chased. Kyle got part of the story from Jaxon when Kyle met him at Brayden's place, and Nathan had gotten a majority of the story from me before I left his house after we slept together, but no one else really knew what happened. Both Jaxon and I had kept our suspicions to ourselves for the time being. Jaxon believed that the men were after Cherri and me, specifically, but we also thought that they had something to do with Brayden's disappearance. Why would they take him if *we* were their quarry, and if they had snatched Brayden, why would he be lying about it now? He made a good point. His parents didn't seem as concerned with his disappearance as we were. We had some of the pieces of the puzzle, just not all of them, and we didn't want to put the rest of the group on edge without knowing for sure.

Kyle seemed to take notice of Brayden's discomfort first. "Let's, uh, change the subject. I don't know how many of you have looked at a calendar, but prom is next week."

Colette choked slightly on her drink. "Oh my god! Are you serious?" She dragged out her phone and clicked through it. "You're right! My god, are we already mid-May?"

"Yeah," Alistair said with an exasperated breath in his voice. "That is *painful* to hear. I feel like it was just yesterday that we all hated each other."

Everyone snickered, and Kyle continued. "Well, in the interest of being slightly normal, we should all go! I think the ticket deadline was last week, but…" He fished into his pocket and came back brandishing a small stack of prom tickets. "Fortunately, I'm *super* responsible and on top of my shit."

"Is that ten tickets?" Jaxon asked, a rarity for him in a large group of people, but he was also the only one who would ever notice something like that. "Who are the other two for?"

He shrugged. "Cherri and Sicily. I was literally gonna just bum-rush Sicily at some point today when Cherri is nowhere in sight, throw the tickets at him, and take off."

"Solid plan," Avery quipped.

"Anyway," Kyle continued, "I know we have a couple of couples." He looked over at Alistair and Avery, then at Nathan and I, but then his gaze turned to Jaxon and Colette. "Or maybe three?"

"Let's not go as couples," Avery said. "Let's just go as a group."

Brayden slammed his hand on the table. "That's stupid. We *know* who the couples are. Nathan will go with Nikita. Alistair will go with

Avery." He pointed at Jaxon and Colette. "Apparently, these two are a thing now."

Kyle chuckled. "You're right. I guess that means you're stuck with me."

Everyone looked over to Kyle, including Brayden, who looked across at him with shock. "What?"

"What do you say?" Kyle held out one of the prom tickets toward Brayden. "Do you wanna go to prom with me?"

Brayden was quiet for a long time in the wake of the question. No one said anything—hardly breathed—as Kyle sat with the ticket outstretched. At first, it seemed like he may just be kidding, but his face held stone seriousness.

Finally, Brayden looked up from the ticket at Kyle, and he seemed like he may burst from anger. "Is this supposed to be some sort of joke? I knew it! You're fucking pitying me!"

Pity?

Kyle pulled the ticket away. "No. I swear. Everyone's pairing up, so I thought we could go together. If you don't want to—"

"What would make you think that I want to!" Brayden stood up. "I don't need any more of your fucking help. Just stay away from me!" he shouted, and with that, he ran off.

Kyle and Nathan both stood up in concern

since the last time Brayden ran off, we didn't see him for two weeks, but surprisingly, Colette stood up. "I'll go after him. Jax, come with me."

Jaxon nodded. "Okay."

Colette and Jaxon stood up quickly and rushed off after Brayden, and the rest of us watched as Kyle completely deflated as if he'd truly been rejected. Nathan looked at me, and I shrugged, but in looking around to see if anyone else saw Brayden's outburst, I happened to notice that Sicily was sitting alone. Where Cherri was wasn't a concern to me, but I didn't want to waste the chance to talk to Sicily alone.

"Hey," I said. "I know this is kind of a vulnerable moment, but can I get those two tickets for Sicily and Cherri? I have to go chat with him anyway."

"Oh, sure," Kyle replied.

He separated two tickets from the stack and handed them over to me. I took them, offered Nathan a quick kiss on the cheek, and then stood up and rushed over to where Sicily was sitting. I dropped down into the seat across from him, and he jumped a little, then let out a sigh of relief when he noticed it was me.

"Cherri making you jumpy?" I asked.

"What? No," he replied, and he was serious. "It's, uh… It's nothing."

I decided to take a shot in the dark. "Have you seen some guys following you?"

Sicily's eyes shot up to mine. "Why would you ask that?"

"We've seen them too. Where is Cherri now?" Sicily nodded toward the windows that gave a view of the courtyard, and I saw Cherri standing out there, working on a cigarette. "She's smoking now?"

"She doesn't even like it," Sicily replied, "but she thinks it takes the edge off. I don't know. Maybe it does."

"Well, we think these guys who are following us may be looking to pull a snatch and grab, so just stay together, okay? Don't ever be alone, and if you can, keep some of us in your sights, just in case."

"Yeah," Sicily said. "I'm sure Cherri's gonna let us start hanging around you guys all of a sudden."

"Look, I said what I said. You do what you're gonna do," I replied and slid the prom tickets across the table toward him. "Here."

Sicily picked the tickets up, his eyes uncomfortably shifting as he did. "I gotta say, Nikita, this is unexpected. You're great and all, but—"

"No," I cut him off. "I couldn't say *no* more if I

wanted to. Those are for you and Cherri. It doesn't have to be romantic. I know it won't be easy, but try to convince her to go. Have fun and be normal. We'll leave you alone. I swear."

"Aw, thanks. I'm the techie between us, so I can convince her to go." He chuckled and slid the tickets into his bag. "Anyway, was that it?"

"No, uh, I wanted to ask about Cherri. Does she… Does she still have feelings for Nathan?"

Sicily recoiled. "No offense to him, but Cherri never had feelings for Nathan. Seems to me that he never had any feelings for her either."

"How do you know that?" I asked.

"I mean, I saw Cherri with Deon, and they…" He smiled. "I've never seen anything like it. And I saw you and Nathan together. You guys are pretty great too. I think it's obvious that you two are much better for each other."

That made me happy, but I kept a straight face. "Do you know how long she's gonna hold this grudge against him for Deon and the rape?"

That took Sicily by surprise. "The rape? What are you talking about?"

For a moment, I thought I'd stuck my foot in my mouth. I'd just naturally assumed that Cherri, or maybe even Deon before he left, told Sicily about what happened. "Um."

"Are you talking about when he attacked her right before Deon left?" he asked.

"Oh." I let out a sigh of relief. "Yes."

"Oh. Yeah, Cherri isn't holding a grudge about that. At least, I don't think she is. I think he's the one of you she's *least* mad at. All her rage comes from losing Deon. It has nothing to do with that attack. She told us straight-up that it wasn't like Nathan to do that to her. She said he wasn't *in there* when it happened. She knows Papa Loche has him fucked up in his head."

"I'm shocked. I thought she was holding that against him. She's mad at him the *least* out of all of us?"

He nodded. "Yeah. She knows how caught up he was in everything. Yeah, he asked you all to take her and run, but it's because you guys listened that she got so upset."

That gave me much more to think about than I thought it would. If Cherri wasn't holding Nathan's attack against him, then why was I?

22

———

NATHAN

Kyle had just about made it to his car when I slipped into his path. The roll of his eyes was the only acknowledgment I got as he side-stepped me and continued to his car. I didn't try to stop him, but I followed behind him, and as he unlocked his car to climb in, I climbed through the passenger's side door.

Kyle let out a large sigh. "Nathan."

"Okay, okay, okay, look," I replied. "I don't expect you to talk about anything you don't want to talk about, but—"

Kyle cut me off. "I don't want to talk about it. Please get out."

I nodded. "That's fair. I told you I wouldn't make you talk about it if you didn't want to, but

I'm your best friend, and I really wish you'd talk about it just a little bit because that was shocking to me."

"What part?" Kyle asked.

"What do you mean?"

"What part was so shocking?" Kyle crossed his arms and looked at me, awaiting my answer with a serious but anticipatory gaze.

Was he just trying to get me to admit to something without asking outright? "Um. Well, you asked Brayden to prom at lunch."

"Yeah." His expression remained unchanging. "That was shocking?"

Suddenly, I felt like maybe I'd been a shitty friend, or rather, maybe I'd been a shitty friend in a way that I didn't realize had been shitty. "It was. Should it…not…have been? Did I miss something, being self-absorbed like usual? I realize that's a thing lately."

Kyle rolled his eyes. "No. You didn't miss anything."

I wasn't quite sure what to do with that answer. I at least hadn't been a shitty friend in *that* regard? Kyle and I had been friends since long before I formed The Royal Court. He hadn't dated many people throughout our friendship. He was with a couple of girls in middle school and then Avery for our freshman and sophomore years, but he'd never shown any interest in men. Not that I had an issue with that, but I would like to think that if he was some sexuality other than straight, I would have noticed.

He'd never been a particularly overtly sexual guy. He rarely participated in your typical 'locker room' talk, and he was the guy who would defend women against guys trying to ogle them or advance on them in a way that they wouldn't like. However, I'd heard him discuss admiration for the female form, and as far as I knew, he and Avery slept together. Their relationship fizzled, not for any physical reason, but because Avery and Kyle just got along better as friends. At least, that was what I'd been told. Maybe it was worth a conversation with Avery.

But then why did Brayden bring up pity?

"I'm not sure what to do in this situation," I said.

He shrugged. "Why do you have to do anything?"

"Because you're my friend, and I kind of feel like you need consoling, but I don't really know what I'm consoling you about. Like, when you asked Brayden to prom, did you want to go with him like how a bunch of you went to prom *last* year or like how Avery and Alistair are going to prom *this* year?"

"Are you asking me a specific question, Nathan?" Kyle asked.

"Um, no. Just, if you're feeling disappointed or want to talk or even just hang out to take your mind off of…stuff, I'm here for you. You know that, right?"

Kyle's shoulders relaxed a bit, and it made me feel like I'd made the right choice in abandoning the subject. Kyle's sexuality was his business, and if he wanted to talk to me about it, he would. If he didn't, then he wouldn't. He obviously was prepared to make *some* sort of statement, given that he boldly asked Brayden to prom in front of all of us. If Brayden had accepted his offer, they would have been going to prom together. It's something we would have all seen. On the precipice of Brayden turning him down, he probably just needed some space to mull it over, space he would most certainly get from me.

"Thanks," he said.

I gave him a supportive pat on the back and then climbed out of the car. With a final look at me, Kyle pulled his seatbelt on, started his car, and pulled out of the parking lot. I turned around, prepared to get into my own car and go home, but

I noticed a small group of The Royal Court members standing off to the side. Nikita, Avery, and Alistair were all lingering around my car, and after the talk with Kyle, which did not make any clearer how I could help him, they were a sight for sore eyes. Avery and Alistair had admitted to coming around to me at lunch, so it was nice to see them waiting for me.

"Wait," I said as I approached my car. "Were you three *waiting for me?*"

Nikita walked toward me with a bright smile on her face. "Don't be a dick. You're going to ruin it."

"Fine," I replied.

Nikita and I walked into one another, meeting with a kiss, and I was happy when she laced one of her hands into mine and held onto it. We walked over to where Avery and Alistair stood. Alistair was leaning against the trunk of my car, and Avery was leaning into him. We felt like two normal, happy, high school couples. It almost felt sinful to enjoy it as much as I did.

"Hey, uh, Avery," I started. "You dated Kyle. Did you ever get the sense that he was, you know, not straight?"

"Oh, yeah!" she replied, much more loosely than I thought she might. "I mean, Kyle likes women. Trust me. He *loves* women."

Alistair squeezed Avery a little. "That's enough."

Avery giggled. "Aw, come on, Ali. You know no one puts it down like you."

"Okay," Nikita whined.

I held up a hand. "*Without* the colorful commentary, please? Let's have some respect for our potentially scorned friend."

Avery still let out a little chuckle before continuing. "Yes, in short. I always noticed it most when we'd go out on like dates and stuff. Sometimes, guys would walk by us, and he'd glance after them. We had this *long*-running joke that Timothee Chalamet was on both of our freebie lists, so if he ever turned up, and if we were presented with an opportunity, then we'd just go for the threesome. I know threesomes are just as much a straight guy thing as a non-straight guy thing, but I made a joke about how the session would last *days*, and he said we could tag out for breaks in between. That was when I really started to suspect it, but I didn't ask."

"So, you think he's bi?" I asked.

Avery opened her mouth, but it was Alistair who responded. "I get more of a pansexual vibe from him. I just don't really think Kyle cares as long as there's an attraction."

Nikita scrunched up her nose a little bit. "I

guess we need to address the bigger issue, then. Is Kyle attracted to Brayden?"

Everyone looked off in their own directions as we pondered it. Kyle hadn't had a ton of dating history, but those few people he had been with were all incredibly beautiful. It wasn't that Brayden was unattractive, and maybe I just didn't know how to gauge it, but Brayden didn't seem like Kyle's type.

"I don't think Kyle likes Brayden like that," Avery said. "I mean, for a while, he couldn't *stand* him. Even when he slowly started to tolerate him, it was still like everything Brayden did sort of pissed him off. I always felt like he was just *dealing* with Brayden. Even recently, you've been going through all your stuff, Nathan, and Kyle's such a wonderful guy. I think that's why Brayden was talking about when he mentioned pity back there. Kyle is just showing Brayden an unusual level of friendship because he feels bad about the ground Brayden's lost with you."

That killed me. Not only had Brayden felt like he'd lost a friend in me, but Kyle had to step *so* far outside his comfort zone just to clean up my mess. Again.

Alistair leaned around and kissed Avery's cheek. "Let's go, gorgeous. I'm exhausted. Let's get some dinner and go to bed."

Avery nodded. "Yeah, that sounds good."

They stood up, said goodbye to Nikita and me, including a warm hug between Alistair and myself, and then they walked off toward Alistair's car. Nikita walked around to face me, tilting her face back to look up at me and looping her arms around my waist. Our relationship, if that's what it could be called, was still new and undefined, but Nikita hadn't been big into PDA so far. That day, however, there was something totally new. Her mood had been good since the beginning of the day and had only improved since lunch.

I didn't ask about it. I figured we'd get around to discussing her feelings at some point, and I was too afraid that if I brought it up now, it'd ruin the moment. I leaned down and kissed her instead, relishing in how easy it was and how amazing it felt. It was awful that I'd denied us one another for so long. I would never be able to repay her for all the pain I'd caused her, but if she'd let me, I'd spend the rest of my life trying.

"I spoke to Sicily earlier," she said. "He's seen the men following them too. That confirms Jaxon's theory that they're probably after Cherri and me. I told him what we thought and told him not to leave her alone. I also lightly suggested that they always stay within screaming range of The Royal

Court, but I'm sure you can guess how well that went."

"Yeah," I replied. "Still. *Fuck.* This has to be my dad. I swear to god, if they try and hurt any of you, I'm going to flip my shit."

"Well, let's not get too up in arms yet. We stick together, we look out for each other, and hopefully, Deon will pick up a scent soon."

"Oh my god," I said. "I completely forgot to tell you."

"Tell me what?"

"Deon's missing. I mean, as much as he *can* be missing. The day after you got into that fight with Cherri, he called me. We were talking about what's been going on, and he told me he thinks people are following him too. Then mid-conversation, the line just went dead. I waited for him to call back, but he never did, and I haven't heard from him since."

Nikita's brow furrowed in concern. "How frequently had he been contacting you before?"

"Every week or so. Sometimes eight or nine days in between, but that was the max. It's been almost two weeks now."

Selfishly, I wished that I hadn't remembered. It'd been such a good, borderline normal day, and all of a sudden, all my stress was back. It *wasn't* a normal day. It was deceptively quiet. I rubbed my temples, and Nikita kissed me, no doubt trying to push my obvious stress away. I let her.

"Dinner and sleeping sounded really nice when Alistair said it," she said.

I nodded. "It really did, didn't it?"

"I'll pick something up and meet you at your place," Nikita said. She craned her neck to kiss me one last time and then reluctantly pulled away from my grip. Before she got too far away, I grabbed her hand. She looked back at me with a grin. "What? I'm gonna see you again in twenty minutes."

"We never made a decision about prom at lunch today," I said.

"No, we didn't."

We'd probably end up going as a group. I knew that, and I could see in Nikita's eyes that she knew it, too, but I still pulled her back to me and set my hand on her face. "Hypothetically, if I *were* to ask you to prom officially, as my date, what would you say?"

The small smile on Nikita's face got larger. "Hypothetically?" She gave me a quick peck. "I'd say yes."

23

NIKITA

I looked at my reflection in the mirror and snarled. "I *cannot* believe you talked me into this."

"Stop whining. Come out here and show us!" Colette called back.

At least a thousand times over the course of my years with The Royal Court, I'd heard Avery and Colette make plans to go shopping with Cherri, and every single time, I had the exact same reaction when they didn't invite me.

Thank God.

But it was the Saturday of prom, and Colette randomly called me up and asked me what dress I was planning to wear, and when I told her I was planning to wear a nice pair of jeans and a button-up, I could hear her fall out of her chair. She immediately patched me through to a call with Avery, called it an emergency, and said she was on her way to pick me up. At first, I got annoyed, telling them I didn't want to be a replacement for Cherri, but Colette lovingly told me that I could never replace Cherri, who "had a sense of fashion."

Avery lovingly told me that she'd always secretly hoped I would go shopping with them because she thought I was cool. Colette jumped in, and they went back and forth for twenty minutes, talking about how amazing they thought I was.

Long story short, I was now standing in a dressing room with a ball gown on.

"Nikki, I swear to fucking god, if you don't get out here, I'm gonna come in there, and it's *not* going to be pretty."

I chuckled at Jaxon's gruff voice and even more at the sound of Colette groaning at his language. It was my compromise when I agreed to go shopping. I wanted to bring my best friend. The truth was, I was absolutely *terrified* to be on my own with Avery and Colette, especially doing something so painfully far outside of my wheelhouse as dress shopping. Colette was over the moon with the idea. Jaxon, not so much.

Taking one last look at the fluffy blue ensemble,

I turned around and unlocked the door to the dressing room. When I opened the door, Colette and Avery screeched with excitement, but Jaxon had to turn away to prevent the projectile soda flying out of his mouth from getting on the expensive number.

"What?" I yelped at him. He looked back at me, fighting back a laugh, and I quickly dove into my cleavage for a blade and flipped it out. "I'll cut you."

"Oh, put that away, *Cinderella*," he hissed.

"Okay," Avery said. "It does *not* look as bad as he's making it seem, but I'll agree that it's not really you."

"Can I *please* just wear my pants and button-up?" I begged. "I won't even wear a leather jacket."

"Nikki, what you're suggesting is an absolute sin. At least wear dress pants and a nice blouse or a suit if you'd prefer. I'm not letting you wear what you'd wear to an *apple orchard* to prom! I couldn't call myself a friend nor an upstanding citizen of society if I let you do that."

"I don't have to wear a dress?" I asked.

"No! There are *tons* of prom ensembles that aren't dresses," Avery replied.

I flopped my arms out. "Then what the fuck am I doing in *this*!"

Given that Jaxon was still fighting back laughter, if not the associated tears, I didn't even wait for a response. I immediately turned around and went back into the dressing room to start disrobing.

"Okay, wait in there!" Colette called. "Jaxy, come on. You know her better than any of us. Help us find something more *Nikita*."

"Jaxy?" I called out. "Cute!"

Jaxon popped his hand over the top of the dressing room door, middle finger brandished before Colette dragged him away. I removed the dress and returned it to the hanger, then hung it on the wall.

"Nikki?" Avery called over the door.

"Yeah?"

"Hey," she said, and her voice was quieter. "Thank you for doing this. She'd been looking forward to this all year, and then when everything happened, she didn't think we'd be able to do it. I swear that every time we talked about prom dress shopping, she included you. You aren't a replacement."

"I can tell," I said. "Thanks for including me."

No other words passed between us, and none were needed. The Royal Court had always been an obligation for us, so learning how to just be friends was taking some serious practice, but we were getting there.

After about twenty minutes of flipping through my phone, Avery let out a yelp. "Oh my gosh! It's perfect, but I've got a new plan." She knocked on the door. "Nikki, close your eyes. We're coming in."

"Why would *I* close my eyes? Shouldn't it be the other way around?" I asked.

"Please. It's nothing we haven't seen before. Just do it," she retorted. "Oh, unlock the door first." Not wanting to argue, I unlocked the door and then closed my eyes. Two other bodies packed into the dressing room alongside me—I assumed Colette and Avery—and then Avery said, "Okay, keep 'em closed. We're gonna dress you."

"What?" I screeched. "No!"

"Come on! I want it to be a surprise. Please! Just trust me."

"Jaxon picked it out," Colette added. "Really, it's gonna be absolutely perfect on you."

I let out a sigh and held out my hands, and an instant later, Avery and Colette's hands were all over me. It wasn't a dress, given that someone was working a top over my head while someone else was working pants over my legs, but from what I could tell of the material, it wasn't the cotton I was planning on. Still, it wasn't entirely uncomfortable, not until whoever was handling the shirt pulled it all the way down. It stopped just above my midriff.

"Is it too small?" I asked.

"Nope, it fits perfectly," Avery said.

I wrapped a hand around my stomach. "My stomach is showing, though."

"It's supposed to be that way, Nikki," Colette replied. "Don't worry. It's *super* sexy."

Sexy wasn't ever a look I was striving for, but then Avery let out a quiet hum and said, "Nathan's gonna lose his mind," and it sent a chill rushing through me.

For Nathan, it'd be nice to be sexy.

Eventually, Avery and Colette's hands left my body, so I asked, "Can I open my eyes now?"

"No, wait!" Avery yelped. She reached forward and undid the two braids I typically kept my hair in. "Oh, wow. Your braids give your hair this natural, beach-curl look."

"It's super cute, but it's still missing something," Colette replied, then screeched, "Oh! I know! Keep your eyes closed." She clamored out of the dressing room. About two minutes later, she came back, and I felt her tying something around my forehead and knotting it behind my head. "That's it!"

"That's totally it," Avery said. "Okay, Nikki. Open."

Slowly, I opened my eyes and looked into my reflection in the mirror. A smile rose to my face without my control. I was wearing a pair of black, flared, sequined pants, but the sequins were small and understated, so it didn't look gaudy. The top was a plain, stain, black top with spaghetti straps that gave a very subtle but very enticing view of my stomach. My blond hair with multi-colored strands dyed in was down in loose beach curls, and they tied a thin rope hippie-style around my forehead.

I looked over at Avery, and I had to imagine that I was blushing. "I look pretty."

Both Colette and Avery cheered, and then there was a knock on the door. "Hey! I picked it out. Let me see!"

Avery and Colette slid out of the dressing room first, and then I followed them. When Jaxon's eyes landed on me, they widened, and he got a bright smile on his face that was unlike anything I'd ever seen.

"Holy shit, Nikki!" He stood up. "You look amazing!"

"Yeah?" I asked.

Jaxon looked at Colette. "Clearly, I need to update my resume to include fashion sense."

"Clearly," Colette replied.

Avery and Colette had a much easier time

picking out dresses. Then we secured Jaxon a last-minute button-up, suit bottoms, and suspenders that deliberately didn't match Colette's dress since we'd ultimately decided to attend prom as a group. We took our bags and drove over to Nathan's house, where we were gathering to get dressed and catch a limo to prom.

Avery, Colette, and I got dressed up in Nathan's bedroom while the boys turned the living room into their dressing central, and after being talked into applying a very, *very* thin coat of makeup, we went back downstairs to meet up with the guys. Avery insisted that she and Colette go first so that I could make a big entrance, and with how much fun they were having, I didn't want to deny them. They fluttered down the stairs, presented themselves, and then made a huge announcement for me.

"Presenting, for the first time ever in formal wear, Nikita!" Colette said.

I walked around the corner, and Brayden and Kyle's jaws both dropped. Kyle started to laugh from how shocked he was while Brayden just stared.

Finally, Brayden clapped. "You *do* clean up well."

"Thanks." My gaze drifted over to Nathan, who

was looking amazing in his navy-blue suit, and he looked dumbstruck. "Well?"

He scoffed. "Are you kidding me with this? I... You..." He looked at Kyle. "You see that, too, right?"

Kyle tapped Nathan on his shoulder and pushed him toward me. "Yes. I see it too."

Nathan walked up to me, took my arms, and held them out. "Baby, you look..." He smiled. "I mean, you always look beautiful, but this is just...unlawful."

I laughed. "You look good too. I love seeing you in a suit." I leaned in a little bit. "I'd love to see you without it even more."

Nathan's eyes darkened a little bit. "Don't do that. If you talk like that while looking like *that*, we *will* miss prom."

"No, no, no," Colette said. "All sex will be reserved until *after* prom. Now, let's go." She clapped her hands. "Our limo is waiting."

The rest of our peers almost seemed irritated with how much we'd managed to gather ourselves in time for prom, but all eyes were on us, and a short fanfare erupted. Two people stood out amongst the crowd as the only two who seemed less than impressed with us, but as our eyes found

Cherri and Sicily in the back corner, we were all relieved that they were there.

We were all so distracted by everything going on that we didn't even stop to see what prom's theme was, but as we walked in, it was clear it was space-themed without being tacky. Different planets and stars hung from the ceilings, and all of the balloons were starbursts in different shades of purple, blue, and white. There was a beautiful, starry galaxy backdrop to take prom pictures against, and the dance floor had been fashioned with a galaxy-painted paneling. It was beautiful.

We found a table to claim as our own and took turns going to the dance floor as couples so as not to rub our couplings in Kyle's and Brayden's faces. We danced and hung out together as a group of friends who were happy to be with one another. A few songs did come on that were perfect for dancing together, so Avery invited Brayden out for a dance. Colette cut into the dance as Avery's and Brayden's was ending, and then after giving Nathan a look, I walked out and cut in myself.

Brayden let out a fake, dramatic groan. "Can't a guy rest?"

"It's your fault for being so light on your feet," Colette said as she left, and I took over, letting Brayden lead.

"I didn't think you'd come over here," Brayden said. "I know you don't like me."

"At first, yeah, I didn't really like you a whole lot," I admitted, "but you've grown on me. Quite a lot. I was sick when you *took a break* without telling us for two weeks. Nathan was sick with worry."

Brayden rolled his eyes. "He had you, so I'm sure he was fine."

I wasn't sure what I had to do with it, but I didn't know how to ask without being weird. "We got into a pretty bad fight while you were gone. I found myself wishing you were around because you could have kept him from falling into too bad of a slump. He always lets you pull him out easier than anyone else."

"Yeah."

"Hey, can I ask you a question that's probably crossing the line for our ambivalent, undefined relationship?" I asked.

He chuckled. "Why not?"

"Why was your reaction to Kyle asking you to prom so visceral? It seemed like he really wanted to come with you." Brayden didn't immediately answer, so I quickly added, "Sorry, you don't have to answer."

"No, it's…" He bit his lip a little bit. "I don't know. I thought he was just fucking around, and it made me mad. It's not the kind of thing to joke about."

"If he wasn't fucking around, what would you have said?" I asked.

Even in the low light, I could see Brayden's cheeks get a little darker. "I don't know."

"Can I give you some advice as someone who has absolutely no business giving *anyone* advice?"

"Sure," Nathan replied.

"I spent a really, really, really long time not being honest about my feelings for Nathan, and now it feels like we're swimming through mud just to get to a clear understanding. If there are feelings there, know that none of us would judge you, know that Kyle wouldn't fuck around with your feelings, and just say something."

The words just kind of came out, and I wished they hadn't. I remembered Avery saying that she didn't think Kyle truly liked Brayden, but then why ask him to prom? The song changed, but Brayden didn't make any movement to stop dancing. Neither did I, so we kept going.

A little smile came across Brayden's face at the change. "Nathan loves this song."

Brayden wasn't even facing Nathan, but I looked over Brayden's shoulder and saw Nathan grooving to it. "Yeah, it looks like…"

Then it hit me like a train. Brayden was *always* running around after Nathan. Brayden idolized him and didn't seem to like Cherri almost as much as I didn't seem to like her. He was ready to trash her when Nathan broke up with her, regardless of what he'd done to her, and when Nathan did openly nice things for Brayden during the past few weeks, it put him on cloud nine.

Brayden had feelings for *Nathan*.

Kyle must have figured it out and was trying to divert Brayden's attention. It broke my heart into pieces. I didn't say anything else to Brayden because I didn't feel like anything that I could say would be enough of an apology. Instead, we danced quietly until the song was over and then stopped.

"Thanks for dancing with me," I said. "Really, we—I—like having you around."

He offered me a weak smile. "Thanks. It won't last long."

"Huh?"

"I'm gonna run to the bathroom. See you in a bit," he said, and then he turned around and walked away from me.

What won't last long? What did that mean?

I walked back to our table, unsure of what to make of Brayden's statement and indecisive about if I should ask the group for help or not. Then I noticed that Jaxon was fixated on something across the room. I followed his gaze over my shoulder and to the wall on the other side of the dance floor.

The two men we'd chased in the van were standing against the wall, and they were brazenly staring right back at us.

24

NATHAN

Nikita seemed really put off at the end of her dance with Brayden, and I was just about to ask what it was all about when I noticed her look at Jaxon and then back over her shoulder. The rest of us at the table noticed that Jaxon and Nikita were focused on the same thing across the room, and one by one, we all looked over. The two men who Jaxon had shown me pictures of back when he first noticed that we were being followed were standing against the far wall, looking back at us. I hadn't gotten the entire story about what happened when Nikita and Jaxon chased them down. I felt like there was something Nikki was keeping from me about it, but I wasn't sure what.

It was Kyle who spoke first. "Are those the guys, Jaxon?"

"Yeah," he responded. "This is different, though. They're being brazen. They know we see them, and they don't care."

He scanned the room, and his eyes landed somewhere else. I followed his direction until I saw Sicily and Cherri in the opposite corner of the room. Sicily seemed to have a bead on the men as well. In a quick moment, Sicily looked over, and we locked eyes. I nodded in the direction of the men, and he nodded at me before returning to his conversation with Cherri while keeping a close watch on the men as well.

"Okay," Avery said. "What's going on?"

Nikita looked across at her and Alistair. They were probably the most out of the loop since Kyle, Colette, and I had all gotten bits of the story due to our associations with Brayden, Nikita, and Jaxon.

"There are two men standing against that wall. They have been following us," Nikita said.

"What?" Alistair yelped and then turned to look at me. "How could you not tell me that?"

"I didn't—"

"It wasn't up to Nathan," Kyle cut in quickly. "I asked Jaxon and Nikita to keep it down. We didn't need the group panicking for no reason, and it was just a hunch until we found Brayden."

"What happened when you found Brayden?" Avery asked.

"Well, the guys came to Nikki's house," Jaxon said, taking over. "I was nervous that they were going to try and snatch her, but I got to her first. We decided to follow them and chased them all the way into North Postings, but right as we were about to catch up to them, we saw Brayden randomly wandering down the road. Obviously, we had to stop for him, so we lost them."

"Do you think they took Brayden?" Kyle asked.

"We don't know if those guys took him, but the two events are definitely related," Nikita said. "There's no reason why Brayden would appear at that *exact* moment. We think wherever Brayden was, whether he went willingly or was taken, the guys in the car were able to somehow contact whoever had him and say to cut him loose as a distraction."

"My dad," I tacked on. "That's my guess."

"Do you think he's here in Postings?" Avery asked. "I thought he would have bolted."

"Me too," I replied, "but when I went to my company's board meeting back in February, his office was decorated with congratulatory decorations for me. He's the only one with a key to the office and who can get in or out, so he's the only one who could have done it."

"Do…" Kyle looked at Nathan. "Do you think Brayden's in contact with your dad for some reason? Like, of his own volition?"

"He just said something super weird to me at the end of our dance," Nikita said. "I told him we really did love having him as part of our group, and he said, 'That won't last long.'"

"What?" I said. "No. There's no way that Brayden would betray us like that."

Kyle stood up and walked away from the table, and without even asking, we knew that he was on the way to see if he could track down Brayden. I watched the two men, but they made no attempt to move. They didn't seem to care that Kyle had walked out.

"That confirms my theory," Jaxon said.

"Which one?" Alistair asked.

"I think that these guys want Nikki and Cherri, specifically," he replied.

Nikita had told me that part, though she'd left out the suspicious coincidence of what had happened right before she found Brayden. Maybe she thought I'd assume the worst and didn't want to upset me, but it would have been nice to know before that moment. I might have kept a closer eye on him.

"What do we do?" Avery said. "Do we just live in fear until your dad decides to leave us alone?"

If I was going to pick a time to tell the table that Deon was alive, this would be it. "I have someone looking for him, so we just have to keep up with each other a little bit longer. Double down on never letting one another out of our sights. Travel in groups, and I'm going to get you guys weapons, I think, and schedule some shooting lessons, just in case."

Jaxon raised a hand. "I have so many weapons."

Nikita didn't say the same, only flipped out one of her smuggled-in switchblades, twirled it in her fingers, and then flicked it away again.

"Okay, I know you two are good," I said, "but the rest of us could use some protection."

Colette meekly raised her hand and pointed at Jaxon. "All of our dates have been to shooting ranges, rage rooms, or battleax-making courses," she said. "He got me a gun for Christmas."

"That's dark," Alistair said.

"What greater gift is there than protection?" Jaxon asked. "I'm not about to let anything happen to this one." He earned himself a kiss on the cheek for that.

I looked at Avery and Alistair. "You two aren't harboring secret firearms, are you?"

"You mean since we all got cornered in your dad's cabin in the woods where he pointed a gun at us and threatened to kill us?" Alistair asked. "Yeah, we both got guns and licenses to carry them."

I looked over at Nikita. "Great. Looks like I'm slow on the uptake."

"Hey, at least everyone is *super* prepared," Nikita replied.

Kyle came walking back to the table without Brayden, looking particularly dejected. "Nope. He's not here, and his car is gone."

"Shit," I said. "I really hope he's not mixed up with my dad. He has no idea what mess he's getting into if he is."

"Your dad wouldn't kill him, right, Nathan?" Kyle asked with honest fear in his voice.

Maybe Kyle *did* have feelings for Brayden. I was caught between not wanting to upset him any further and wanting to be honest. "Uh, as long as he does what he is told, he should be fine. My dad knows how to use a good tool until it's useless."

"What if Brayden is supposed to spy on all of

us and tell these goons the best time for a snatch and grab?" Colette mused.

"I really don't think he'd do that," I said. "Brayden may have felt like an outsider, but he still cared about us. *If* he's caught up with my dad, I don't think it's willingly."

There was an air of tension at the table. It seemed like no one believed me, and I couldn't blame them, but I had faith in Brayden. The Royal Court meant everything to him. He wouldn't risk everything like that. I believed that from the bottom of my heart.

We spent the next hour or so enjoying a little bit more of the food and drink, and we all made our trips out to the dance floor once more, but we were all tense. Everyone made their own attempts to track down Brayden to ask him to come back to the party, but he wasn't answering anyone's calls or texts, just like when he disappeared last time.

I kept a close eye on Cherri and Sicily, and fortunately, Sicily always seemed to have the two men clocked. They didn't move much, only occasionally shifting to the left or right when the rotation of people on the dance floor and at the tables obstructed their view of us. Jaxon was right. They were not being subtle about watching us. If and when we decided to leave, we were going to need to go as a group, and it was going to have to be fast. I was already considering inviting everyone to my house so that we could all stay together, but Avery's words rang true in my mind. I didn't want to live in fear of these men forever. They would only know where to find us for another few weeks. We'd graduate soon, and tracking us would get considerably more difficult for the goons.

I was hoping everything was sorted out by then. I didn't want my friends' anxiety to drag on into our last summer together before we all went our separate ways for whatever we had planned for the next legs of our journeys.

"Maybe we should all go," Nikita said, reading my mind. "We're not having any fun here with these guys stressing us out."

Colette frowned. "Senior prom ending with a bang."

It was just another thing my family's drama was costing my friends. Thanks to me, their *entire* senior year had been ruined. They would never get another chance to fall in love with their high school sweethearts or dance at their senior prom. Hell, even graduation was going to be ruined at this point.

"You guys, I'm—"

Alistair slapped the table. "Yes!" He showed his

phone to Avery. "Check that out, baby. Nine-thirty-two. You owe me dinner."

"Goddammit, Nathan," Avery hissed. "You couldn't have gotten self-reflective five minutes ago?"

"Um. What?" I asked, shocked.

"As soon as everything took a turn, Avery texted me, betting me that you'd apologize to the group before nine-thirty. I said you'd wait until a little after," Alistair explained.

"You meant like ten o'clock," Avery said.

"Hey, a little is a little," Alistair quipped back. "I will take Pork Rolls tomorrow."

Avery fake gagged. "Oh my god. Even the tables there are deep-fried."

"Yep. That's what I want."

"Am I missing something? Why is that worth betting on?" I asked.

Avery smiled. "Because you're still so convinced that everything is your fault and that you owe us the world and that you're carrying everything on your shoulders. We could have left, you know? We're still here. You said it yourself. We have to stick together."

"Yeah. If you guys hadn't hitched your horses to my wagon—"

"Yeah, but we did," Kyle said. "None of us *had* to be in The Royal Court."

Alistair raised his hand. "I did."

Kyle rolled his eyes. "Okay, none of us other than Alistair had to be in The Royal Court. Then you gave us all a free pass to go, but we stayed. We're all here. We're part of this. We know what it means, and we're part of it anyway."

"Yeah, Nathan. You disappeared last semester," Colette said. "The second we heard that you disappeared and that your mom died, we panicked, and then when Nikki tracked you down, we got together with Cherri and Deon and came to find you. Even the two people who liked you the *least* at that time broke their backs to get to you. You think that we were all tied to you for the perks or out of obligation, but maybe, *just maybe* we like you a little."

That was true. When my dad took me and drove me up to our cabin, the entire Royal Court plus Deon showed up to save me. They rushed in and fought with my dad, risking their lives to fight for me. People who hated you didn't do that kind of thing.

"I'm so dumb," I said. "Friendship has never really been like this for me. Well, I never really had friends. I made a bunch when Deon lived with my family, but when he left, all of them left except for

Kyle, and of course, Nikki has always been by my side."

"Wait," Colette said. "You've been comparing us to *those* shitty friends this entire time? Kyle! Hit him for me!"

Kyle didn't hesitate. He reached over and whacked me across the arm. Though he put some force behind it, and though it hurt a little bit, all I could do was smile. "I love you guys," I said.

"I am *not* telling you I love you back," Alistair replied, and the table laughed. I could feel it in the unspoken. I was loved by my friends. It made me think of what Nicole said to me about forgiveness. I could give as much as I wanted, but it would only be when they truly wanted to forgive me that it made any difference.

"Do you guys wanna get out of here?" I asked. "We can all crash at my place if we want to stick together, or I can call us a limo to get us home."

"No offense, but I kind of want to be in my own bed tonight," Kyle said.

"Me too," Alistair said, and Avery nodded with him.

"Besides," Nikita said, side-eyeing me. "It's better if we have no visitors."

My entire lower half tingled at the look in her eyes, and I turned to face everyone else. "Oh, never mind. Invitation rescinded. Go home or wherever you want. I don't care. You just can't come to my house."

"Perverts," Kyle huffed.

"Where is Cherri?" Colette suddenly asked.

"Huh?" I replied. "I mean, feel free to invite her if you want, but talking to her hasn't gone well for us as a group."

"Went fine for me," Nikita huffed under her breath, and I glared at her before snickering. I may have stuck up for her, but Cherri lost that fight.

"No!" Colette yelped, pointing across the room. "There's Sicily, but where is Cherri?"

I looked over, and Sicily was looking down at his phone. Cherri was nowhere in the vicinity. He seemed unaware that she wasn't there. He looked up in the direction of where the men stood against the wall, but when he did, he looked slightly panicked. I looked over and realized that they weren't there anymore. Sicily jumped up and looked over in our direction. Our eyes locked, and we realized that we'd gotten too distracted and made a terrible mistake.

"Shit!" I yelled, jumping up. "Outside!" No one asked why, and we rushed away from our table, rattling it as we moved. "What happened?" I barked at Sicily as he ran up beside us.

"I think she gave me the slip on purpose. She knew that I was keeping her close, but I wouldn't tell her why," Sicily snapped back. "I was *just* talking to her, though. She couldn't have been gone longer than thirty seconds."

That was all it took. We rushed out through the front doors and didn't see anything. I was terrified that we were too late and terrified that I was going to have to tell Deon that I let Cherri slip through my fingers, but then we heard screaming. It sounded like it was coming from the back of the building, so we bolted around to the back just in time to see Cherri entangled with the two men as they attempted to drag her off. Cherri was a small girl, but she was putting up quite a fight, and she had a small blade in her hand that she was swinging wildly, keeping the men from getting too much of a hold on her.

"Cherri!" I screeched.

The men saw us running over and tried their best to drag Cherri toward an unmarked black SUV parked a little bit away, but her fighting was enough to give us time to catch up. Nikita had a knife out in five seconds and jumped in swinging, but it seemed like the men were going to try to take the opportunity to snatch her too. One abandoned Cherri and started trying to wrap around Nikita, but it turned out to be a grave mistake. The second he wrapped his arms around her, she sliced him across the arm, cutting straight through his suit. Then she flipped around and clocked him right in his nose. He fell backward, and Nikita turned on the other guy, who Jaxon was already pulling off of Cherri.

Jaxon shoved Cherri away, and Sicily and I took each of her arms to pull her back as she tried to jump back in. She was swearing like crazy and trying to fight her way out of our grip, but we held position. Jaxon headbutted the guy that grabbed Cherri in the face, and the guy, too, fell backward. At that moment, the person who was meant to be driving the car climbed out with a gun brandished. He pointed it at Jaxon and Nikita, who both stopped advancing.

"Get in the car, you fucking idiots. They're kids," he huffed.

The two damaged men got to their feet, stumbled over to the car, and climbed in. The driver, who clearly had no intention of fighting us, backed up until he was at the door. He climbed in, keeping his gun on us until the very last second, then pulled away with a loud screech.

I ran over to Nikita to make sure she was okay, as did Colette to Jaxon, but everyone was unharmed. Cherri was jostled but otherwise okay, but it didn't stop Avery from rushing over to her.

"Are you okay?" She reached out to try and touch her, but Cherri smacked her hand away. "Cherri."

"What the fuck are you guys doing out here?" she spat.

I rolled my eyes. Maybe it was my recent breakthrough, but I was in no mood to deal with Cherri's attitude after we just saved her—again.

"Guys, let's just go. If she's not gonna be grateful, this is only going to get ugly," I said.

That seemed to take Cherri back a bit, but she quickly recovered with an evil glare. "Grateful? For what? I had it covered."

"Sure," Jaxon said. "That's what halfway to the kidnap car looks like."

"What?" Cherri asked, looking as if she was going to advance on Jaxon, but he didn't even flinch, and neither did anyone else. For the first time, The Royal Court looked down at Cherri with nothing but disappointment and disgust. That is, everyone apart from Avery.

Alistair walked over, wrapped his hands around his girlfriend, and pulled her away. "Have a nice night, Cherri."

Avery didn't put up a fight, just sadly looked

back at her best friend as she was led off. I waited for everyone else to walk away first, then I looked back at Cherri. I could see the calculation in her face—the realization that we'd all reached our limit with her. Part of me wanted to ask how that made her feel, but the rest of me just wanted to take my beautiful Nikita and leave.

"I feel bad for you, Cherri," I said. "The Royal Court…" I looked ahead at them, watching them walk away. "We're going through this amazing transformation, and we really wanted you to be a part of it, both of you," I said, including Sicily. "I'm so sorry that us giving a damn about you has created such a huge rift, but that consideration won't be a problem for you anymore. We're done."

With that, I wrapped my arm behind Nikita's back and led her back toward the front of the building where everyone else was waiting. We called a set of Ubers, chatted a little more while we waited, and then it was time for the couples to all go their separate ways, with Kyle heading home alone.

"Come with Avery and me," Alistair said to Kyle. "I know the rabbits over here," he said, nodding his head at Nikita and me, "have naughty plans, but our idea of a sexy night is sleeping until we've drooled so much that the bed sheets need to be changed."

Colette nodded. "Hot," and everyone laughed.

"We mostly stay at my house since my parents don't mind, and we have, like, three guest rooms."

Kyle shook his head. "Thanks, but Brayden was right. The couples here are pretty evident. You guys go, and please, for the love of god, do something more exciting to celebrate your senior prom night than sleep."

We all got into our individual rideshares to head back to our homes after reminders for everyone to take special care and be vigilant. When Nikita and I were in our car, I rested my head back against the seat, and everything washed over me.

"You okay?" Nikita asked.

"Yeah," I said. "That was hard. I still feel like I owe Cherri the world, but you're right. We can't just continue to stand around while she hurts us."

"Yeah."

"I wish I had a way to contact Deon. He needs to know that these guys made a move," I said. "He still hasn't called yet."

"We have to be patient. Our fates are in his hands now. Our job is to keep ourselves safe, and as long as we can do that, the rest is up to him."

The car dropped us at my house, and we

walked in and straight up to my bedroom. I flopped down on my bed and looked over at my laptop, just thinking about the number of unread emails I probably had.

"Oh, don't you dare," Nikita said, straddling herself over me. "It's my senior prom night, and I'm having sex with my boyfriend."

I looked up at her with shock in my eyes. "Boyfriend?"

25

NIKITA

Nathan's hands slid up my stomach and slipped under the base of my shirt. He didn't pull it off, but instead, he continued up until his hands were cupped around my breasts. I let out a huff as his cool skin gave me goosebumps, and he smiled at my reaction. He looked so good in his suit that I almost didn't want to take it off, but while his hands journeyed over my chest, mine dropped down to undo the button of his suit jacket. He pulled his arms out of the sleeves one by one so that he never truly had to stop touching me, but once I started to work on his button-up shirt, he broke contact with me so that he could strip it off. He shoved both the jacket and the button-up off the side of the bed and then placed me down on my back on the bed.

He anchored his hands on either side of my face and leaned down to kiss me. It was a soft peck at first, just enough to give me a taste of him, but then my arms slid up his chest and wrapped around his back, and he parted his lips slightly to let his tongue slide out. Mine entangled with his for a bit before he pulled my bottom lip between his teeth to nip it. He pulled away just enough to kiss me on my cheek and down my neck. Then his head dropped against my shoulder.

"Man, Nikki," he huffed in my ear. "I love you so much."

"I…" It got caught in my throat a little bit.

They were words I'd thought so many times before, but I'd never said them out loud. The past week had been so good, though, and after talking with Sicily and seeing Nathan worry about me over Cherri during the fight at prom, I realized how important it was to say. He meant so much more to me than even myself, and at that moment, I was overwhelmed with the need to be honest with him about how I felt.

"I love you too, Nathan," I said.

He leaned on his forearms so that he could look down over me. "Really?"

The purity in his eyes was so heartwarming. "Of course, really." I reached up and put a hand on his face. "I figured it out."

He grinned. "You did?"

"Yeah." I craned my head so that I could kiss him. "I'm sorry it took me so long."

"No. Don't apologize. Honestly, it gave me a lot of time to figure out who I really am and who I want to be. I still don't think I have it totally figured out, but there is one thing I know for certain, and that's how much I love you."

"Me too," I said. "Since I was a shut-down, abused little girl, you've always been by my side. It was painful to watch you with Cherri, but I held out hope that it would work itself out. I feel selfish, and I feel like I shouldn't get to be so happy while other people are suffering, but I do get to be happy. I love you."

It was all that needed to be said. Nathan smoothed his hands along my sides, nesting them into the bend of my waist. My body burned all over, most warmly where he touched. He bent over and kissed my stomach, and then when he slid his hands up, he pulled my shirt with it.

He laid a line of kisses up my stomach and along my sternum. He alternated between kissing me and licking me until I was little more than a puddle in his hands. His breath blew in warm puffs across my skin, leaving a feeling behind like a blazing iron had been dragged across it. I could feel my ears burning, and my legs trembled with anticipation as he worked.

It was usually around that time that I would try to lock some of myself away, tethering myself to some reality that eventually I'd have to give Nathan up. I'd try desperately to keep my feet on the ground while he was trying to drag me into the clouds.

This time, I let him pull.

Every time his lips pressed to a new spot on my skin, it felt like I was getting higher and higher. His mouth traveled further up until it pressed against the front clasp of my bra. He snapped it free and pulled my bra away, almost immediately closing his warm lips over one of my waiting breasts. His hands massaged while his mouth worked my sensitive nipple, and I let out a sigh of pleasure, writhing beneath him and anticipating what was yet to come. One of his legs kicked between mine to push forward and apply gentle pressure to my heat below. I found myself grinding against it as he switched from one breast to the other and back again.

Eventually, he sent one of his hands between us

toward our legs. He undid the button of my pants and dove beneath them until he was able to rub over me through the fabric of my panties. A moan sang out of me, and Nathan took it as a sign of satisfaction and became rougher with his movements. He bit at my nipples, and the fingers between my legs pulled aside my underwear to poke directly at my sensitive spots.

"Nathan," huffed out of me before I could stop it. "That feels good."

He lifted his head from my breasts and looked directly into my eyes. His rubbing below grew faster. A finger sank inside of me while his thumb continued to flick my bud, and my mind started to simmer. My lips were held slightly open, with only my breathless moans coming out, and my vision blurred as an orgasm started small and then ricocheted all over my body. I lifted my back into the feeling of Nathan's hand, but he held eye contact as he rubbed me through. I dropped back to the bed, trying to catch my breath.

Nathan stood from the bed and undid his pants. He continued to look down at me with a dark, starved expression that sent chills blanketing my body. He'd taken on a new alpha-aura that I'd never seen before but wasn't unhappy to see. Kicking his pants off, he took his hard length into his hand and stroked it as he looked down at me with apparent admiration.

Nathan held out a hand, which I took, and he dragged me up to stand. He flipped me around so that he could push me against the bedroom door, and moments later, his hands were on my pants, pulling them down. He trailed kisses up my legs as he stood back up, then attached himself to me and buried his mouth against the crook of my neck. He used a hand to brace himself at my entrance, then slowly pushed into me.

Our moans matched in desire and desperation as he thrust in, and when he was settled inside, he stopped moving. "Shit." He laughed against my shoulder. "I'm clearly going to have to figure out a way to deal with how good you feel." He pulled almost all the way out and slid all the way back into me. His hands braced on my hips, and he said, "I love you."

"I love you too," I replied.

In the wake of that, Nathan picked up the pace as he moved in and out of me. It took him no time at all to find the spot inside of me that made my brain fuzzy and fogged over. All I knew was Nathan's closeness and the feeling of him stoking me, stirring me up, forcing my body to memorize and remember him. I loved him so much, and as the thoughts of all the times we had ahead of us flicked through my mind, I came again. It snuck up on me, but when it hit me, it was monumental and all-encompassing, causing me to scream out. One of Nathan's muscular arms slammed against the wall next to me, tensing to survive the feeling of me spasming around him.

"You're not helping," he growled.

"Blame yourself."

He pulled away from me, dropping out and leaving me desperate for more, but he grabbed my hand and turned me around. He pulled my head to him and mashed our lips together in a deep, passionate kiss. He sat down on the bed and pulled me down to straddle him, and I wasted no time in guiding him back into me. He was searing hot and slick as he went in, and I shuddered as he clasped his mouth over my breast to suck. I started to ride up and down with fervor, chasing more of the ecstasy I had found in freeing myself to enjoy him.

The way he flicked his tongue over my nipples and sucked with gentle firmness threatened to drag me over again. Nathan grew ever larger inside of me, and eventually, he released himself from my breast. With his hands digging into my hips, he pumped in a few more times. Another orgasm hit me, causing my entire lower body to shake, and

Nathan repositioned to pull out of me just in time to release, shaking and moaning as he did so.

With my hands curled behind his neck, I kissed Nathan one more time. It was almost like I was trying to make up for lost time or like I was still operating under the impression that there would be an undefined amount of time before I'd be able to be this close to him again.

Nathan traced circles across my lower back. "What, Nikki?"

"Nothing, just, when I said boyfriend, that's what I meant, you know?" I said.

"When you said it, my heart started beating triple time. That's what I've been waiting for this whole time. I want to be yours, and I want you to be mine."

"You're nothing like my father, Nathan. I know I couldn't separate the two for a while, but you care about Cherri. You showed remorse, and you showed guilt. You apologized and tried to do the right thing. Cherri doesn't hold it against you. She knows that wasn't part of who you are, and I know that too."

He squeezed me a little tighter. "So this is it? Me and you?"

I nodded with a smile on my face. "Yeah. Me and you."

26

NIKITA

The last week of May brought finals, which meant that on top of all of The Royal Court's run-of-the-mill stress, we also had the additional stress of nailing our final exams. It wasn't as if any members of The Royal Court weren't particularly intelligent or prepared to ace their exams. The issue was the added stress of being sequestered from one another, leaving us alone or *maybe* in pairs for a vast majority of the day. The biggest issue was not being able to keep an eye on Brayden. After our hypotheses from prom, we were surprised to see him return to school and continue hanging out with The Royal Court as he always had, but everyone kept him in sight and mind.

However, Brayden was a junior. They had final

exams, too, but they weren't as important or as intense as the senior's final exams. He had much more free time during the day, so there were several chunks of the day where not only was he not with any other member of The Royal Court, but he also had a lot of time to get into something he shouldn't. Nathan was pretty convinced that Brayden would never work with Connor to harm us in any way, and I wanted to believe that was true, but I wasn't so sure. If anything, I knew how conniving Connor could be.

There was something that curbed the darkness of Brayden's lack of supervision, though. Cherri was present for the finals. Several members of The Royal Court reported seeing her in their classes in the little bits of time we had between classes to check our phones and used the bathroom, and at least in the one class Cherri and I had together, she appeared to legitimately be trying. How she was managing the course material after skipping class nearly all semester, I wasn't sure, but even the teachers seemed to be shocked at her presence.

The students of whatever class you were in during the lunch hour were the ones with whom you ate, and the food was delivered directly to your class to prevent cheating. The only other member of The Royal Court in my class during lunch was

Kyle. As soon as lunch was delivered, he made his way over to my desk and sat down. His eyes were certainly a bit wearier, and I was wondering how much he'd talk to me about Brayden if I asked. Kyle and I had been friends since before Nathan even conceived The Royal Court, so it was oddly nice and calming to have a one-on-one meal with him.

"We should probably all get together tonight, huh?" Kyle offered. "I feel weird being separated from everyone all day. Do you think they would all go for dinner?"

"Yeah, I think it's a good idea. It'll be nice to relax and have some good food. If we go to Colette's mom's place, she'll let us drink wine."

"Oh, that's a good idea. I'll send a text." He typed on his phone, and I heard the message notification as he sent the message to our group feed, but I didn't bother to check it. "There. Everyone will see it when they can, and we can figure out the specifics after school."

"Hey," I started. "Can I ask you a question that you totally don't have to answer?"

"Okay," he said, tilting his head to the side.

"So, I have kind of gathered that Brayden maybe has feelings for Nathan, and I get the sense that you figured that out too."

Kyle rolled his eyes. "Ah. Busted."

"So prom was what?"

"Nathan was going through so much, and he was trying to fix things with you and make things right with Cherri, and he didn't need Brayden in the mix, muddying things up. Plus, Nathan is obviously straight, and I just felt bad having to watch Brayden go down that road. I thought I could maybe serve as a distraction for him and put both him and Nathan in a better spot." He took a sip of his juice. "Can I admit something to you, though?"

I smiled. "You like him?"

He shrugged his shoulders. "I don't know why. It really was supposed to just be something to get them through the rest of this year, but then I started to really get into it. All of a sudden, I'm dreaming about him and can't get him off my mind, and all this shit with him and what's going on with Nathan's family keeps me up at night. I'm terrified that he's going to get hurt."

"So why don't you say something?" I asked.

"I mean, it's pretty obvious that he's not into it the way I am."

"I don't know," I replied. "I think it could be less black and white than you think."

"Maybe once all of this is all over, once there's less mud to swim through, I'll tell him how I feel."

I tilted my head to the side as I imagined it. "Though, if I can be honest, I feel like you guys would be a weird couple. Not bad, necessarily, but weird."

"Whose fault is that? You all paired up and left us alone! Flirting spreads, you know? You all made cuffing season look *real* good."

I laughed. "Sorry, not sorry."

"Man, it doesn't really feel like it's been eight years since we met, does it?" he mused.

"Eight years?" I thought back and realized that it was true. It had been eight years ago when we met. "Wow. No, it doesn't."

"Do you remember how excited he was when we first all went to play basketball together?" Kyle asked.

I smiled, remembering the wide, dopey smile on Nathan's face as he ran at me with a basketball in hand, screaming at me that he was going to show me his jump shot. "He was elated. All it took was for Deon to spend one day teaching him how to play. Then he wouldn't put a basketball down."

"It's so weird. I doubt many people even know how much he loves basketball," Kyle said.

"I was just thinking about that recently. There are all these things about Nathan that got pushed beneath the surface and hidden because of his dad and the pressure of The Royal Court. He loves the outdoors, he's really into classical music, and he *hates* technology. His computer is as old as dirt. Every time his dad forced him to get a new phone, he complained to me for hours about it."

Kyle started to laugh. "Yeah. I had to have a whole tutorial to show him how to use his phone." He smiled at me after that. "I'm happy he has you, Nikki. I mean, I know he says it, but he's, like, *always* loved you. When we first met, I told him that I thought you were cute, and he flipped his shit. He told me to stay away from you. And you could do anything, literally anything, and he'd get excited about it. After everything that you've ever done for as long as I've known you that's even been mildly impressive, Nathan would call me to talk to me about how cool you were. He really, really loves you, Nikki."

That made me happy to hear. "He's been around for me ever since I was a little girl. I suffered abuse by my parents, and my grandma wanted to move me out of Postings, but she let me stay here with my foster mother because it was obvious how good he was for me. When he started dating Cherri, I was crushed."

"I can't even imagine how hard that must have

been, but I need you to know exactly how hard that was for him too."

"I know that his dad made him do most of it, but I'm not dumb. Cherri is beautiful, and I'm sure he enjoyed having her on his arm."

Kyle bobbled his head. "I guess a little, but at the end of any day, he was always looking at you."

That gave me a warm feeling in my stomach. I liked thinking that it wasn't just a trip to paradise for Nathan when we weren't together. I'd made a promise to myself not to look back on what happened before we got together, but it didn't stop the insecurities from seeping in. Kyle, whether he was doing it on purpose or not, was helping to ease some of those insecurities.

We finished our finals and then met up with everyone outside of school. Everyone was really excited about spending some time together to celebrate, so we paired off to head to Colette's family's sushi restaurant to end the day. Brayden hadn't disappeared during the day, which was good, and he joined us to celebrate the conclusion of the finals and officially being graduation-bound.

We were ushered to the back of the restaurant, where a private room had already been set up for us to sit in, complete with congratulatory balloons and a few bottles of wine to share amongst us. We placed different orders for a variety of sushi combinations to share, and the staff delivered a bunch of appetizers to the table for us to enjoy while we waited. Nathan popped open the first bottle of wine and poured everyone a glass.

"We're gonna make it," Nathan said with a sigh, lifting up his glass of wine. "Fucking toast to that shit." Everyone lifted their glasses and clinked them together. "You guys, we *have* to have a massive graduation party. I know your parents are all throwing you your own graduation parties, and obviously, I'm gonna be there, but I want to throw a big, insane graduation party. I'm gonna spend, like, a hundred grand on it. I don't care. The odds were stacked against us this year, and we still made it, and that's a huge deal."

"I certainly have a lot to celebrate," Avery said. "Ali got a job in New Haven, and I got my official award letter for my full ride. I'm Yale-bound."

"Officially," I said. "I'm going to be heading up the new debt collection division of LCE, with the help of my grandmother, of course."

"And I'm gonna be taking my position as president once I graduate," Nathan said.

"Aw, I'm sure those adults are gonna love having two teenagers running things," Alistair joked.

"Well, we decided that we are both going to get our degrees in business," Nathan replied. "Nikki wants to get her master's degree."

"Hell yeah!" Colette said. "Well, I've kind of played close to the vest, but I've been accepted to Postings Proper University. I guess I'm gonna be sticking around here," she said and looked over at Kyle. "I'll even have a friend close at hand."

"Your acceptance letter came in?" Brayden asked.

Kyle nodded. "It did."

Brayden grinned. "I told you it would."

A warm smile found Kyle's face, and it gave me butterflies in my stomach. "You did, and you were right," Kyle said. "Thank you."

"I'll be working with my dad," Jaxon said simply. Everyone waited for him to say more, but he didn't.

"You'll have to excuse him. He's not a man of many words," Colette said, and everyone laughed.

His family owned a very successful real estate company. I couldn't see Jaxon selling houses, but that didn't mean that he couldn't find a way to work it out.

"See? We *all* have post-grad plans, even though we were all hopeless in January. That's impressive. We're doing this party," Nathan said. "Leave it up to me." He looked over at Brayden with a smile. "You're expected to come too. I know you're not graduating, but if you hadn't been there to keep us all sane, who knows what would have happened."

None of us immediately responded to Nathan. Clearly, we all shared the same fear that Brayden was involved with Connor, but Avery smiled and said, "Of course, it wouldn't be a party without our best friend there."

Brayden smiled at everyone and nodded. "Oh, none of you have to worry. I'll *definitely* be there."

27

NATHAN

Nikita had her arms crossed in the passenger's seat of my car, so I reached over and stroked her cheek. "Baby, I know. I know that you don't like this, but I already said that I would do it. Besides, she tried to do her finals. Doesn't that stand for *anything?*"

Nikita didn't respond. It was the Saturday before graduation, and I was finalizing the down payment on D.J. Motley's house in order to ensure that Cherri would graduate. I'd told Nikita everything, and I even felt better about it after Cherri seemed to suddenly give a damn and do her finals, but even if she *had* found a way to pass them, which I doubted, there was no way she got good enough scores to pass.

"It's my final act, Nikki. I swear. After this, I'm done with Cherri for good."

"Really?" Nikita asked, looking over at me with a raised eyebrow.

"I swear."

She rolled her eyes. "Fine."

"Thank you. I'd ask you if you want to come in with me, but I'm afraid you'll cut me, so I'll be quick. I promise." I leaned over and kissed Nikita on the cheek, then hopped out of the car with my briefcase in tow.

I entered Postings Proper National Bank, the bank that was underwriting the loan for D.J. Motley's house, and one of the greeters immediately approached me. "Good morning, sir. Can I help you?"

I pulled out my phone and navigated to the email from D.J. with the name of the specific loan writer who was handing her documents. "Yes, I'm here to see Miss Dee Hart."

"Oh, yes, of course. She's expecting you. Follow me."

I followed the woman through the bank, toward the offices in the back. The one that was marked *Dee Hart* had the door closed, but the greeter knocked a couple of times and then ushered me in. Dee, a redhead with a towering height, stood up out of her chair and held out her hand to me.

"Mr. Loche, it's good to meet you."

I shook her hand with a smile. "You as well. Thank you for squeezing me in today. I promise I'm not going to take up too much of your time."

She motioned to the chair across from her desk, and I sat down in it, setting my briefcase up on the desk and immediately opening it. I pulled out the check and smiled at the devious move I pulled at the last second. I handed the check and verification form that D.J. had signed over to Dee, and she took it and looked at it. Her eyes widened, and she looked up at me.

"You're co-signing on this home?" she said.

"Yes. That's part of the reason I'm offering the down payment. D.J. and I go back, so I just want to see her have her dream home," I said.

Of course, D.J. had no idea of the change I'd made. I'd played my cards right and made sure that all her paperwork was already signed. All that was left was to hand the check over. Thankfully, the Loche name has a lot of weight behind it, so they bent the rules a little to make it work. With D.J. not there, I was able to add myself discreetly to her deed as a co-signer. I had no plans to take her house or plans of reneging on my deal, but I wanted to have a vested interest, just in case. Connor Loche may have taken my childhood from me, but being a business shark was the product I got for the price I paid. I was well versed in how to make sure a deal always benefitted me more, and this was exactly how I planned to do it.

Dee gave me all of the necessary paperwork that already had all of D.J.'s signatures on it, and I signed as the co-signer in all the appropriate spaces. By the time D.J. realized what I'd done, it'd be too late, and she would be in no position to cause a fuss because if she did, I'd let the world know she'd taken a hefty bribe for a hefty cheat in the system.

Once I'd signed everything and the check had been accepted, I shook Dee's hand and saw myself out of the office. A smile crossed my face as I walked out. I was proud of the leverage I'd gained in that situation. I *almost* wanted to tell Nikita about it to try and improve her mood about the situation, but it was probably best to just drop it with her and tell her if the situation ever came up.

Heading back out into the fresh sunlight, I walked back over to my car and got in, leaning over to kiss Nikita as I did. Despite her frustration, when I got nearer to her cheek, she turned her head suddenly, kissing me on the lips. As she tried to pull away, I set my hand on her cheek and pulled her back to me to kiss her once more.

"I really don't want to take you home, but it would ruin the surprise to keep you with me," I said.

Nikita chuckled and rolled her eyes. "I know. It's okay. I'll see you again tomorrow."

My stomach twisted with frustration. I'd never spend another day apart from Nikita if I didn't have to, but I had a plan in my head, an important one, and it was going to have the greatest effect if no one saw it until its big reveal. That meant Nikita had to go home for the remainder of the day.

Reluctantly, I started my car back up and pulled away from the curb, bound for Nikita's home. Every time we got near the block her house was on, I would turn and head down a different street and circle the block until Nikita started laughing. The sound was such a beautiful and happy one that I was almost tempted to do it all day, but eventually, I did turn down her street and park my car in front of her home. I looked around for the guys that tried to snatch Cherri, but we hadn't seen them since they got their assess handed to them after our prom, so they were likely laying low for a little bit after such a close call.

"I don't wanna go," Nikita complained.

"I know. I don't want you to either." I reached over and took her hand, linking my fingers into hers. It was so easy to do now that it almost felt unfair. "Just come back with me. Fuck the surprise."

She snickered. "You've been so excited about whatever you're planning. Don't throw it all away just because we're grossly in love."

She was right. I'd mentioned needing the afternoon to plan things out half a dozen times or more, maybe because I knew how difficult it was going to be to say goodbye to her when the time came. She tugged on my hand, and I leaned across the seat and into her so that I could kiss her. We lingered that way for a while, just being with each other for a moment. Finally, Nikita pulled away, pinched my cheek, and climbed out of the car. I let her go, as frustrating as it was, and after she got safely behind her front door, I pulled away again and made my way back home.

All the joy that spending the morning with Nikita gave me was gone by the time I stood in front of my parents' house on our property. I'd made a handful of absolutely necessary trips in for no more than a couple of minutes over the course of the last six months, but I hadn't gone in with the intention of changing or moving anything. It'd been the subject of conversation in my therapy sessions as of late since I realized I'd been avoiding going in. Did I think they were suddenly going to come back somehow? Did I think my mom wasn't going to be dead, that my dad wasn't going to be a psychotic murderer?

But I had a new plan in mind now. Something that was going to take the house of horror and turn it into a place of warmth and love. There were people in my life who meant the world to me, and I wanted the main house to be a tribute to that fact. So I stepped up to the front door, ignoring the shake of my hands as I set the key in the lock, and finally stepped through the door for the first time in over six months.

It was dusty and dank inside, which was to be expected. The overwhelming smell of cleaning products still dominated the space, likely because with no windows or doors opened, the ones that had been used to clean the carpet after my mother's murder hadn't had a chance to properly ventilate. It was weird, almost like I'd expected the place to have changed somehow, but the living room was still pristine and untouched—a place I was *never* allowed to go as a kid. The kitchen still had pans stacked on the oven, likely prepared for a new day's meal before I fired the chef.

I spent about thirty minutes walking around the house. When it was my home, before my parents had my own house built on the land, there were several rooms that I was *never* allowed into. One was my parents' plush, well-appointed bedroom on the third floor, complete with a gaudy four-poster bed. Another was my dad's office, with its stacks of papers and the only thing he ever truly loved—his work.

Then there was my mom's studio.

A lot of my memory of my childhood was filled with her disappearing into the room for hours on end, doing god knew what. I always thought that she was doing something untoward inside, but when I walked in, I was presented with some of the most beautiful paintings I'd ever seen. There was even a painting that looked like she was trying to paint me from memory, but it looked much more beautiful than I felt like I looked. I loved my mom a lot, but thanks to my dad's oppressive reign over me, we were not allowed to bond the way any mother and son should. People thought she was evil, but she was just another of Connor Loche's victims, hanging on by a thread.

As I looked over the collection of stunning pieces, tears slowly started to slide down my cheeks. Everyone kept telling me that it was strange that I hadn't seemed to have mourned my mother, but the feelings never really hit me. It didn't feel like she died, more like she'd gone on vacation, and she'd come home one day.

She wasn't coming home.

For all her talent, the only mark she left on the world was the nasty reputation she earned as an extension of my father. She didn't deserve that. Over the course of the next hour or so, I collected all of the paintings in the studio. She had a closet in the back of the studio with hundreds of paintings in it, all various paintings of landscapes, people, and close-ups of objects. There was enough to fill an entire gallery, which was what they'd do.

I kept the painting of myself. It felt a little too narcissistic to hang it up anywhere, but if my mom saw me in that beautiful light, I couldn't just sell it or give it away. I selected an additional ten or so paintings to hang around the house, and the rest I stacked to be wrapped. I'd commission a gallery somewhere and get my mom the notoriety she deserved, even if even post-mortem.

Wiping my eyes and wishing that I had kept Nikita with me, I finished my tour of the house, taking stock of all the rooms. Then I went back down to the living room to lay out my plans. I could never sleep in my parents' bedroom, but that was fine because we'd mostly be staying in my house behind the main house. That room would be turned into a club room, which would work fine since it had an attached sitting room, and the massive walk-in closet could be turned into a room for drinks and snacks.

My dad's office space would be turned into a utility office with multiple desks and computers, and my mom's studio would remain there as a homage to her incredible skill. My old room would be modernized and made comfortable for Nikita and me when we wanted to be in the main house with our friends instead of at our house. I earmarked four of the guest bedrooms for my friends. One for Jaxon and Colette, one for Avery and Alistair, and so as not to make too many assumptions, Brayden and Kyle each got their own room.

There were still extra guest rooms, so I'd be sure to make sure each one of them was equipped to take additional people if any of the couples split and needed an additional room, or for when Brayden expanded The Royal Court in his senior year. Mostly, this house was for my friends and me, but if Brayden surprised me with his choices, and I had a feeling he would, there would be extra space for visitors.

I set aside a room for Sicily, as well, and chuckled to myself as I imagined asking him to legitimately join The Royal Court. We were probably beyond titles, but if I were to give him one, what would he be? The baron? Baron Sicily? I planned to put some sort of placard to the extent in the bedroom as a joke.

I went down to the room that had been Deon's for the year that he was there. It hadn't been touched since he left it, which I always found odd. Learning that my father had made Deon an officer at his company suggested that he was hopeful that Deon would come back at some point. He aided me so much in my vengeance against Deon that I wasn't dumb enough to think it was out of love, but his master plan was still unclear to me. That room would be updated for Cherri and Deon to occupy —hopefully, together.

It was well after midnight by the time I was done. I'd ordered food and decorations for the graduation party and would have to come back in to set everything up the day of, but that was after the walls were all painted, the new furniture was moved in, and the carpets were pulled up. I'd always been a natural wood floor kind of guy.

As I locked the door behind me as I left, the feeling in my gut was much different than the one I walked in with. It was anticipation and excitement. I was excited to offer my friends a place to stay, a place where they could be comfortable and, more importantly, where we could all be together. Alistair and Avery wouldn't be there a lot of the time since they'd be in New Haven, but they could come home for holidays and have a nice, relaxing place to stay.

That's when it hit me.

I felt like I'd done so much for everyone else, but Alistair was still the one person that eluded me. Avery said that he got a job in New Haven, but they hadn't mentioned a place to live yet. Neither of them was short of cash, and they probably planned to take care of housing when they got there, but I had a better idea in mind.

I called my family's accountant, wincing as I heard the sleep in his voice and remembered what time it was. "Shit, Lindsey, I'm sorry."

"It's fine, Nathan," he replied. "What's up?"

"Well, you can do it in the morning, but I'm hoping you can look into nice apartments in New Haven, Connecticut."

28

NIKITA

My heart was beating significantly faster than I expected.

I looked in the mirror with my hair down, loose from its braids, and smiled. Ever since Colette and Avery talked me into wearing it down for prom, I'd been doing it much more. It had a certain luxurious look to it that I didn't often associate with myself, but I was growing fonder of it. Braids always felt much more muted, but I found that I didn't necessarily think I needed to do that anymore. I could just relax and be myself more lately. It was nice.

Colette walked into the dressing room where I was and smiled. "Here you are. Hiding from us?"

"No," I replied. I smoothed down my graduation gown and liked the look of it on myself. "Just taking a few minutes."

She walked over and set her head on my shoulder. "I love your hair down. It's kind of weird, but it just feels like it's more you."

"I was just thinking that," I said. "Although it's a little too long. I might cut it soon."

"Oh, that'd look cute." She grabbed the edges and tucked them under so that it was closer to being shoulder length. "Oh yeah. We're doing this, like, first thing this summer."

Maybe that was why there were so many butterflies in my stomach. It was graduation day, and after the wild ride I'd had with The Royal Court, it felt like a definitive ending to a story, but Colette's words reminded me that it isn't the end for us, just the end to this part. It was the end of a chapter. Starting tomorrow, we'd be on to what the rest of our lives would hold, and even though things weren't finished with Nathan or his dad, I was excited to get to the next stage for us, even if it was a little scary.

I looked at Colette and smiled. She somehow made her graduation gown look fashionable. Her typically pixie-cut hair was starting to grow out more, but it didn't really matter how she wore it. It always looked good. She'd finally made her way back to professional-grade makeup application and looked like a goddess. I almost didn't want to stand near her.

"You look amazing," I said.

She knocked her hip out to one side. "Naturally." Then she winked. She looped her arm through mine and started pulling me out of the dressing room. "Come on. We're going to line up soon."

Colette pulled me out of the room and into the bustling lobby of Postings Proper High, a packed room filled with graduates. Everyone was giggling, chattering, and cheering in their individual groups while teachers circled the space and made sure everyone looked presentable and ready to go. Principal Hix stood at the front of the room in a suit and tie, talking to D.J. Motley and a couple of other teachers while they waited to be called in.

We made our way through the throngs of students and over to where The Royal Court was standing, save for Brayden, who was still a junior. He had already made an appearance and was somewhere out in the stands, cheering us on. I reached down and laced my hand into Nathan's, and he brought it to his lips and kissed it.

"You okay?" he asked.

"Yeah," I said. "I think I'm just shocked that this day is finally here."

"I know what you mean," Kyle said. "It really feels like we got here by the skin of our teeth. In January, you two," he said as he pointed to Avery and Colette, "were a mess. You," he said, pointing to Nathan, "were in that pit of self-loathing. You two," he said as he motioned to Alistair and me, "were exhausted by trying to keep the rest of these guys together. I thought to myself, 'Well, at least they'll all flunk together, so they'll have each other next year.'"

We all laughed, and Nathan gave him a light punch on the arm. "You held yourself together surprisingly well. I mean, we had some shit going on, like some *shit* going on, and you kept your head up and served The Royal Court way better than I ever did as king. You got us through this shit, Kyle. I'm serious. We would *not* be standing here without you."

I nodded. "I have to agree. You've been our rock. Thanks for remaining so level-headed."

Kyle grinned. "Hey, I couldn't just let you guys crash and burn."

"Nathan, is the party ready for after we're done?" Avery asked. "I told my parents *not* to expect me back home tonight."

A huge smile crossed Nathan's face. He had apparently prepared the surprise he was working on, but I'd been to his house a couple of times in the week between finals and graduation and hadn't seen anything out of the ordinary. "Oh yeah. It's all ready. I was just staring at it before coming here today. You guys are gonna love it. I can't wait."

Not long after that, Principal Hix called for the students to line up alphabetically, which effectively pulled all of us apart. We gave our final hugs and kisses and congrats before lining up, and my stomach rumbled with anticipation. Only about five spaces in front of me, dressed in a gown and with a look of anxiety on her face, was Cherri. Her hair had been curled, looking similar to how it used to look when she was with The Royal Court, though it was still shorter and dyed. Beneath the base of her gown, I could see that she was wearing heels, similar to something I might have expected to see her in a year ago as opposed to the tennis shoes or combat boots I was expecting from her in the past six months. She had makeup on, again similar to what she used to wear, and though she was fidgeting back and forth, I could see that her nails were done.

It seemed that the members of The Royal Court weren't the only ones getting back to normal, but if she was finally coming down off her high and mighty attitude, did that mean she'd try to get back into The Royal Court?

Almost as if she sensed me looking at her, she turned her head, and our eyes locked. My gut reaction was to look away, but I held her gaze, and to my complete shock, she lifted a hand a little bit and waved at me. My lips parted in surprise, but nothing came out, so I just lifted a hand and waved back. After that, she looked away from me, and I glanced around to see if anyone else in The Royal Court had seen it, but everyone seemed tangled up in conversations with the people who were nearest them in line.

Then the call came. Principal Hix and the teachers walked out first, and then after a short welcome from Principal Hix, the processional started. Pomp and Circumstance boomed over the sound system as we filed out onto our football field under the cheers of our friends and family. I spied my foster mom, Sistine, my foster father, Charlie, and my grandmother, Hannah. They started to jump up and down and cheer as our eyes met, and I chuckled and waved a hand at them.

A few seats down the way was Brayden, and he was frantically trying to wave at each specific member of The Royal Court as they passed. When our eyes met, he held up a thumbs-up and screamed, "Congrats, Nikki!" It made me feel good to see that he seemed to be in high spirits, and I waved at him as I passed. We all took our seats, and I turned and looked into the row behind me, where Nathan was sitting almost directly behind me. He stepped out of line briefly to kiss me and then returned to his spot, winking at me as he did so. I turned to face forward again, and then we were seated so that the ceremony could begin.

I was grateful that Principal Hix committed to keeping things short and sweet. The longest part of the ceremony was Colette's speech. Though she'd missed her final chance to be Valedictorian and Class President, no one took the positions in her wake, so when she applied for the chance to be the Class Speaker at graduation, she snagged it without issue. Her incredible skills for writing showed in a moving and emotional speech that she ended by calling out each member of The Royal Court, Cherri and Sicily included, and saying, "Thank you for making me who I am."

Walking across the stage left me lightheaded and buzzing. The screams of my family from the stands and of The Royal Court from amongst the students rang in my ears long after the ceremony had ended. I wished I could have recorded it for when I felt sad in the future, but the memory would have to suffice. I found my family after the ceremony and enjoyed the flowers they gave me along with their hugs. It was nice to see my grandma again after almost a year.

"Um," my grandmother said softly. "Where are Nathan's parents?"

I looked over my shoulder and saw Nathan standing off to one side alone. Occasionally, different students and their families walked past and congratulated him, but Nathan had made sure to tell us the night before not to try and drag him into any of our family interactions because he thought it would be too hard.

"It's complicated," I responded. I scanned the crowd for Brayden. He had to be somewhere around and could keep Nathan company while the rest of us hung out with our families. "Sorry, I'll be right back."

I handed my flowers to Sistine and slipped away from the group, sliding in and out of the thick sea of people, looking for Brayden. Finally, I spied the back of his head and slipped my way through the crowd to get to him. I was almost to him when I noticed he was talking to Cherri, and I stopped.

"Yeah," he said, and it was clear I'd come in mid-conversation, "but only if you come. Sicily too. I know that Nathan would really want you there. He's been planning it for a week and is really excited to share it with all of us."

The graduation party? He was inviting Cherri and Sicily.

"I'll be there. It's not a question," Cherri replied, and it was the first time I'd heard her speak to a member of The Royal Court without any ire. "At his house?"

"His parents' house, technically, but yeah."

"Okay," Cherri responded. "Yeah, we'll definitely be there. Will you tell him for me?"

"Yeah," Brayden said. "Thanks, Cherri."

"No," she said. "Thank you."

With that, she turned around and walked over to her parents and extended family, who were all talking and laughing.

That was weird. Nathan had promised me that he was done dealing with Cherri and begging her to come back around, so I highly doubted he wanted her at the graduation party. Cherri did seem to be showing more of her old self, though, so maybe Nathan saw it and wanted her to be included? That wouldn't bother me so much, but I still wished that he had told me.

Before Brayden could turn around, I weaved back through the crowd toward where I had last seen Nathan. He was still standing there, still sadly looking out at the socializing families, and it broke my heart. Connor had isolated his own parents and siblings and had forced Nathan's mom to do the same, so he didn't have any extended family there to support him either.

"Hey," I said, sliding over and giving him a kiss. "I know you said not to drag you into anything, but my grandma did ask about you."

"Yeah, she came over a couple of minutes ago," he said. "Just hugged me and said she expects me to get dinner with you guys while she's here."

"She's always loved you," I replied. "So, um, hey. I'm not angry, just curious. Did you invite Cherri and Sicily to the party tonight?"

Nathan recoiled. "No. Why?"

"Oh. I just overheard Brayden inviting them. He said that you really wanted them there, and I just thought maybe you passed a message through him to be discreet."

"No, Nikki. I didn't lie when I told you I wasn't keeping stuff about Cherri from you anymore, but..." He smiled. "That's funny that Brayden did that. He knows me pretty well. I *did* want to invite them, but I never mustered up the courage. Things have been relatively calm since prom. Cherri seems to be doing a little better, and I didn't want to break it. I decided stasis was better than the risk, so I left it alone."

"Hey, guys." Brayden excused his way through the group and walked up to where Nathan and I were standing. "Congratulations! I know I'm biased, but you looked the best out there of anyone. I'm pretty sure your graduations count more." Nathan walked away from me and pulled Brayden into a huge bear hug. Brayden seemed shocked at first, eyes wide, but then his arms slowly came up to wrap around Nathan. "Uh, okay?"

"Nikki told me that you invited Cherri and Sicily to the party tonight," he said as he pulled away. "Thank you *so* much. I really want them there, but I couldn't muster up the courage to invite them."

Brayden looked at me, and the look on his face was not of gratitude or happiness for having made Nathan happy. It was pure, unfettered fear. "You heard that? All of it?"

"The tail end," I said. "Why?"

Nathan shook his head. "Why doesn't matter. What matters is that you never cease to be so considerate of me, Brayden. Thank you." Nathan pulled him into another hug.

And I saw it, a look that sent a chill down my spine and shook me to my core. The look on Brayden's face was one of life-ending, absolute guilt.

NATHAN

It made me happy when we could barely make it up the front sidewalk to the front door of the main house. Avery and Kyle, flower aficionados, kept stopping along the pathway to talk about the different colorful flowers I'd had planted there, and Alistair was impressed with the hedge work and new cobblestone pathway. Nikita seemed fine to just hold my hand and follow along as everyone buzzed about the house's new look. I'd planted a few fresh trees that would grow over the course of the next decade and had all the stonework power washed so that it looked fresh and inviting.

"It's *so* nice," Colette said. "I never really realized how dreary it seemed until I saw it like this. You really made it much more inviting."

"Thanks. That was the goal," I said. "This isn't even the best part, though. Come in."

I unlocked the front door and led the members of The Royal Court into the renovated house, where they were met with several dozen bundles of gold, silver, black, and white balloons, sashes in the same color scheme, and a *Congrats Class of 2020* banner hanging across the front entryway. The kitchen was jam-packed with everyone's favorite foods, and there were now colorful, welcoming pillows in the living room, where each of our senior portraits was placed on the mantle of the fireplace.

"Wow!" Nikita said. "You completely redid it."

"Yeah. I won't say I was trying to get the feeling of my parents out of here, but I wanted this to be a place I could love and feel good about. I wanted it to be a place where all of you could come and be comfortable, which is why…" I walked over to the table in front of the fireplace and held out my arm toward the bags on the table. "In these bags, you'll find a variety of fun things, including a key to the front door and a fob for the front gate. I want you guys to come and go as you please."

Everyone walked over and fished into their bags, and though they all seemed excited about the contents, it made me happy that they all immediately went for their keys and started adding them to their key rings.

"What about your dad?" Avery asked.

"I had all the locks on the place changed, and the gate is being replaced in a few weeks, at which point I'll have new fobs for you. I wanted it done sooner, but the people who installed the original gates are no longer in business, so I had to contact new people, and they have to install new doors." I shook my head. "It's a whole thing. There had been enough employees floating around who had fobs before I let them go, so there were enough to go around. When the new gates are installed, we'll be the only ones who have the fob, except for maybe some new housekeeping staff."

Brayden flipped his key over in his hands a few times and seemed taken aback. "You good?" I asked.

He jumped a little, but then he looked up and smiled. "Yeah. I'm good."

"Okay. Stay close. I have a lot of exciting stuff to show you." I smiled, and Brayden smiled back before sliding his key into his pocket. I locked eyes with Nikita, who'd admitted on the way home that she thought Brayden was up to something. We were staying on high alert, but I thought his emotions were simply related to not being a senior and feeling distant again. "Come on. This is just the start of it."

With everyone in tow, I started my tour of the house, showing everyone the common areas first, including the fully stocked kitchen, the game room where my dad's sitting room used to be, and the modernized library with room to add books as we needed to. Then I led them up to the second floor and showed off their bedrooms.

Colette's and Jaxon's room was done in opposing pink and red themes to match their starkly opposite personalities. The colors on the walls blended into a nice magenta right around where the bed was situated to symbolize their bond as a couple. There was a writing desk in there for Colette, and a punching bag for Jaxon, with plenty of room to add things as they saw fit.

Avery's and Alistair's room was very understated to match the pair. I'd given them the room with the best view of the garden, complete with a nook for them to curl up in like a couple of cuddly cats. Over the course of their budding relationship, I'd learned that their favorite thing to do was just be together, so even though I'd put an old-fashioned record player in there for Alistair and a classical piano for Avery, the bulk of the space was dedicated to different ways the two could simply be together.

The room that Nikita and I would share was also very simple, though it had a few high-end swords on the wall that held Nikita's attention for much longer than I expected them to. We'd sleep most frequently in our house on the back of the property, but I made sure we had a plushy, comfortable bed for when we wanted to drink coffee and spend a few more minutes lounging around, and it also had an attached rolling desk for mornings where I had to work.

Kyle's room had tons of closet space and a large ceiling to floor mirror. Just as he was about to comment that I'd themed his room around his vanity, I stopped him to tell him that it was so he could help me with *my* fashion sense since, apparently, it sucked so badly. There were also a few succulent plants scattered around for him to tend to, and I added an aquarium because I knew he really enjoyed fish as a low-maintenance pet.

Brayden's room had a large entertainment system with all three major gaming appliances affixed to the wall. His television was theater-style and projected across his entire wall. In front of his bed were two haptic gaming chairs for when he and I wanted to get into some gaming sessions. He was responsive and thankful, but he was not as happy as I expected him to be. I'd work on figuring out what was wrong with him later, but I didn't want to ruin the mood in the group.

After everyone got to their rooms, I let them all spend some time in them and then brought them down to the living room.

"Nathan, those rooms are beautiful," Avery said. "It makes me sleepy just thinking about falling asleep in Ali's arms in that window seat."

"Well, there will be plenty of time for that, but for now…" I plucked the small remote for the stereo system from the mantle in the living room and pressed play, and music started to fill the room. "We're going to party like our lives aren't based on one of those teen dramas!"

"Yeah!" Colette yelped.

Everyone helped themselves to the food and the kegs of the personalized drinks Kyle had made for everyone, and then we all walked out back to the pool. Our decorations spilled outside, including beach balls in each color of the scheme that floated on the water, and we situated ourselves around the pool, all kicking our feet in for now so that we could hang out and talk.

"I have a couple of things to admit," I started

again after a while. I wanted to spread out my announcements so that we could have some fun.

"Okay?" Alistair said.

"First of all, you," I said, pointing right back at him. "You've been evading me this whole time. I've gotten everyone else something worth-while in some form or fashion, but you're a slippery one."

"I told you already—"

"Shh," I cut him off. "So, here's what I've done. There is a fully furnished, penthouse apartment waiting for you in New Haven if you want it. I know you could have gotten one for yourself, but Avery told me where you're working, and it's nearby. It's got a ton of space, and once Avery is ready to move out of the dorms and in with you, you'll still be more than comfortable there. The complex has tons of really nice amenities, and I've taken care of rent and utilities for four years, so all you have to do with your money is pay for the rest of your costs to live there."

Alistair's jaw dropped. "Wow, Nathan, that's…huge."

"I know that you guys probably could have afforded something between you just fine, but I wanted to do something for you, especially since you guys have forgiven me for all my shit." Avery and Alistair both opened up their mouths to protest, but I cut them off. "Ah! Let me finish." They both closed their mouths. "This brings me to the second announcement." I took a deep breath. For some reason, my heart was pounding as I thought about it, but I knew it had to be done. "The gravy train is ending. As of this party, all the gifts are coming to an end, at least the excessive stuff. Of course, I'll still celebrate how much I love you guys from time to time, but you've all forgiven me, and I no longer feel like I need to buy you guys in a guilt-ridden attempt to earn back the friendship I never lost. If you ever need anything, I'm here, but I'm going to be the president of my dad's company soon, and the past six months have been one bad financial decision right after the other. I've got to be smarter soon, so there you go."

"Uh, if you're not paying for shit anymore, I'm out," Alistair said with a stone serious face, but almost immediately, he cracked a smile. "No, I'm kidding, but seriously, Nathan, thanks for the place. We'll take it. The cost of living near Yale is expensive. Also, I'm glad you finally figured out that we aren't going anywhere. We wouldn't still be here if we thought who you were this past year was who you really are. We knew the stress you were under and decided to see you through it."

"Don't get us wrong. You've *always* been an

ass," Colette tacked on, "but not *that* much of an ass."

"I've felt like so much more of the person I'm supposed to be in these past six months, and that's thanks to you guys. I promise to be a better friend."

"Congrats," Kyle said, slapping a hand on my back. "We're with you."

I smiled. "Thanks."

Not long after that, the doorbell rang. We all looked over in the direction of the door, confused at first, but then I exchanged glances with Nikita and then Brayden.

"Um, I'm pretty sure that's them," Brayden said. "I'll go let them in since I invited them."

"Okay," I said. "Thanks."

"Them?" Kyle asked.

"Yeah," I said. "Brayden pulled a last-minute clutch move."

Everyone fell quiet while we waited, and eventually, Sicily and Cherri came walking through the back door. Sicily was his typical self, but Cherri looked a little closer to normal, wearing light blue jeans, roman sandals, and a striped tank top. It was comforting to see, even though she did still have a punkish scowl on her face.

"Hey," I greeted, standing up to walk over to them. "Thanks for coming."

Avery jumped up out of the pool and ran over to stand next to me. "Hi, Cherri! Are you back?"

Cherri looked Avery up and down, and I could see the longing in her face to greet her best friend, but she didn't. Instead, she looked at me, crossing her arms. "I'm not here to buddy up." Her tone was closer to the dark Cherri we'd been battling with for the past few months. "I'm here to hear what you have to say about Deon."

"Deon?" Avery asked.

I could hear the water sloshing behind me as everyone climbed out to walk over. "What about Deon?" I asked.

I'd been battling with whether or not to come clean to Cherri about Deon, but no one knew that I was considering it, not even Nikita.

Cherri shrugged. "I was promised information."

"By who?" I asked as Nikita reached my side.

Cherri recoiled a little bit. "Brayden."

"Brayden promised you that? I didn't tell him anything like that." I walked around Cherri and into the house. "Brayden?" I poked my head in and out of all the rooms, and Kyle was just behind me, rushing up the stairs. When I was convinced that he wasn't in the house, I turned around and peered up the stairs. "Kyle?"

Kyle came back to the top of the stairs, looking frustrated. "He's not up here."

"We should leave," Nikita said. "I don't have a good feeling about this."

I heard the footsteps behind us before a man said, "No, you shouldn't."

I slowly turned around and saw that one of the two men who had been following us was standing behind Nikita with a gun directly to her head. My whole world screeched to a halt at the look of fear on her face.

The other man took a few steps past them with his gun pointed toward the rest of us. He smiled at me with malice. "Your father sends his regards."

NIKITA

Fear was bouncing through me like a loose ball. It was less for myself and more for the rest of my friends. We foolishly believed that we were safe at Nathan's house. I should have expected that whatever Brayden was up to was nefarious and been more vigilant. I had blades on me, as I always did, but if I went for them, I was going to get a bullet through the brain.

Cherri took a few steps forward, and the guy who didn't have his gun to my head stabbed his gun in her direction. "Stop!"

"No," she hissed back, then looked at me. "They need us alive. He's not going to shoot you."

"I'll fucking kill you, you little bitch," the other guy said.

"No, you won't," she spat, and with that, she leaped out and tackled the guy to the floor.

His gun discharged, firing straight up, and the rest of The Royal Court scattered up the stairs, likely to gather their own weapons, except for Nathan, who stood still, staring at me. Seeing Cherri tackle the man to the ground, I developed some confidence and quickly ducked down. The gun fired just over my head, and I jumped, thinking he maybe *did* intend to shoot me. Maybe Cherri was just banking on false confidence. When the bullet missed me, I quickly stood back up, headbutting the guy in the head.

"Fuck!" He drove his fist down into my rib cage, and I crumpled sideways.

I was a fighter, but a grown man was still a grown man and had far more power than a teenage girl. Nathan rushed forward and got between the guy and me. Acidic sludge filled my stomach at the thought that an unarmed Nathan was going to get shot. I got to my feet as quickly as I could, but while Nathan was battling with the guy who'd attempted to shoot me, Cherri was struggling to overpower the man she was up against. I was about to run over and help her when I heard a piercing battle cry, and Sicily came flying out of the kitchen with a bag of flour. He reached his hand in and grabbed a clump of it, dropping it in the man's face. Cherri used the distraction to put some distance between her and the guy. All the members of The Royal Court came bolting back down the stairs with guns, and they looked at him in shock.

"What? It's what I can do," he said.

The man wiped his eyes clean and made an irritated charge for Sicily. Cherri jumped in and tangled up with the man, just as the one Nathan was fighting with reached out and grabbed me by the arm. We all got twisted in together, and it felt like déjà vu. It was so similar to what happened back in Nathan's cabin, almost like it was purposeful. As long as no one could get a clear shot on either of the guys, they couldn't shoot, and the men knew it.

The one that Nathan and I were mixed up with cocked his shoulders back and got his arms free. He socked Nathan in the face, knocking him to his back, and I could see the daze in Nathan's face. The man quickly pivoted behind me, rolling an arm around my waist to take me. He started to drag me toward the door, and because he was behind me, I was struggling.

The Royal Court charged forward, but the man put his gun back to my head, and everyone stopped short. That time, I wasn't brave enough to duck out of the way. He fired last time, and though he missed me, it was clear that whatever confidence Cherri had that they wouldn't kill us wasn't entirely accurate. I needed an opening to make a move but wasn't sure where it would come from.

Suddenly, I went flying forward onto the ground. I heard the clatter of the gun as it went skidding across the floor and watched as someone ran over to pick it up and kick it away. I twisted around, trying to get free of the man on top of me, but then my brain stuttered. Suddenly, I was back in my childhood bedroom. My dad was there, and my chest caved in. My breathing started to get short, and just like so many nights back then, I wanted to scream for help, but no words would leave my lungs. All the fight left my body, and all I could do was curl into a ball. I was inhaling and exhaling as much as I could, trying to force air to enter and exit my body when someone dragged me away from the fray.

"Nikki." The voice was barely able to reach me. It was warm, comforting, begging me toward it, but it was so far away that I was afraid to look. "Nikki." It was closer to me. Arms wrapped around me, arms that didn't want to hurt me. Arms that loved me and wanted to keep me safe. "Nikki." The voice was right in my ear.

I finally clawed my eyes open and looked into Nathan's eyes. "Nathan?"

"It's okay. You're okay. I'm here." He kissed my forehead.

I looked over my shoulder and saw Jaxon tangled up with the man who had been dragging me toward the door moments before. Jaxon was fighting with him, and fortunately, the man didn't have his gun, though it didn't look like Jaxon had one either. Not far from them, Cherri was still fighting with the other guy, keeping her body between him and Sicily, who was still only armed with a bag of flour. It didn't make sense to me that we were still struggling so much with two men when we all had weapons, but then I scanned The Royal Court and noticed for the first time the looks of fear on all of their faces. They *had* guns, but they didn't have what it took to shoot. It was one thing when it was a target, but when you were faced with having to hurt or potentially kill someone, it was a whole different ball game.

It poured confidence back into me. Most of my friends were still leagues away from being able to defend themselves, but fortunately, a few of us had the experience we needed. I got to my feet, and Nathan tried to stop me, but I pulled free. I flipped a blade out of my sleeve and started to advance on the guy who was fighting with Jaxon when the guy who was fighting with Cherri shoved her away. She fell back against Sicily, and the guy pulled out his gun and cocked it.

"All right. I've had enough of you."

He pointed his gun at Cherri, and I heard a shriek. It shocked the guy enough to cause him to hesitate as Avery rushed out and jumped between Cherri and the guy who was pointing the gun at her.

"Avery!" Cherri and Alistair yelled in response, and I reflexively jumped forward.

I collided into Jaxon, who collided into the guy he was battling with, who collided into the guy pointing the gun at Avery and Cherri. The gun went off, and I heard Avery yelp. The stream of blood I saw first made me panic, but then I noticed that the bleeding spot on Avery's arm was very small. I'd just sent the trajectory off enough for the bullet to barely graze Avery's arm. I threw out an elbow toward the guy who was still pointing a gun at Avery, and it slammed into the guy's face. In a flash of color, Alistair was next to me, pointing his gun down, but I shoved it away.

"We don't need it, and you'll never come back from killing someone," I barked. Alistair cocked back a fist and brought it down hard against the man's face, and his entire body went limp. His head dropped back to the floor, and he lay there, unconscious. "Oh, okay. That's not what I meant, but that'll work." With the blade in my hand, I walked over to the guy who was tussling with Jaxon and stuck my knife to his throat. "You're outnumbered."

The guy froze, looked back over his shoulder, and noticed that his partner was out, and then he held up his hands. I was prepared to keep him standing, but all of a sudden, a pan flew out of nowhere and slammed against his head. His eyes rolled back, and he dropped to a heap on the floor.

Jaxon and I looked over in shock as Colette turned the pan over in her hands. She looked up at Jaxon with concern. "Are you okay?"

"Yeah. Are you?"

She smiled, holding up her frying pan. "Hell yeah. I think I just found my new favorite weapon."

"Shit, Nikki," Jaxon murmured. "I think I fucked around and fell in love."

I chuckled. "Yeah, buddy. That's been evident for about three months."

It was useful but frustrating that both guys were out cold. I was hoping to ask them some questions, but whatever. They were down, and that was what mattered.

Everyone converged on them at that point,

using whatever they could find to tie them up. We propped them up against the wall when they were properly secured. Nathan was frozen in place, and I thought it might have been from fear, but when I walked over to him, he whispered, "Brayden set us up."

My heart broke as Nathan, once again, lost a friend that he'd fought to keep. He would have some trouble bouncing back from that one, but the rest of us would be there for him every step of the way.

I looked over at Avery and saw that she was holding her arm. Alistair crouched next to her, and Cherri stood in front of her. Despite the fact that it was Avery who was bleeding, she looked up at Cherri and smiled. "Are you okay?"

Cherri dropped to her knees with tears in her eyes and threw her arms around Avery. "Yeah. I'm much better now."

NATHAN

"I gotta say," Alistair said, "this is *not* what I was expecting when I imagined this moment."

All of the members of The Royal Court except for Brayden were sitting on the couches in the living room, watching as Kyle and Cherri sat in the middle of the floor, sobbing at one another while attempting to blubber out words. They'd been at it for about twenty minutes and were showing no signs of stopping.

"Yeah," Avery said. Her arm was now wrapped, but that wasn't stopping Alistair from holding her as gingerly as he could to keep from jostling it. "I'm the heartbroken best friend, and Colette got her ass kicked."

"I'm sorry!" Cherri screeched.

"It's okay," Kyle whined back, and they hugged and continued sobbing.

"Why are they the ones?" I asked. "It doesn't make sense to me."

"Remember how we were talking about Kyle being the one who held it together and kept us all in line? Remember, we said he didn't break down like the rest of us did?" I asked.

"Yeah," Nathan responded.

I held a hand out toward Kyle. "This is what happens when you repress your emotions."

"I guess that makes sense," Colette said. She was sitting on Jaxon's lap side-saddle with her head resting on the top of his head. He hadn't let her go since the fight ended. "Cherri's been repressing all of her emotions, too, so they're just a superstorm right now."

"Oh my god!" Sicily screamed from upstairs, his voice echoing through the house.

"I guess Sicily likes his bedroom," Nikita joked.

"What's in it?" Jaxon asked.

I leaned against Nikita, and she opened her arms so that I could lay back against her. One of her hands combed into my hair to scratch my head. "One wall is lined with computers, and I got him the best CPU I could find. It's also all noise canceling in there because he has a fuck-ton of siblings, so I figure he'll probably enjoy some peace and quiet from time to time."

"That's so considerate, Nathan," Avery said. "I really wish those idiots hadn't ruined everything."

"Are you sure you can trust the people who you got to pick them up?" Alistair asked. "Aren't you worried that your dad still has control over everyone you've worked with in the past?"

The people I'd called to come and take the goons who attacked us were a woman by the name of Anisa and a man by the name of Cobalt. They were former undercover agents for the FBI and were the same two people I called to help discreetly take care of my mom after her murder. Anisa specifically had hung around my family a lot since she was one of my dad's cleaners, but she saw the way he treated me and hated him for it. As I got older, she would frequently tell me that if I ever needed her help with anything to let her know, and I often thought she was referring to just killing my dad for me.

"No, the people I called have no loyalty to him. In fact, they hate him," I said.

"So why didn't you just tell them about the guys following us as soon as we noticed it and let them deal with it?" Colette asked.

"Because they're cleaners, not fighters. Until

there was a mess to clean up, they weren't of a whole lot of use to us," I explained.

"I've been thinking about this for a while," Alistair said. "Is your dad a mafia don?"

I snickered. "What?"

"Well, you're using fucking words like *cleaners* and *fighters*, and everyone in this goddamn town is terrified of him. Hell, by extension, they're terrified of you and all of us. I mean, he uses his money to get what he wants, and when that doesn't work, he resorts to violence, even killing people. He killed his own wife and was about to kill his own son," Alistair explained. "Sounds pretty mobster to me."

"Uh, I think we might be close cousins of the mobster. We are white-collar crooks," I said, and everyone chuckled. "Yeah, my dad uses intimidation tactics, but he's a coward. That's why I haven't seen his face. We're learning how to fight back and defend ourselves, and he doesn't know what to do. All that power my dad exercised over me came from his ability to terrify me into falling in line, but I'm not doing that anymore, and I have all of you guys with me, so he's panicking. He's upset that I picked a woman who knows how to swing a blade better than I do."

"I'll slice his fucking throat when I get the chance," Nikita growled in response.

Cherri wiped her eyes, then wiped Kyle's eyes, and she turned to face us. She seemed exhausted, but for the first time in months, as we looked at her, she seemed closer to her normal self. "Fuck, you guys, I'm sorry. I'm so sorry for everything. I'm such a shitty person. I'll do whatever I have to do to make it up to you guys."

"Oh my god," Alistair moaned. "No. We just went through this with Nathan, and it took him like six months to get through it." He looked over at Avery with legitimate concern on his face. "I don't want to have another self-pitying friend. I can't do it. I'm so tired."

Avery burst out laughing as she wrapped an arm around Alistair's head and gently patted it. "It's okay, honey. Calm down."

Colette started to laugh too. "Oh my god. We are so destroyed from this year. We *all* need therapy and lots and lots of sleep."

"I don't get it," Cherri whimpered.

I smiled at her. "Let's just say I've pretty much tapped out their reserves for patience in that particular area. We're gonna say we forgive you and leave it at that."

As the words left my lips, I thought about Brayden and wondered if I would feel the same about him. I was still refusing to think about the fact that he'd betrayed us because if I thought about it too hard, I was going to fall into another deep, dark hole.

"I just feel like that's too easy," Cherri replied. "I mean…" She looked over Colette. "I hurt you so badly."

"Yeah, but Nikki got to kick your ass back, so that's good enough for me," Colette said, then looked over at Nikita and flashed her a wink.

"Oh my god," Jaxon said breathlessly. He stood up, slinging Colette over his back. "Sorry. We'll be back."

Colette giggled as Jaxon carried her off toward the stairs. Alistair pointed up after them. "You *did* say that Sicily's room is soundproof, right?"

"Yeah, but down here isn't," I grumbled back.

"So, they're a thing now?" Cherri asked. "Like, a real thing?"

She looked at Avery for the answer, and Avery smiled. "Yeah, they're crazy about each other. She's made him a bit more sociable, and as you can see, he's made her a bit tougher. It's *really* sweet."

Cherri frowned. "I'm sad that I missed it."

"I said you were missing out on a lot," I replied.

She nodded. "Yeah. I was just so angry and sad. I miss Deon, and I wanted to blame someone for everything that happened. Not just with Deon, but with Miss Abrams and with Deon's disappearance to begin with."

"Disappearance?" I asked. "What do you mean?"

"Back when Deon first got arrested, we were having a picnic for our first date, and this body, quite literally, fell from the sky and splattered in front of us. Deon walked over to see if the guy was okay, and some cop started screaming at us, saying we did it. We had no choice but to run, and I guess Deon doubled back to protect me."

"Oh, wow," Avery said. "I didn't know that."

"Yeah. I didn't find out until right before shit hit the fan."

Kyle looked up at me from where he was sitting. "So some guy just randomly splats on the ground in front of your half-brother, and then he goes to prison for it. Then, four years later, some woman jumped out of a building that also had nothing to do with him, and he got blamed for it again?"

"Shit," I hissed.

I didn't know everything about what had happened, but it was becoming clearer that my father was to blame for *all* of our troubles, not just recently, but even back then. What didn't make sense to me was that if my dad did set Deon up four years ago, why would he have done it? I thought he was waiting for Deon to come back, judging by the preserved room and the spot at the company. Now it seemed more like he was trying to take him out.

"Nathan," Cherri said weakly.

I looked up at her. "Cherri, I'm so sorry for everything that I've put you through and that my family has put you through. I can't beg your forgiveness forever, but—"

"You're forgiven. I know what happened back then wasn't you, and now I see the pressure you were under. I don't know how you didn't break sooner."

"I've made peace with the stain I'll always have, so I can't just be a stool forever while I try to make it up to you, but is there anything I can do? Anything?"

"Yeah," she replied. "You can tell me if Deon is alive."

I looked back at her, trying my best to maintain my poker face. I could see Kyle eyeing me and could feel Nikita's gaze on the back of my head. My mind drifted to the bedroom upstairs, Deon's old room, the one I'd prepared for Deon and Cherri to stay in together one day if it became possible. It wasn't that I didn't understand why Deon wanted Cherri out of the loop, but if my relationship with Nikita had taught me anything, it was that the love that two people share is strong enough to overcome any obstacle. The way Cherri loved Deon and the way he loved her was the kind of force that was going to get us through whatever challenges and traps my father had set up for us in the days ahead, but only if they were together.

"Yes," I said finally, and Cherri doubled over. She let out a sigh of relief, and I could see tears dripping from her eyes.

She looked up at me, and grief and desperation were written all over her face. "Where?"

"Wait," Avery said, looking over at me. "Deon's alive?"

"Yeah," I said to her and then looked to Cherri again. "I don't know where he is, though. I swear. He and I have been communicating on and off, but…" My stomach churned as I prepared to tell her the next part. "About, I don't know, four weeks ago—maybe more, I can't remember—Deon called me to check in. We were talking, and the line went dead all of a sudden. He hasn't called back since. Kyle can verify."

"You knew?" Alistair barked at Kyle.

Kyle pointed at me, and I held up a hand. "Deon and I both *swore* Kyle to secrecy, and he only knew because of unavoidable circumstances. He said very clearly that he thought it was a bad idea and wanted to tell Cherri right away."

Cherri looked over at Kyle. "Thank you."

He nodded. "Yeah."

"Why don't you call him?" Cherri asked.

"I don't have a number for him," I replied. "He calls me on an unknown number every single time, and it just rings and rings until I pick up. It never goes to voicemail."

Cherri's eyes widened. "What?"

"What?" I asked.

Cherri jumped up and bolted for the stairs. "Sicily!"

The rest of us exchanged looks and then stood up and ran after her. We rushed down the hallway, past the room with some suggestive sounds coming out of it, and down to Sicily's room. Cherri opened the door, bursting through it. Sicily was sitting in front of his wall of monitors, clicking away at the keys, playing some game where he was a little green astronaut running around. A lot of other multi-colored astronauts were running around too. Right as we walked in, he appeared to get killed by one of the other astronauts.

"No! Lime!" he screeched. "Dammit."

"Sicily," Cherri barked. "Quit playing that dumbass game."

"I knew he was sus," Sicily replied and then turned and saw that we were all standing in the room. "Oh. Hey, guys."

"Sis, remember that time that I got a phone call. It just rang and rang and rang, and for like fifteen minutes, it rang, but we never answered it. Finally, you just made me turn my phone off."

"Yeah," Sicily replied.

"You said that you kind of wished we'd answered it because then you could have tracked it?" Cherri said. "Nathan has gotten calls like that too. They were from Deon."

"What!" Sicily snapped, then jumped up and ran over to me, slamming his hands on my arms. "Do you still have the phone?"

"Yeah." I shoved my hand into my pocket, pulled out the phone, and handed it over. Sicily took it and sat back down at his computer. He exited out of the game and started aggressively clicking through websites and programs that I didn't understand. "Are you going to be able to find him?"

"If nothing else, I'll get a lead," Sicily said.

"Good. Work as fast as you can. Time is of the essence," I replied. "We need to find Deon so that we can track him down. Then we can find my dad together and end this mess for good."

DEON

Gunshots ricocheted off the wall as I bolted for the door. My ribcage wanted to give out. I still hadn't fully tended to it since my last gunfight ended in disaster, but that didn't matter for now. I had to keep running. If I didn't, they were going to kill me.

I turned the corner and saw a nice little couple on their summer vacation who were pulling out their card key to get into their hotel room. Either they hadn't heard the gunshots or thought they were something else, but I didn't have time to consider it. I raced toward them, yanked the card from the man's hand, scanned the door, and pushed us all into the room, slamming the door behind them.

They were just opening their mouths to scream, and as much as I hated to do it, I lifted my gun and pointed it at them, putting my finger to my mouth to tell them to keep quiet. Tears slid down the woman's face, and I didn't stop her when she curled against her partner. He wrapped his arms around her, and I took a step toward them, motioning for them to move over so that I could look through the peephole out into the hallway.

"Shit! Where could he have gone that fast?" Briscoe asked. "He was just right fucking here."

"You idiot," Dante snapped. "How could you let him get past you? All we had to do was keep him here one more day, and then we were moving him."

I gave the couple a quick look. My gun was still outstretched, and I set my finger to my lips again, begging them to keep quiet. They both nodded that they understood, so I pulled my gun down. Eventually, Briscoe and Dante walked past the room, and I slid out of the sight of the peephole just in case. I stepped back from the doorway so that the shadows of my feet wouldn't show beneath the threshold of the door. We stood in silence for a few minutes until the sounds of their footsteps had fallen completely out of earshot.

I turned around and looked at the couple, motioning for them to walk further into the hotel room. They did as I told them to, and I followed, flipping the brass door latch as an extra measure of security, just in case. The woman started to cry a bit harder at this, so I walked over and held up my hands.

"Shh, I'm not going to hurt you, okay? I am not going to hurt either of you. I don't want to. I just need your help, okay?" I asked.

They both nodded their heads, and the man dared to ask, "Were those guys looking for you?"

I nodded. "I know I don't look like it, but I'm only eighteen, and those men had kidnapped me. I'm just trying to escape. Do you have a car? A rental? Anything?"

The man and woman exchanged looks, and then the woman slowly stood up and walked over to the safe. She entered the code and pulled out a purse, out of which she pulled a set of keys. She pulled off an electronic key fob and then handed it to me, saying, "It's a keyless start." She walked toward the window, and I walked over as well, keeping the guy in my eyeline to be safe. She pressed the unlock button, and an army-green SUV down in the parking lot beeped a few times. "It's a rental. We have insurance."

"I'll try not to total it. You can report it missing in three days. I'll have ditched it by then," I said. I took the key fob from her. "Thank you. I under-stand that you may completely turn around and call the cops, and I wouldn't blame you, but you just saved my life."

With the key fob in one hand and the gun in the other, I slid open the sliding glass doors of the balcony and slipped outside into the night. I looked around, making sure no one was looking. Then as quickly and as quietly as I could, I made my way down the fire escape. I rushed over to the SUV once I got to the parking lot and jumped into the vehicle, immediately pressing the button to start it. I was grateful for the hybrid, which had a near-silent engine and a built-in navigation system, and it seemed my luck was finally turning around.

I waited until I was free of the parking lot to press the button to initiate the navigation. "Where would you like to go?" it asked in a robotic tone.

"Emmesk Penitentiary," I said out loud, and the navigation immediately hopped to attention, calcu-lating the directions. I was about two hours away, but that was fine. Putting that distance between my babysitters and me would ease my tension bit by bit.

Traveling back into Maine put a knot in the pit of my stomach. I imagined the bright red *At Large* stamp next to my mugshot in the Maine Offender

Database and knew that if I got caught by so much as a mall security guard, I'd be going back to prison for the rest of my life. If I had any other choice, I wouldn't be doing this, but it was the only option I had left. Briscoe and Dante had taken everything from me, and I ripped up my contact list to keep them from getting it.

The only number I had memorized was Cherri's, but she didn't answer when I got the chance to call, not that I could blame her. She thought I was dead, so it probably just looked like a solicitor call to her.

I made my way further and further upstate until I was driving into the parking lot of Emmesk Penitentiary, the place that had been my home for the past couple of years. I swore on my life that I wouldn't come back to this place, and I wished to any god listening that I had another choice. The only person who was bound to be more upset with me for being back here than I was upset with myself was the one person who I promised would never see me again.

Hopefully, he'd forgive me.

My heart pounded as I walked up to the front door of the building. Everything about it felt wrong, but I also knew that I was entering a sphere of influence that might keep me safe for a little bit longer. Still, I threw up my hood and kept my head down as I entered.

Inside, the place was as cold and unwelcoming as I remembered. It gave me a sense of dread, just standing in the lobby, and my anxiety was through the roof, knowing that if I made one wrong move, they would drag me back to a cell. Yet, I walked with confidence, right up to the front desk.

"Good afternoon, welcome to Emmesk Peni—" The man at the desk looked up, and his jaw dropped. "Deon."

"Hey, Lupe," I replied. "I need to talk to Venom."

"He's going to rip your throat out if he sees you here," Lupe responded. "You're on my fucking wanted list. What kind of balls do you have, man?"

"Do you think I'm here to take a walk down memory fucking lane?" I hissed. "It's important."

Lupe let out a deep sigh. "Fuck. You're gonna cost me my job."

"No, Venom will look out for you. Just bring me back."

He stood up and motioned me toward the metal detectors. I held out the key fob. I didn't have anything else on me or to my name. Lupe murmured a few words to the guards who were handling the metal detectors, and then one of them motioned me through. I passed through the metal detectors, and only after getting a thorough pat-down was I eventually ushered through the heavy, concrete doors. When they slammed behind me, my stomach lurched, and my head started to hurt. The murmur of prisoners and the tension of the guards settled around me, and I felt like I was going to be sick. It was familiar in the worst kind of way.

Eventually, though, I got to the visiting room. Lupe knocked on the door, and a guard opened it and looked out at me. He rolled his eyes, whispered, "Shit," and then yelled into the room. "All right! Visiting hours are over. Say your goodbyes!"

A few people tried to protest, and I felt bad, knowing how much I yearned for visits from my mom. I hated it when they got cut short. Desperate times called for desperate measures, though.

I kept my head low as other guards led the outgoing visitors through the exit, and then I was led in and instructed to sit in the chair at the centermost visiting station. I was separated by a piece of plexiglass from the hell I'd lived in for two years, and it was doing a variety of things to my stomach and head. Even my vision blurred.

After about five minutes, the door on the other side of the plexiglass opened, and Venom came waltzing in. He was cuffed at the wrists and the ankles, and when he looked over and saw me, his eyes narrowed into a steely glare, but I smiled. For all the awful sensations, Venom's tall, thick build, chocolate brown skin, and bald head were a sight for sore eyes.

They sat him down across from me, and he reached forward, pushing the maximum reach his chains and cuffs allowed to grab the phone and put it to his ear.

"Son, I don't want you to think I ain't happy to see ya, but I thought I told ya to stay away from here."

Behind bars, people sometimes forged pseudo-families. My pseudo-dad was Venom.

"What's goin' on, Pop?" I asked. "And I know, but I need some help. I tried to use some of your contacts, but I had to come directly to the source."

"What do you need?" he asked.

"Someone's hunting me, but I need to find him first."

"Who's that?" Venom asked.

My eyes narrowed. "My father."

IMPORTANT AUTHOR'S NOTES:

Thank you for reading Evil Queen! Don't miss the

final book EVIL VILLAIN from Deon and Cherri's point of view. And if you loved this book, consider leaving a review on Amazon. Just 1 or 2 lines would be amazing. **Thank you!**

WANT MORE?

Check out my author page for a full list of my books.

Get an alert when I release a new book:
SMS: Text REBEL to 77948 (US only)
EMAILs: join at www.RebelHart.net

WANT TO BE A REBEL?

Join my Group of Rebels to chat with me and other fans. I'd love to have you there!

ABOUT THE AUTHOR

Rebel Hart is an author of Contemporary and Dark Romance novels. All her books are FREE in Kindle Unlimited. Check them out at author.to/RebelHart.

NEVER MISS A NEW RELEASE:
Follow Rebel on Amazon
Follow Rebel on Bookbub
Text REBEL to 77948 (US only)
Sign up at www.RebelHart.net to get an email alert when her next book is out.

authorrebelhart@gmail.com

CONNECT WITH REBEL HART: